K-PAX IV

OTHER BOOKS BY GENE BREWER

K-PAX
K-PAX II: On a Beam of Light
K-PAX III: The Worlds of Prot
K-PAX: the Trilogy, featuring Prot's Report
Creating K-PAX
"Alejandro," in *Twice Told*
Murder on Spruce Island
Wrongful Death
Ben and I
Watson's God

K-PAX IV

A New Visitor From The Constellation Lyra

Gene Brewer

Copyright © 2007 by Gene Brewer.

ISBN: Hardcover   978-1-4257-1889-3
            Softcover   978-1-4257-1890-9

All rights reserved. No part of this book may be reproduced or transmitted in any form or by any means, electronic or mechanical, including photocopying, recording, or by any information storage and retrieval system, without permission in writing from the copyright owner.

This is a work of fiction. Names, characters, places and incidents either are the product of the author's imagination or are used fictitiously, and any resemblance to any actual persons, living or dead, events, or locales is entirely coincidental.

This book was printed in the United States of America.

To order additional copies of this book, contact:
Xlibris Corporation
1-888-795-4274
www.Xlibris.com
Orders@Xlibris.com

Anything is possible.

—prot

PROLOGUE

This book can be understood and enjoyed by those who have not yet read *K-PAX* (1995), *K-PAX II: On a Beam of Light* (2001), and *K-PAX III: The Worlds of Prot* (2002). To fully appreciate the context, however, I urge you to read the trilogy prior to, or immediately after, reading *fled*.

The aforementioned series describes the appearance, in 1990, of a man who claimed to have arrived "on a beam of light," from the planet K-PAX, some 7000 light-years from Earth in the constellation Lyra, and records my attempts, as a staff psychiatrist at the Manhattan Psychiatric Institute, to determine his true origins and treat his apparent delusion, which continued until the time of his final "departure" in 1997.

For those of you who *have* read the first three K-PAX books, it should be mentioned at the outset that prot makes no further appearance in the present work. This should come as no surprise, however, as he himself stated that he would not be making a return trip to Earth.

Six months after prot's departure I retired from active practice, and my wife and I moved out of the suburbs and into a lovely cedar-shingled home in the Adirondack Mountains in upstate New York. I did continue to visit the hospital from time to time, and occasionally gave a lecture at Columbia University, where I held the rank of professor emeritus. Aside from those forays back into the clinical and academic worlds, my wife and I have enjoyed doing all the things we would have liked to do earlier but never had time for–travel, reading, gardening, socializing with family and friends. I finally took up flying, a hobby If enjoy very much (to the horror of my son Fred), but which turned out to be far more expensive that I had imagined. (Q: What makes an airplane fly? A: Money.) And–owing, no doubt, to prot's influence–astronomy. For a retirement present Karen gave me a four-inch reflecting telescope, and over the past seven or eight years I have become quite familiar with the planets, moons, and stars in our galactic neighborhood. I even found time to write a couple of novels (see *www.amazon.com* or *www.amazon.co.uk*).

The entire family, incidentally, is doing fine. Karen is totally free of cancer cells and is more active, if possible, than ever. Abby is now the mother of college men, Rain (Princeton) into computers, while Star (NYU) wants to be an actor, like his uncle Fred. The latter has found a comfortable niche in Broadway musicals, and has appeared in two major films as well. He's confident a starring role will come along soon. Jennifer is the busiest of the brood, intimately involved in the testing of the first vaccine against AIDS. Will runs a close second, though, as the newest member of the psychiatric staff at MPI, and he loves to discuss his patients with me as do I, of course, with him. He even takes my advice from time to time! I have been told that he looks a lot like me, and I suppose that's one of the reasons most of us have children: to do it all over again, in a sort of vague and distant way. (On the other hand, I've also been informed that anyone with a beard looks much like me.)

I should also mention that we have another member of the family, a mixed-breed dog obtained from the local animal shelter. Flower is seven now, in the prime of life, and she's a clumsy, hilarious, canine oaf, whom we love dearly.

As an aside, the excellent film version of *K-PAX* didn't do as well at the box office as had been expected and, as of this writing, a sequel is still up in the air. (If you know of a studio or producer who's interested, please ask them to contact me through my website.) There's a ray of hope in the strong videotape and DVD sales and rentals, however, and as prot pointed out on numerous occasions, anything is possible. Whatever happens, I think the movie was a good adaptation of prot's story, and brilliantly played by both Kevin Spacey and Jeff Bridges (as well as Mary McCormack and the rest of the cast). Karen and I were privileged to meet the stars during the filming (look for me at the end of the "bluebird" scene), and both are fine gentlemen as well as great actors.

But the point I was making is that when prot departed the Earth at the end of 1997 I was pretty sure we would hear no more about K-PAX, certainly not in my lifetime, and especially not from an entirely different visitor from that faraway planet.

As usual where alien visitors are concerned, I was wrong.

CHAPTER ONE

On a lovely spring day in 2005, while I was answering some e-mail, there came a knock at the back door. Actually, it was more like someone was banging on it. Flower ran from the study, barking as usual (she even barks at falling leaves). Karen was out doing some shopping, and I thought it was probably *her* standing there, arms full of grocery bags. I left a note unfinished and hurried to open it. But when I looked through the window in the upper part of the door I saw something so strange, so unbelievable, that I froze, unable to turn the knob. I attributed the apparition to some ordinary portobello mushrooms (i.e., not the psychedelic kind) I had eaten the previous evening. I love the things, but they sometime make me feel a bit peculiar and see things a little off-kilter.

The hairy creature standing outside stared grotesquely in at me. I stared back. Finally she yelled, over Flower's barking, "I have a message from prot!"

Still stunned, I opened the door a crack. That was all she needed. With an enormous foot she barged her way into the kitchen and gazed around with interest, as if we weren't even there. Flower, for her part, gave her a good sniffing and ran hopefully to get a toy to play with, as she does with every visitor we have. I couldn't help but notice that this one was wearing nothing. Finally she looked at me with her huge black eyes and said, "Prot told me you would put me up."

I managed to squeak, "Put you up?"

"That's what he said. It means you will give me food and some space in your dwelling for a while."

"I *know* what it means."

"Well?"

"All right, all right—I'm thinking about it." She was literally covered with hair. Except for her face, and even that was quite fuzzy. She resembled more than anything else a large, talking chimpanzee. "Are you from K-PAX?"

"Of *course* I'm from K-PAX. Otherwise I wouldn't know prot, would I?" She spoke quite loudly and *very* fast, much faster than prot. It was hard to keep up with her.

Despite her hirsute appearance and somewhat belligerent manner, I found myself drawn into the conversation whether I liked it or not. Apparently K-PAXians of whatever nature had this effect on people. "Not necessarily," I countered. "You could have met him on one of the other planets he has visited."

Flower came back with her squeaky rabbit, which this . . . being . . . grabbed and tossed into the living room. "Not likely. He's retired from traveling, remember? Says he's seen enough."

"So he sent you."

"I didn't say he sent me, you doofus. I said he sent a message."

At this point Karen drove up. I told our new guest to make herself at home, that I would be right back, explaining, "I have to help my wife with the groceries." Of course I also wanted to prepare her for what she would find inside. Our visitor stared out the window for a moment—evidently she had never seen anything as primitive as a motor vehicle—before shrugging and wandering on into the house, Flower following eagerly with her toy.

I ran outside. Karen was already opening the car door. "Just a minute!" I yelled.

"What? What's the matter?"

"There's something I need to tell you."

She got out of the car. "Fine, but help me with the groceries first, will you?"

"We have another visitor from K-PAX."

She seemed amused. "Really? Who is it this time—prot's mother?"

"She's not related to prot, as far as I know. I don't think she's even the same species."

"No kidding! Well, help me with these bags and let's go in and meet her." I should mention here that nothing on Earth fazes my wife. Even something from a different galaxy, forty feet tall and with seventeen eyes, would have to work hard at it.

I grabbed a couple of sacks and started toward the door. There was no point in trying to describe the alien creature. She would see for herself soon enough. "I should warn you—she seems a bit more outgoing than prot."

"How refreshing."

We set the groceries down on the kitchen cabinet. Karen looked around. "Well, where is she?"

"She must be in one of the other rooms."

"This isn't one of your mushroom dreams, is it?"

"I have a feeling I'm going to wish it were."

At that point our visitor reappeared, Flower at the heels of her huge feet. "Why do you need all those rooms?" she demanded.

"Because we have a big family."

"Oh, yes. Prot told me about your attachment to 'families.' Very peculiar, don't you think?"

My wife was still unflapped. "What should we call you?"

"Call me ishmael."

Neither of us responded.

The ape-like creature burst into laughter, or what passes for laughter in her species: a piercing, hoot-like giggle. "He *said* you had no sense of humor! Actually, my name is 'fled.'"

We stared some more.

"You were expecting someone else?"

Karen said, "We weren't really expecting anyone. But please—sit down. Are you hungry? Has Gene shown you the facilities?"

"No, but if you mean the excrement catchers, I found three of them. Isn't one enough? And yes, of *course* I'm hungry. I haven't eaten in months. *Your* months, of course."

"Of course," I murmured dismally. I was already contemplating a long period of disruption, confusion, and possibly even debacle. I excused myself to make use of the facilities.

* * *

While I was sitting there I ran over in my mind some of the ramifications of what I had just seen. K-PAXians seemed to sleep wherever they found themselves and eat whatever was around. So what did she mean by our "putting her up"? Would she want a room of her own or, since the weather was already growing warm, would she prefer to sleep outside in a tree? What did her species (whatever it was) eat? Could we get her to wear clothes, and if so, would she look as silly as a performing chimp? (I should mention that her genitalia, like her face, were not covered by hair, and were quite noticeable.) But, if not, would she be subject to stares and ridicule for running around naked?

More importantly, perhaps: why did she come here? And how long was she planning to stay? I remembered her opening statement: "I have a message from prot." What was the message—another attempt to get us Homo sapiens to behave ourselves? No, that's wrong; prot never made such an appeal. In fact, he didn't seem to care much what happened to us. He was, he said, merely observing the Earth and its inhabitants (see "Prot's Report to K-PAX" in *K-PAX: The Trilogy*, Bloomsbury, London, 2003).

It briefly occurred to me to wonder how we would know whether she really came from K-PAX. But of course she couldn't have come from *here*—we have no talking (in the usual sense) apes on this planet, as far as I know. I laughed, hollowly to be sure; I was going around the same circle I had traveled with prot nearly fifteen years earlier (God, has it been that long?). While reaching for the toilet paper, I came to an understanding with myself: this time I wouldn't fight it. I would just accept her statements at face value and see what came of them.

When I got back to the kitchen our unannounced guest was digging into a large bowl of uncooked kidney beans. Not with those long, hairy fingers, but with her protruding lips. She was obviously enjoying them, washing them down with loud swigs of apple juice. Flower was sitting beside her chair patiently waiting for something to fall, as if our surprise visitor had been living with us all her life, while I tried to take it all in—her rapid movements, the air of self-assurance. It occurred to me that she could take care of herself in any situation. I certainly wouldn't want to tangle with her.

While I waited for her to finish her simple meal, Karen filled me in on what I had missed. Fled had told her that Robert and Giselle were as happy as gonks (clamlike beings on K-PAX), and that "baby" Gene, almost eight years old now (in Earth terms, of course), was becoming, like his father, quite an expert on the native flora and fauna. He even had a girlfriend about his age, formerly from Ukraine. Oxeye, too, was still fit and energetic at fifteen, having a whole planet to run around in. He, too, had a playmate, another Dalmatian prot had rescued from a pound "nine thousand jarts west of MPI."

Bess and Frankie were fine, too, though fled didn't see them much. Bess, our former psychotic depressive, spent much of her time visiting other worlds. As a retired psychiatrist I suspected that this was her attempt to make up for her childhood years tied to the family tenement, endlessly cleaning and cooking for her parents and siblings and rarely leaving the place. But who knows how the mind works, human or otherwise? During prot's visit it became painfully obvious to me that I certainly didn't.

Frankie, on the other hand, never did much of anything, though she, too, had apparently been able to shed much of the bitterness she had accumulated on her former world. Indeed, all the hundred beings prot had taken back with him to K-PAX were doing very well. There was a little homesickness, of course, but not one person (mammal, insect, whatever) wanted to return to Earth. Since the publication of *K-PAX III*, we've (the hospital and myself) received literally thousands of e-mail messages requesting a placement on the passenger list for the next trip to that idyllic planet. Thus, it occurred to me to ask fled, when she finally finished crunching the bowl of beans, whether she planned to take anyone back with her if, and when, she returned.

She sat back and—you guessed it—burped loudly, as though she were a character in some bad movie. From somewhere—an armpit, maybe—she pulled out a small device of some sort. It appeared to be made of a soft metal, or hard plastic, and shaped like a cone. When she set it on its flat end, an apparition immediately flashed into the kitchen. Here, in the dim light, were Robert and Giselle and their son Gene, running naked in a field of flowers and grains among several kinds of animals. The sky was filled with birds, and behind them stood a row of purple mountains. Eventually they headed toward the camera, or whatever it was, waving.

"Hi, Dr. B," Giselle shouted. "You should come here for a visit. It's unbelievable!"

Robert added a few words of thanks for my part in getting him there, and finally my godson said something in pax-o. His mother whispered a request in his ear and he repeated, in English, "I want to come and visit *you*, too!" But it wasn't like watching a movie. It was as if they were actually in the kitchen with us, except that the walls had disappeared and we were all sitting in the–well, it's hard to explain. But then something even more magical happened. Giselle stepped up and *hugged* me! As did Gene and, finally, Robert. Everyone hugged everyone else.

Finally, just before the "materialization" ended, prot appeared, as if in a cameo role. Neither of us said anything, we merely shook hands. I found myself tearing up a little–I thought I'd never see my old friend again.

Then the walls reappeared and K-PAX was gone. Fled stuck the device back under her arm. "Prot said you wouldn't believe me unless I had proof." The only thing I had difficulty believing was that they had all been here (or we had been *there?*–it was impossible to tell the difference). All I could think to say was, "You don't have another one of those things to give away, do you?"

"I'll leave this one with you when I go. Until then, I'll just hang onto it in case I need to use it again."

"When you go back to K-PAX, you mean."

"Yes, I will definitely be going back to K-PAX. And to answer your question (I hadn't asked it yet): when I do I will be taking 100,000 of your beings with me. If that many want to go, of course."

"A hundred–I presume you mean mostly bugs and worms?"

"No, this time it's people."

That I had trouble believing. "Did you say *people?*"

"Prot told me your hearing was going. I repeat for the deaf among us: I can take 100,000 people back with me when I go."

"But– But how?"

"Well, I'm happy to see that you're still curious about math and science, doctor b. It's simple, really. All I need is a place big enough to hold everyone."

"You mean . . . a football stadium or something like that?"

"Something like that. The dimensions have already been programmed, and there's a comparable place on K-PAX waiting for our arrival. It's just a matter of setting a time."

"And may I ask when that might be?"

"Sure. Why not?"

"All right, dammit, what date have you selected?"

"I have reserved six windows for the trip, each about twenty-six days apart, in case we don't make the first window. Do you think we can gather together everyone who wants to go in three weeks?"

We? I thought. "I haven't a clue."

At this point the telephone rang. Karen answered it. It was Will, just checking up on the old folks on a Saturday morning in May. It suddenly occurred to me that perhaps fled might be more comfortable living at the Institute while she was on Earth. They could keep an eye on her, she would be safe, there would be food and a place to sleep, and patients who would be delighted to learn that the "legend of K-PAX" had come true again (though none of them had ever doubted it would).

"Sure," fled agreed. "I'll stay where prot did when he was here."

But I hadn't asked yet. "You– You can read minds?"

"Of course."

"But prot couldn't do that, as far as I know."

"Don't tell him I said this, but we trods are a little more advanced in some ways than the dremers."

"How do you do that?"

"Well, the brain gives off electromagnetic waves–that's how your encephalographs work. Of course you have to know how to interpret them . . . ."

I asked her a bit apprehensively, "Can you project your thoughts into other people's minds?"

"Not exactly. But we could influence your *own* thoughts so you would think whatever we'd like you to think."

"You could, but you don't?"

"Spoken like a true homo sapiens," she snorted, and a glob of mucus (or something) plopped onto the table. "Your governments and your clergy would love to know how to do that, wouldn't they?"

Trying unsuccessfully to ignore the snot lying on my usual eating place, I got up and took the receiver. "Will," I said, probably a bit too desperately, "How would you like a new patient?"

"I don't think I can fit in a new patient right now, Dad, but bring her in, anyway, and we'll find someone to look after her. Let me talk to Virginia (Goldfarb, the hospital director) about it."

I promised to bring her in the next day and, for the time being, we left it at that. As for fled, herself, I told her the hospital would "put her up" on condition that she cooperate with Goldfarb and Will and the rest of the staff, quickly adding, "and that you would be willing to meet with my son or another staff member two or three times a week to talk about your visit to Earth and the problems of the patients there" (we needed all the help we could get).

"Seems like a fair exchange."

For the rest of the afternoon and evening fled slept in the backyard, Flower alternately standing guard and curled up beside her.

* * *

She hooted when we started for the city, presumably at the primitive type of conveyance she was riding in. "You just sit here in this little room, is that it?" she asked me, "and the thing moves along by itself on those little round feet?"

"Well," I corrrected her, "it's not quite that simple." I started to explain how a car operates, but found that I had forgotten most of what I had learned in driver's ed half a century ago. I did mention, however, that the energy came from the oxidation of refined hydrocarbons, which pushed down on the pistons, and somehow this turned the crankshaft, and then the driveshaft, and finally, through a system of gears, the "feet."

She laughed again. "And I suppose one of your 'airplanes' works the same way?"

"Uh, not exactly. The fuel part is similar, but the propeller or jet engine pulls the plane forward."

"So what makes it fly?"

I started to tell her, but she interrupted: "Besides money, of course."

"It has something to do with the shape of the wings. Actually, there are a couple of different theories on that . . . ."

I had given her the stack of e-mail messages I had received from people who had professed an interest over the last several years in going to K-PAX, and she perused these for a few minutes. When we merged into traffic on the interstate, I glanced over at the passenger in the pickup truck passing us on our left. I couldn't hear anything, but I could see that she was screaming. She turned toward the driver and suddenly the truck accelerated to about 90 mph and pulled away from us. Fled chortled again as she tossed the mail into the back seat. "We won't need these," she explained. "It's a whole new ball game."

I was still trying to collect my thoughts on how the shape of the wings lifts a plane into the air.

"Never mind," she said. "I get it." After a moment she added, "One day I'll take you for a ride in the sky with me."

A chill shot up my spine. What effect would that have on the physiology of a sixty-six-year-old human? Even John Glenn had some medical problems with his final trip into orbit. I realized that Karen would go with her in a heartbeat.

"Her, too," fled promised.

Since we were on the subject of light travel, and not knowing whether I'd ever have a chance like this again, I started to bring up some of the questions I had about cosmology. For example, if the universe recycles over and over again, where did it come from in the first place, and when would the reverse process begin?

She yawned. "That stuff doesn't interest me."

Thoroughly disappointed, I asked her what did.

"Life on other PLANETS. EARTH, for example." (NB: For a K-PAXian, only heavenly bodies are deemed worthy of capitalization. Everything else, including people, are lower-case entities.)

"Why the Earth?"

"Who knows? I'm not a shrink." She glanced at me accusingly before continuing. "Some of your beings study the biology of your oceans, right? I'm interested in the biology of other PLANETS. Besides," she added matter-of-factly, "I wanted to come to EARTH before it was too late . . . ."

"Too late for what?"

"Too late to find any sapiens."

I didn't like the sound of that. "Is that why you're planning to take 100,000 of us back to K-PAX with you? To sort of 'preserve' us? Put us in zoos, maybe?"

"Not at all. We're not *humans*, gino. Prot informed me that most of you want to get off this WORLD. I thought: what the hey? As long as I was here, I might as well help some of you out."

"What kinds of people will you be taking?"

"If I told you that up front, it wouldn't be much of a book, would it?"

"What makes you think I'm going to write a book about your visit?"

"You can't help yourself!"

"Well, what about *you*? Aren't you writing a report about us?"

"Nope. Most K-PAXians know all they care to know about you."

While she gazed at the suburban landscape, I thought: how could she possibly determine which of us to take out of so many possibilities?

"Well, you can eliminate anyone with a cell phone in her ear, for example."

We "talked" on about prot and Robert and Giselle, and I learned that my namesake was going to have a little sister in a few months. "That must be quite a rarity on K-PAX," I noted. "Given your reluctance to have—uh—sexual relations."

"Oh, that only applies to the dremers. And a few other species. The rest of us can't get enough of it."

I changed the subject. "When you got here, you said you had 'a message from prot.' What was it?"

"Nine suggestions."

"*Nine*?"

"Yes, nine, o deaf one."

"What are they?"

"Prot advised me not to tell you until later."

"Why not?"

"He thinks I should tell everyone at the same time."

"You mean go to the UN?"

"Unless there's something better."

"That's awfully 'science fiction,' don't you think?"

"Except in sci-fi they never make it to the UN."

The city of New York came suddenly into view. "Whoa!" she exclaimed. "It's just like prot said. Except that the world trade center is gone now, of course."

I shrugged defensively. As we were crossing the George Washington Bridge I began to think about fled's visit and what we might learn from her. I didn't want to screw it up and find myself remembering to ask her something after she had gone.

Despite her brusque nature she must've felt a little sorry for me. "Okay, gene," she sighed. "I'll answer one question about cosmology. What will it be?"

There were so many that I had to ponder for a minute or two. Finally, I came up with: "Is there a Grand Unification Theory?"

"You mean to resolve the apparent dichotomy between relativity and quantum mechanics."
"Yes."
"No."
"You mean no one will ever—"
"Forget quantum mechanics and superstrings. It's all fantasy. Mathematical farting."
There was only one appropriate response to that. "You would know."
As we turned onto Amsterdam Avenue she told me, "Albert lives on K-PAX. As a 'hologram,' of course. He's still mad at himself for wasting so much of his time on Earth with the GUT, as you call it. A fascinating guy with a childlike curiosity. He's great pals with Wolfgang."
"Mozart?"
"No, you twit. Wolfgang Schwartz, the physicist."
"Oh." I wanted to hear more, but we were almost to the Manhattan Psychiatric Institute. "And Robert Porter's father—is he there, too?"
"Oh, yes. Rob talks to him all the time."
I parked illegally right in front of the hospital and hustled fled past the gate and into the building as quickly as possible, informing Officer Wilson that I had an emergency case to admit. The elderly guard's mouth was still open when we hurried inside.
Fled was far more demonstrative than prot had ever been. She waved and smiled (at least I think it was a smile) at everyone milling on the lawn or in the main (first-floor) lounge. A few of the inmates waved back, including Phyllis,[*] who thinks she is invisible, but most of them seemed confused by what they were seeing. A couple of the patients tried to follow us into the elevator (fled was greatly amused by this contraption), but I admonished a bug-eyed nurse to take them back to what they had been doing.
Goldfarb knew who was coming, but even she was shocked by the appearance of our guest. Nevertheless, she managed to return fled's grin and offered a hand, which our newest visitor enthusiastically shook. Evidently fled had been coached by prot on the proper protocol with respect to introductions.
After we had all sat down and fled was gawking at everything around her, I put it right to Virginia: did she have someone to look after prot's K-PAXian friend? I presumed Will had spoken to her about the matter. By now she had regained her composure. "I was thinking *you* might take care of fled."
It hadn't even occurred to me that she would come up with this nutty idea, and I told her so. I protested further that I was retired, and didn't even live near the city anymore. Goldfarb wasn't daunted. She's never daunted. "That's precisely it. No one on the staff has room for another patient. You do, and you come in once a week anyway just to hang out and get in everyone's way. Why not do something useful while you're here?"

---

[*] As always, the names of the patients have been changed to protect the anonymity of their families.

"What about—?"

"Your son has more than he can handle. So does Chang and Menninger and Rothstein and Rudqvist and Roberts. We have more patients than we've ever had, and none of them seems to want to leave. They're all waiting for someone from K-PAX to come and get them. And who knows more about alien visitors than you do?"

My last feeble defense: "I don't have an examining room."

"You can use mine. It has a separate entrance and I don't have that many patients anymore."

She had me and she knew it. And the truth is, I rather missed the direct interaction with the residents of MPI, though, technically, fled wasn't a patient. "I'll have to clear it with Karen." But I knew my long-suffering wife would have no objection to getting me out of the house a couple of days a week.

When I turned to see how fled was taking all this, I found that she had fallen asleep again, her feet curled around the legs of her chair.

I whispered to Virginia, "We're going to have to do something about the front gate. If people see a large chimpanzee loping around the lawn they're going to think this is a zoo."

"I'll take care of it," she promised.

* * *

As usual when visiting the hospital I decided to have lunch in the faculty dining room. Several of the staff psychiatrists were there and they greeted me warmly when I came in. I thought that rather odd, as I had been showing up fairly regularly almost since my retirement. It turned out that they were all relieved and happy that I had taken fled off their hands and they didn't have to deal with her.

I sat down with our two most recent arrivals, Cliff Roberts and Hannah Rudqvist. The latter had arrived only three weeks before, on a sabbatical leave from the Karolinska Institute to work with Ron Menninger. (As part of an international exchange, Arthur Beamish was on leave in Stockholm for the year. Carl Thorstein, incidentally, left the Institute for good four years ago.) I didn't yet know Hannah very well, but I wasn't especially fond of Cliff, the hospital's only African-American staff psychiatrist, who seemed to personify the unappealing self-centeredness of the younger generation of whatever race or ethnic origin. He was rumored to be a womanizer as well. On the other hand, he was a bright young doctor who had taken on some of the institute's most difficult patients, including Howard, "the toad man of Milwaukee," and Rocky, who cannot forget a slight, regardless of how miniscule, until an apology is made or revenge taken.

As do most psychiatrists, Hannah has her own little neuroses, and for reasons of her own, blushed when I sat down. In an attempt to put her at her ease, I asked her about invisible Phyllis, who is one of her responsibilities. Phyllis's affliction, though rare, does occur occasionally, and it's a difficult one for both patients and staff. If someone comes up and stares right into her eyes, for example, or punches her on a shoulder, she is convinced that the offender is merely looking at himself in a mirror, or shadow-boxing, or whatever. As with most delusionals, nothing can persuade her of the unreality of her situation. I mentioned that Phyllis seemed to wave at fled when we came in.

"Maybe you could get your monkey friend to help us out with her," Cliff interjected brightly. Obviously he already knew something about our alien visitor.

"I'll check with her, but I think it's a little early to know whether she has the same chairside manner as prot. In fact, she seems to have different interests entirely."

"That's too bad," he said. "I was hoping she could do something about our ridiculous workload."

Another reason I didn't like Cliff: he seemed more interested in his own personal well-being than in helping the patients. I noticed that his teeth could use some work, too. Perhaps I would ask fled if she had any interest in dentistry....

But a light seemed to click on in Hannah's head. "Perhaps she knows fled can see her!" she exclaimed. (Though her English was flawless, she spoke with a lilting Swedish accent.) "Maybe Dr. Roberts is right: maybe we can get Phyllis to tell your new patient what troubles her!"

I pointed out that fled was a visitor from a faraway planet, and not a new patient. But Hannah was undeterred, and her enthusiasm was infectious. I was starting to get that feeling I had whenever I talked with prot. What could fled do for us, for the patients—for the world—that we couldn't yet imagine?

At this point Ron Menninger and Laura Chang pulled up chairs. Both tried to speak at the same time. Ron finally gave way to his more persistent colleague. "Will you ask her to speak with Claire?" she pleaded. "Sometimes I think I've gotten somewhere with her, and the next thing I know we're right back to square one."

"Yes," Menninger piped up," and Charlotte has suddenly gone into a deep depression for no discernible reason." Anticipating my next question, he added, "No, it's not a side effect of her medication, which she's been taking for some time. But all of a sudden she doesn't seem to care about anything. I think she's just lonely."

"And Jerry," Chang interjected. "Prot got through to him. Maybe fled can, too."

"Hey, take a number!" Roberts shouted out. "Let her take a look at Rocky first!"

"Whoa!" I said. "Slow down! Give me a chance to talk to her. She may not want to practice Earth-bound psychiatry. She's only here to study turtles and trees, as far as I can tell."

They all backed off for the moment, but I knew they would be waiting impatiently for a verdict, and considerable help, from fled. And who can blame them? The Manhattan Psychiatric Institute takes only the most difficult patients, often those that other mental hospitals have given up on. Many have been here for years. I, too, hoped with all my heart that fled could relieve them of their suffering, help bring a measure of peace and happiness to their endlessly tormented lives. But that depended entirely on her willingness to cooperate with us and take an interest in their problems.

CHAPTER TWO

I spent the weekend listening to the tapes of my conversations with prot in 1990, 1995, and 1997. Not to refresh my memory of those sessions—I would never forget them—but to reconsider all the mistakes I had made in dealing with our first K-PAXian visitor. There were plenty, foremost of which was my reluctance to accept anything he had been telling me. Yet, how many psychiatrists would have done otherwise? All of us have encountered patients claiming to be from the reaches of space, from another time, even from the corridors of heaven or the depths of hell.

For those who have not read the previous books, a very brief review: prot had been brought to MPI from Bellevue Hospital, an apparent delusional amnesiac (eventually diagnosed with dissociative identity disorder). With the help of Giselle Griffin, a freelance reporter who had come to the hospital to do a story on mental illness, we were finally able to track down his Earthly origins to a small town in Montana, where his wife and nine-year-old daughter had been brutally assaulted and murdered. That, of course, could drive anybody insane (though technically, it was an alter ego, Robert Porter, who was the severely traumatized patient).

But prot was different from most multiple personality sufferers. Not only did he know certain things about astronomy that even astronomers (like my son-in-law Steve) didn't know, but was demonstrably able to see light in the ultraviolet range. At first I didn't believe he could travel at light speed, and even much faster, until he eventually demonstrated that ability on national television, and even then I thought it must be some kind of hallucinatory trick.

With fled, on the other hand, it seemed clear that we wouldn't have to waste time determining whether she was also from K-PAX and came here on a beam of light. For one thing she knew prot and had brought holograms of him and Robert and Giselle, and, for another, she certainly couldn't have come from Earth. I wondered whether she liked fruit; she might have looked like an ape, but that wasn't actually the case. Who knew what her wants and needs might be, or exactly what she planned to do with her time here. I would have to spend at least a couple of visits just getting to know her.

Superimposed on all this was the urgent question of what effect fled might have on the other patients at the hospital. Would she be sympathetic to their plights, as prot had been? Or indifferent, as she was to my cosmological questions? Or perhaps even antagonistic toward them (and vice versa)? Her edges seemed considerably rougher than prot's; would this propensity for directness (she reminded me of former patient Frankie, now a resident of K-PAX) put off the other inmates, as well as the hospital staff?

I certainly hoped not. Some of the patients had been waiting years for another visitor from K-PAX; many of them, in fact, were depending on her to take them back with her when she returned. These included Cassandra, our long-time resident prognosticator, and the aforementioned Jerry, our autistic engineer, who was working on a large matchstick model of the Institute itself, including the new Villers wing, named for our former hospital director and his wife (and rather unsympathetically dubbed, by Cliff Roberts, "The Screaming Hilton"). Other, newer residents, including some of the "Magnificent Seven," were also patiently waiting for a voyage to the stars. Most wanted nothing more than to try their luck on another planet.

Two of the latter, incidentally, have been successfully treated and released, and a third, the "female Jesus," was transferred to our sister hospital, "The Big Institute," at Columbia. (We sometimes exchange difficult patients, hoping that someone can come up with something the other staff has not; in any case a change of venue is often salutary for everyone involved.) The other four were still with us. Besides Howard and Phyllis these include Rick, who is constitutionally unable to tell the truth, and Darryl, who thinks Meg Ryan is in love with him. Other recent denizens include "Dr. Claire Smith," who believes that she herself is a psychiatrist, rather than an inmate, and Barney, who has never been able to laugh at *anything*. It was patients like these whom we all sincerely hoped fled might be able to help—something that none of the staff has been able to do, even with years of dedicated effort.

I hoped that these and our other residents would give fled the benefit of the doubt. In her favor was the notion most of them shared: that she held the key to departing our hostile planet, the direct or indirect source of their problems. Some of the issues responsible for the patients' troubles would, indeed, be left behind if they could but reach escape velocity—oppressive parents, onerous duties, unwanted obligations, endless guilts and frustration, and all the other baggage that, they believed, would no longer harass them. Even some of the staff would probably go with fled in a New York minute.

But first, before any of that could be sorted out, I needed to determine what she really wanted from us in order to try to head off any problems that she (or anyone else) might encounter during her visit. And beyond all this, I hadn't forgotten that I would be shouldering an enormous responsibility in talking with another visitor from the planet K-PAX, both to the hospital and to society at large. Who knew what she might come up with that could be of tremendous benefit to everyone, if only I were astute enough to recognize it?

On Saturday night I went out to look for K-PAX in the constellation Lyra, but of course I couldn't find it–it's too far away. Nevertheless it was prominent in my imagination, as if it were the full moon. Prot was there, and Robert and Giselle and Gene and Oxie and all the others who had made the journey eight years ago, and all the memories came roaring back....

I couldn't wait for Monday to come.

* * *

I went up in my rented Cessna on Sunday morning. It always gives me a sense of perspective to go flying on a beautiful spring day. No telephones ringing, no one knocking on the door–only the sky above and the ground below. And I suspected it might be the last chance I'd have for a while to get away from the events that were sure to engulf us at home and in the hospital.

That afternoon the phone started to ring. Daughter Abby and her husband Steve had decided to come up for a visit, and I was pretty sure I knew why: Abby had told my astronomer son-in-law that fled was here, and he wanted to talk to our alien visitor. Though Karen had already explained that she wasn't interested in astronomical matters, Steve, as always, was undeterred–he wanted to learn whatever he could from her.

Will and Dawn, with daughter Jessica, arrived about the same time. I think Will felt a little guilty about offering to take on fled, only to be rebuffed by hospital director Goldfarb. At the same time, he expressed a sincere interest in discussing her "case," and in helping in whatever way he could. I reminded him that psychiatry is an overworked profession and that his other charges would appreciate his not diluting his efforts on their behalf. He reluctantly agreed, but I could see that the wheels in his head were still turning. I assured him I would consult with him regularly. He is really quite knowledgeable and thoughtful, and I value his opinions very highly. Whatever his motive for showing up, it was wonderful to see our seven-year-old granddaughter, who had just lost an incisor. "When will it grow back in, Grandpa?"

"When you're twenty-two," I told her.

Her eyes became as big as saucers. I laughed so she'd know I was joking.

Even Fred, the actor, called. He couldn't make it because he was doing a matinee and learning his lines for yet another show; he was just curious about fled. I wished I had more to tell him. He had plenty to tell *us*, though, primarily about his finally deciding it was time to settle down. "It gets monotonous, Dad, a different girl every other night. Sometimes juggling two or three at once," he lamented. Karen and I, who have been married for more than forty years, had a good laugh over that.

Jenny was still in California, and presumably didn't yet know about our most recent visitor. But, even if she had, she undoubtedly wouldn't have joined in–she was completely immersed in her long-time obsession, a vaccine against HIV. As always, she had high hopes ("We're getting closer all the time, Dad," she reported in her last call), if not yet an effective serum.

Abby and Steve brought their son Star with them (Rain was busy with his studies at Princeton), and even he hit me for information: "Is she really a talking chimp, Grandpa?" I explained that she wasn't a "chimp," at least as far as I knew, but he wasn't convinced and wanted to come to the hospital to see for himself. Thinking he might be showing some interest in psychiatry, I asked him why. "Talking to a chimp would be 'sooooo cool.'" I refrained, as usual, from asking him if he knew any other adjectives. But what he meant, I think, is that he would be able to favorably impress his friends if he could show them a video or the like. Or perhaps a hair from her head. In any case, he didn't try to push his luck, though he spent a good bit of time videotaping everything that was going on around him–practicing, I suppose, for his directorial debut with fled–and he earned some points by giving Flower a pretty good workout. He is clearly a dog lover, a trait he inherited from his mother.

Abby, who loves all animals, wanted me to encourage fled to visit Africa. She has long been interested in learning what chimpanzees and gorillas really thought about and how they communicated with one another in the wild. In her view, they are far 'smarter' than they're given credit for. "The sign language thing is only the tip of the iceberg," she informed me. "There's a lot they know and understand–and feel–that we can't possibly determine by talking with them in such an unnatural manner."

I tried to explain to her, too, that fled wasn't actually a chimpanzee, or an ape of any kind, though I don't think she heard me.

But it was Steve who was, by far, the most excited. Usually pretty taciturn, my son-in-law, who never fully accepted prot's alien nature despite the latter's profound knowledge of cosmology, reasoned that fled's presence on Earth confirmed our earlier visitor's K-PAX connection, giving them both an added measure of credibility. He wanted to know *everything* she could tell him, especially about the elusive graviton.

I tried to tell *him* that fled didn't seem to be interested in those things. "Ah find that hard to believe," he whined, pressing me about when he could speak with her. I told him I didn't know what her plans were or how much time she had, but would let him know if she would be willing to meet with him.

When everyone was preparing to leave I beseeched them all to be patient. At this point I hadn't yet talked to her in depth myself, and I promised them that they would all get a chance to present their cases when the time was right. Nobody was entirely satisfied with this arrangement, but for once I was holding all the cards, or so I thought. It wasn't long before I learned that fled would be making all the decisions about entertaining visitors and giving interviews, not me.

* * *

Almost as soon as my family had left, the doorbell rang. I figured someone had forgotten something. When I answered the bell I found two men standing at the door. One was quite tall, perhaps 6'6" and very thin, the other maybe a foot shorter and much stockier. Both wore crewcuts and ill-fitting blue suits. They identified themselves as Mr. Dartmouth and Mr. Wang. I had met them before, when they had come to MPI to talk with prot about his knowledge of light travel. Nevertheless, seeming not to recognize me, they waved their badges to identify themselves as Central Intelligence agents, and asked very politely, almost humbly, whether they could come in. Unfortunately, Mr. Dartmouth promptly stumbled on the door sill, plunging forward and banging his face on the tiles. At that moment Flower loped into the living room, barking, surprising agent Wang, who sprung into a defensive crouch. When all the commotion had settled, and Dartmouth had wiped the blood from his nose and the entryway with a huge red handkerchief, they proceeded smartly to the sofa as if they'd been here before, Wang keeping an eye on our dog in case of another surprise "attack."

When they were seated, and had declined my offer of beverages, they got right to the point: what did I know about prot's return?

"*Prot*?"

"Please don't pretend ignorance, doctor. We have our sources."

I was tempted to stonewall, but thought better of it. "I think you mean fled. She's another visitor from K-PAX."

Dartmouth, still dabbing at his nose, pulled out a thick, worn, notepad, with pages sticking out everywhere, and consulted it. He leaned over and whispered something to Wang, who turned to me. "Our sources tell us that prot has returned."

"Your sources are wrong. Who are they, anyway?"

"That's classified."

"Well, he hasn't. Her name is fled."

He nodded to Dartmouth, who crossed out something and penciled in something else. Bits of paper flew from the notebook. He patiently retrieved them and carefully shoved them back in while tweaking his nose from time to time, to determine whether it was broken, presumably.

"My apologies, sir. Can you tell us why she's here?"

At this point it occurred to me that they might have already bugged the house and were merely trying to confirm what I had told Abby, Will, and the others. I repeated that I knew very little about her plans. They wanted to know what little I knew. I told them she had come to study us as alien life forms, and wasn't interested in light energy or weaponry. I declined to mention that she was planning to take 100,000 people with her when she departed, unsure of what they might think of such an idea. Perhaps their sources would fill them in on that. They asked the exact same questions in various other ways until suddenly, as if able to communicate with each other through telepathy or the like, they leaped simultaneously to their feet. "When will you be seeing her again?" Wang pleasantly inquired.

"Tomorrow."

"Thank you, doctor. We'll be in touch." Despite his courteous demeanor, I felt a sudden chill when I looked into his granite eyes.

Flower, a toy in her mouth, escorted them to the front door, Wang shouting, "Back! Back!" They stumbled out of the house and quickly closed the door behind them.

* * *

I was up early on Monday. It was pouring rain, and ordinarily I would've picked a better day to go into the city. But, like the rest of my family (and the federal government, apparently), I couldn't wait to see fled. After all, I didn't know how long she would be on Earth. At least a few weeks, presumably, but who knew? Maybe she had earlier departure opportunities she hadn't mentioned for one reason or another. Emergency escape options, as it were.

I almost couldn't find the front gate of the hospital. Someone had put up one of those plywood walls used by construction crews to hide what was going behind it. Obviously Goldfarb had already made sure that curious onlookers wouldn't see too much.

As I entered the old, familiar building and shook off my umbrella as I had done countless times before, I couldn't believe I was coming in again to *work*. Well, it wasn't work, exactly, I was just chatting with a special visitor. Nevertheless, it was a rather nice feeling, a sort of Indian summer in the winter of my professional life. And as prot would have reminded me, it wasn't really work anyway, not when you're doing something you love. I had been lucky. What I had done for a living was actually fun, a game, little different in its way from being a professional athlete, perhaps. Except, of course, for the money. But for something you love, that's relatively unimportant, isn't it?

A lot of memories flooded my mind as I strode through the first-floor lounge—memories of special breakthrough moments when the veil is lifted and a pure ray of sunlight illuminates the mind of a sick patient. These, unfortunately, are very few, but they're the ones that keep us going, like a great golf shot brings us back to the links. And I remembered the staff members who have since departed but were here when I first arrived at MPI, including my one-time secretary, Joyce Trexler. Even Betty McAllister, our exceptional head nurse, had taken leave to raise her family (triplets are a lot to handle), and Jasmine Chakraborty, our chief clinician for many years, had returned to India. Of course I, too, was no longer on the faculty, and I wondered whether Will and the others ever thought of me as they passed through this venerable corridor....

My first stop was Goldfarb's office to pick up the key to her examination room. I also wanted to ask her how fled had spent the weekend, how she was getting along with the patients, what she thought of them and of humans in general, what her immediate plans were. Virginia's ebullient young secretary, Margie Garafoli, escorted me right into the inner sanctum. "She's been waiting for you," she reported cheerfully. I nodded and watched her go. It's hard to take your eyes off Margie—she's not only pretty, but quite shapely as well. Margie always makes me feel younger somehow.

Goldfarb wasn't much help. Fled had disappeared early Saturday morning and hadn't returned until a few hours ago. There wasn't much point in asking her how our alien visitor had managed to leave the hospital—we both knew the answer to that—but I was somewhat miffed that fled hadn't told me she was planning an early escapade.

"Why?" she demanded. "What would you have done about it?"

I had to confess that I wouldn't have done anything, but added that, if I were to be her "host," I needed to know what she was up to in order to co-ordinate—

"You'll find out soon enough. She doesn't seem to be reticent about telling anyone what's on her mind."

And neither, I thought with an inward smile, are you.

Goldfarb showed me a chart describing fled's physical parameters. Basically, she seemed to be just about what she looked like: her facial features, tooth structure, and blood type were amazingly like those of our earth-bound cousins, the chimpanzees. But her eyes, like prot's, were capable of seeing UV light. Her sensitivity to visible light, however, was considerably less than his, and she apparently had no need for sunglasses, which would have given her an even more comical appearance, like that of a circus performer. The results of the DNA and detailed blood analyses, of course, would have to wait for the lab reports.

I handed back the chart and mumbled something like, "Well, here we go again," as I got up to leave.

"Not quite," she said, with dead seriousness. "She's a different animal, so to speak, from prot. If I were you, I'd watch my back."

* * *

I found fled in the Ward Two (the floor that houses patients with serious neuroses and nonviolent psychoses) game room playing darts with Howard (not to be confused with Howie, a well-known chamber violinist and former inmate). She was wearing a loose-fitting yellow shift, but had nothing on her feet. Perhaps the hospital hadn't been able to find anything big enough to fit them. To my surprise she wasn't surrounded by a cadre of denizens eager to go off with her to K-PAX, as I had expected. The room, in fact, normally filled with a couple of dozen patients engaged in various activities, especially when it was raining outside, was empty except for fled and Howard. "Where is everyone?" I asked him.

The "toad man" candidly informed me that the other inmates, as well as most of the staff, were staying away from fled.

"Why is that?"

"They're repulsed by her."

"Repulsed?" Fled was standing nearby, but for once was keeping her big mouth shut.

"She acts like a talking ape."

"So?"

"They don't want to talk to an ape who can talk back. Especially one who is smarter than they are."

"Why not?"

His bulging eyes took careful aim at the board. "Because she reminds them that they are part ape, too. Nobody seems to be able to deal with that image."

I had imagined many difficulties accruing from fled's visit, but nothing like that one. "What about you, Howard? How are you able to deal with it?"

The dart fluttered toward its target. When it thunked into the wall a foot from the board, he turned back to me. "Dr. Brewer, I'm the ugliest man alive. I have no image to protect."

Even Howard's parents and siblings were repulsed and disgusted by him. He had not been a cute baby—his eyes and mouth, as well as his head itself, were way too big, while his nose and ears were almost nonexistent. "But fled isn't an ape," I reminded him. "She's not even an Earth being."

"No," he agreed, "she's a beautiful orf. But to most people she would be considered ugly. Humans hate ugliness. 'There but for the grace of God . . .' and all that shit." I was afraid he was going to break into tears. His extreme sensitivity to that truth was, in fact, the reason he was with us.

But I didn't want to get into that just then. Instead, I turned to fled. "Do you want to talk here, or would you rather go up to Dr. Goldfarb's examining room?"

"I can't go anywhere. My heart is broken . . . ."

"Listen: you shouldn't take anything the patients—"

"Just joking, doc. Let's go and let the patients have their playroom back." Without looking at the target, she flung a dart sidelong into the bullseye. "Will you excuse us, Howard?"

He nodded dismally and clumped toward the board.

On the way to the elevator (I headed that way; fled turned toward the stairs and I hurried to catch up with her) I asked her what she thought about his observation. "Beauty is truth, yet it's a mystery. It's inseparable from sex, though it's only skin deep in the mind of the beholder. Of its own beauty is the mind diseased, but beauty and virtue rarely go together. It provokes—"

"All right! I get it!"

"Are you sure?"

"Let's talk about something else, shall we?"

"Like what, may I be so bold as to ask?"

"Like where you went over the weekend."

"I visited the place you call Congo."

"Congo?" I panted. "Why Congo?"

"Prot said it was a beautiful spot to visit. Did you know it was called Zaire when he first came here?"

"Was he right?" I wheezed.

"Yes, the government changed its name following—"

I gasped, "I meant was he right about its being beautiful?"

We finally made it to Five. "You know the answer to that, doctor b. Anyway, it's the most beautiful country I've visited so far."

"How many have you visited?"

"Two."

"What's the other one?"

"The United States."

"Oh." Still breathing heavily, barely able to focus my eyes, I unlocked Room 520. As if she wanted to prove she could do it, fled turned the knob with a flair and pushed open the door with her foot. She sprang into the room and promptly nosed around the few papers on the back of the desk, as if she were trying to find something. When she was finished she sat down, not on the patients' chair but on the back of it, her huge bare feet resting on the seat. After contemplating her hairy toes for a moment, I took the one behind Goldfarb's desk.

Fled grinned at me, apparently amused by my awkward situation. "Where's the produce? Prot promised there would be produce!"

"Sorry. I'll try to have some here next time. Bananas will work for you, I presume?"

"I prefer vegetables."

"But I thought—your being a—"

"I'll say it one last time: I'm not a chimpanzee, you numbskull! Get it?"

"I know that."

She glared at me. "It's because I don't look human, like prot, isn't it? You're not a speciesist like most sapiens, are you, doctor b?"

I ignored that absurd comment. "Before we go any further with this, I want to ask you something. Why do you keep calling me disparaging names impugning my intelligence? We consider that to be pretty impolite on our planet."

"Oh, yeah, prot told me about your aversion to the truth."

"But he never called me a numbskull!"

"Yes, the dremers are more tolerant of fools than the rest of us, I'm afraid." She slipped down to the seat of the chair and thrust a huge bare foot on the desk. "All right, I won't call you 'stupid,' unless you say something stupid. Fair enough?"

"For your information, even stupid people don't like to be reminded of their shortcomings."

"Why not?"

"Just take my word for it, all right? Now let's get on with it."

Readers of the *K-PAX* trilogy may remember that I used a tape recorder when interviewing prot. The Manhattan Psychiatric Institute is a research hospital, and I wanted to have our sessions accessible for later study, both for myself and for my colleagues. And the tapes turned out to be invaluable in writing the books that came out of our sessions. Nevertheless, I chose not to be encumbered by such a device during these informal discussions with fled. She wasn't, after all, a patient, and I wasn't actually a practicing psychiatrist any longer. Moreover, at the time these conversations began, I wasn't really contemplating writing a book about her, despite her smart-ass assumption.

I cleared my throat and began the short speech I had prepared on the way in. "I thought we would just establish some ground rules today. So we don't get bogged down in extraneous details or go off on wrong tangents."

"You don't want to waste any of your precious time on 'tangents,' is that it?"

"Well . . . no, I don't. Or yours, either."

"Time is very important to you, isn't it?"

"Yes, I suppose it is. Particularly at my age, when one doesn't know how much of it he has left."

"A very human thing to say."

"And you never think about that?"

"No species but yours thinks about that, gino. Ironic, isn't it, that you waste so much of it worrying about how much you have, rather than living your lives as fully as the other animals on your planet, who never think about it?"

As was often the case with prot, I had already lost control of the situation, which was exactly what I didn't want to do. "Okay, that's one of those tangents—can we just stick to the ground rules?"

"Sounds boring. What are they?"

"There are several. First, can I depend on you to be here when I come in?"

"Depends on when you come in."

"Let's say Mondays and Fridays at about this time."

"Let's say I'll let you know if I won't be here those days."

I had learned enough about aliens to know it was a waste of time to argue with them. "Fine. But can you minimize your absences?"

"When I'm here, I'm absent from somewhere else."

I sighed. "Second thing: I'll ask the questions and you answer them. Fair enough?"

"Depends on the questions. And what if I have questions for *you*?"

"What if you wait until I've asked you all my questions before you ask yours?"

"What if we take turns?"

"Damn it, fled, you promised to cooperate!"

With that she leapt from the chair onto the desk. I admit that this startled me, and I jumped. But it didn't take me long to notice that her shift was pulled up, her legs were spread wide apart, and underneath her garment she wasn't wearing anything.

I turned my head away, but I wasn't sure whether it was from modesty or disgust. "Okay," I stammered, staring at the door, "here's another rule: I sit on this chair, you sit on that one."

She leapt back to her chair, crossed her hairy legs, and placed her chin in her hand, obviously faking a demure seriousness. And with that, our series of discussions began, though most of the time I wasn't sure who was interviewing whom.

"All right. The first thing I want to know is: what were you doing in Congo? Besides sightseeing, of course."

Picking her nose, she replied, "I was looking for the nonhuman apes."

"Nonhuman?"

"Humans are a part of the ape family. Didn't you know that, doc?"

"I'm not an ape."

"Spoken like a true speciesist." She rolled the contents of a nostril between her fingers and popped it into her mouth.

Though unable to fully conceal my disgust, I nevertheless forged ahead. "And did you find—?"

"Not many. Most have been exterminated."

"Most of what?"

"Chimpanzees, gorillas, baboons, monkeys—you name it."

"Who exterminated them?"

She snorted. "You're playing dumb again, aren't you, gene? That might work for your human patients, but not for the rest of us."

"No, I mean, isn't it illegal to—uh—exterminate an ape?"

"You ever hear of the bushmeat trade, doctor? Not to mention murdering the parents so you can kidnap their babies to sell for pets? Or anything else that's profitable?"

"Bushmeat??"

"Why don't you just get a hearing aid and save the rest of us a lot of grief?"

This particular K-PAXian seemed to annoy me more and more by the minute. "All right, goddamn it—I'll try not to repeat myself! By 'bushmeat,' you mean—"

"That's it exactly. Ape brains for supper."

"Would you *please* stop reading my mind? It's quite disconcerting to a human being, you know."

She saluted. "Sure, boss. Just trying to save you some precious time."

"Thank you!"

"That's how aids got started, you know. Humans eating monkey brains."

"Yes, I've heard that."

"And now you've got mad cow and bird flu. Not to mention heart disease, cancer, and on and on. Leave the animals alone, doc—you'll live longer."

"Thanks again. As I was about to say, there are still millions of apes and—uh—other things in Africa, aren't there, even with this 'bushmeat' trade?"

"Try 'thousands.' Maybe a few hundred thousands if you include all the great apes on EARTH, but their numbers are decreasing by the minute. It's only the sapiens who are forever on the increase."

"Well, did you run across a few apes? And if you did, what did you find out about them? You *did* come to *study* them, didn't you?"

"No, you cretin. I came to *learn* from them. Something most of you humans haven't opted to do yet."

"All right—what did you learn from them?"

"Plenty. They're sick and tired of trying to hide from the 'naked beasts,' as they refer to you. Especially since they haven't done anything to justify your endless persecution."

Suddenly she grinned and a leg shot up to the desk. Are you sure you don't want to—"

"No, I don't."

"You must have read my mind."

"Never mind that! If you don't stop coming on to me I'm going to throw you out of here and you can find someone else to 'put you up.'"

"It's because I'm an 'ape,' isn't it?"

"No! I mean—well, yes, that's part of it. We don't have sex with animals on this planet."

"I'm no more or less an animal than you are! What you mean is that you're a *speciesist*. Aren't you? *Aren't* you?" She began to play with herself.

I turned away again. "No, damn it! I just don't want to have intimate relations with a— With a goddamn *ape*!"

"Speciesist! Speciesist!"

I stood up. "That's all the time we have for today. I'll see you on Friday." I started toward the door before adding, "But only if you promise to behave yourself!"

"I *am* behaving myself, doc," she shouted back. "On K-PAX it would be impolite for an orf not to make the offer. If you don't like great sex, that's your problem."

I sighed. "Good-bye, fled. Until Friday." I shuffled out and down the stairs, leaving her to amuse herself in whatever way she found polite.

* * *

Hoping that fled wasn't following me I ducked into the quiet room to collect my thoughts and plan my next discussion with her. Instead, I ran into "Dr." Claire Smith, who believes she's a staff psychiatrist. She was reading a journal. The problem with a patient like this is that she, in fact, knows a lot about psychiatry—in some areas, more than most of the staff, perhaps. Certainly more than I, retired and beginning to fall out of touch with the literature and the latest developments. Claire loves to offer advice to her "colleagues," and yes, we often humor her in this to avoid triggering a severe depression.

I sat down beside her at the reading table and brought up the subject of fled. She gave me a knowing smile and pointed to a recent article she was reading, "The

Non-Human Psychiatric Patient." At first I imagined a doctor with a pig or a cow lying on his examining couch. But it was about patients who believe they are not human, and I must confess that I hadn't yet read it. Nor would I have been likely to had "Dr. Smith" not brought it to my attention. "So you've met her," I deduced.

"Yes, I have," she admitted. "What do you think of her?"

Claire had a way of turning the tables like that. "Well, I really don't know *what* to make of her. But some of the patients don't seem to like her much. Do you have any thoughts about that?"

"She's new here. Everyone is suspicious of a new patient. You never know what's going on in their heads."

"It doesn't bother you that she seems to be some kind of ape?"

"Well, she smells a little funny, but you know the olfaction theory. We all smell a little different from everyone else. It's genetic, of course."

"Of course." I pointed to the journal lying in front of her. "What's the gist of the article?"

"I wasn't aware that certain mental patients are convinced they're animals of some sort, were you? For the most part, it's an extreme type of inferiority complex. When you're treated like a dog, you eventually begin to act like one, and finally you become one. Fascinating, don't you agree?"

"So you think that's what's happened to fled? That she's become an ape because she was treated like one?"

She pondered this for a moment. "Not exactly. I would say that she's got some sort of condition–maybe an overabundance of one or another steroid–where she grows hair all over her body. When that happened, she became more and more apelike. It's a defense mechanism, you see. So people wouldn't laugh at her for being so hairy."

This made perfect sense, and I had to admit she could be right, except for one thing. "What about the fact that she's from another planet?"

"She's no more from another planet than you are, Gene."

I was stunned by this assessment. Although I had been convinced of her extraterrestrial origin by fled's apparent acquaintanceship with prot, it suddenly occurred to me that she had done nothing to demonstrate this fact. True, she had left the hospital for a couple of days, and she had shown me a device something like a 3-D movie projector, but– Shit! I thought. Will it ever be possible to know whether these endless visitors are really telling the truth? Even with all the evidence that had accumulated for prot's otherworldly nature, I still wasn't 100% convinced that even he had come from K-PAX. Ninety-nine, maybe, but can we ever be totally sure of *anything*?

* * *

My confidence took another jolt when I stopped in to see Will. I found him sitting at his desk staring at the wall, contemplating the solution to some problem or other, presumably. I didn't realize it was the same one as mine.

Normally when I stop in we chat about the family, as well as some of his patients. This time he wanted to talk about fled. I told him about Claire's suggestion that she might be one of the rare "animal" patients. But what he came back with was even more startling than that. "I've been thinking, Dad. Prot was an alien, or so it seems, but he also fit the pattern for a dissociative identity disorder, right?"

"No question about that, at least."

"So here we have fled claiming to be from the planet K-PAX, and I think she is. But at the same time, could she have some other personalities as well, like prot did? Could there be someone on Earth who may or may not look much like her, but who nevertheless has had similar life experiences?"

I don't know why I hadn't thought of such an obvious possibility myself. "Son, you may be right! But if you are, how would we go about finding her? Or him? In prot's case, we had an idea of where his roots on Earth were planted, and eventually what kind of person Robert Porter was. In fled's case, we haven't a clue."

Will's eyebrows curled into a deep frown, as they do when he is thinking. He jokingly suggested we put her image on milk cartons to see if anyone recognized her. More seriously he wondered, "Do you suppose all K-PAXians have an alter ego somewhere on Earth? Or to look at it the other way, do all of us have an alter ego living a similar life to our own on some faraway planet? It's pretty mind-boggling, don't you think?"

"So how would you suggest we go about finding the right person among the six billion or so candidates?" I asked him.

His eyebrows relaxed. "Same as with prot," he said. "Dig into her mind, find out exactly who's lurking there."

"You mean hypnosis?"

"It's the only way. Unless you want to drug her."

It didn't take long for me to realize that Will was absolutely right about that as well. The answers to all our questions about her were hiding somewhere in fled's brain. I wasn't sure I was the right person to go digging for them, but I sure as hell wanted to try. The old excitement was coming back. Maybe I wasn't as far over the hill as I thought. Wishful thinking, perhaps, but so what? As far as I've been able to tell, life itself is, in large part, wishful thinking.

While driving up the Henry Hudson toward the GW Bridge, however, I experienced a revelation of my own. Based on fled's promiscuous behavior, it seemed quite likely to me that her alter ego(s), if any, could well be a prostitute. That, I assumed, narrowed down the field somewhat. But if milk cartons were out of the question for such a search, what should I do: put a notice on the Internet advertising for ugly whores to send in their résumés?

* * *

When I got home at about lunchtime, Karen told me Goldfarb had called. The first thing that occurred to me was that our alien visitor had come on to another staff member or patient, and she wanted me to speak to me about fled's wantonness. I was as concerned about that as she was, and returned the call immediately. But it wasn't fled's sexual impropriety she was worried about, at least not at the moment. A couple of requests for interviews had already come in, one for network television and another for a British magazine.

"How the hell did they—"

"I don't know, Gene. But that's irrelevant now, wouldn't you say? The question is, what are we going to do about this?"

"Hey, I'm retired, remember? The question is, what are *you* going to do about it? If you want her to talk to someone else instead of me, you have my total consent." I already regretted saying this, but, like prot and fled, Goldfarb sometimes seemed to push the wrong buttons.

"Hold on, Dr. B. You always were too excitable." I detected a little snort. "I suppose that's why your patients all liked you. Made you seem more human."

"Thank you. I think."

"Here's the deal. The network is offering us $200,000 for a live production. The magazine 10,000 pounds sterling, which is around $20,000, I believe. We can't afford to turn down manna like that. All I'm asking is that you coordinate the thing so the hospital isn't totally disrupted by these extracurricular activities."

"Retired. Retired."

"Will you think about it?"

I caught my wife out of the corner of my eye. She was frowning in the manner that I recognized as: *listen and don't say anything stupid until you've thought about it.* "Okay," I told Goldfarb, "I'll think about it. But I should remind you that prot wouldn't let us take any money for his TV appearance, and fled probably won't, either."

"I won't tell her about the money if you don't. So when will I see you again?"

"I was planning to come in on Mondays and Fridays."

"Can you make Wednesday an administrative day? To take care of this sort of thing?"

"I'll think about it."

"Would a regular paycheck help you decide?"

We needed some remodeling done. "Might."

I could see that knowing smile beaming all the way up from the city. "See you Wednesday," she said, and hung up.

During lunch I filled Karen in on what had just transpired, followed by a report on my conversation with Will. She was almost as fascinated as I was by his suggestion that perhaps our visitor had an alter ego somewhere on Earth. "You're hooked again, aren't you?"

I had to admit I was, and that I was eagerly anticipating getting to the bottom of the "fled story," wherever it might lead. "But there are a lot of negatives creeping into it, too," I pointed out. "It's not only the demands on my time that bother me about going back to the hospital a few days a week, it's talking with fled herself. She wants to have sex with me!"

After a momentary frown, my wife burst out laughing.

"What—you don't think I can do it?"

We both laughed at this absurd notion. When we slowed down a little, I added, "Given her promiscuity, it occurred to me that her alter ego might be a prostitute. What do you think?"

"Don't jump to any conclusions, Dr. B," she advised.

* * *

That evening Dartmouth and Wang called on us again. "May we come in, Dr. Brewer?" they begged simultaneously, brandishing their badges and promising, "We won't take much of your time," as if they had been in on my conversation with fled.

I stepped back. Dartmouth eyed the entryway suspiciously, as if it were mined. Wang, for his part, quickly covered his crotch when Flower appeared, wagging her tail hopefully. We proceeded to the living room sofa as before. The government gazed around, apparently searching for anything out of the ordinary. I thought I heard one or two clicking sounds, like the opening of a camera shutter hidden in a button or tie, but perhaps it was only a wisp of wind being passed.

Wang got right to the point. "Sir, we can't let your—uh—visitor take 100,000 people with her when she goes back to K-PAX." If I still had any doubt about fled's origins, they certainly did not.

For some reason, I became annoyed by their assumption that I had any control over fled. "What's that got to do with *me*?"

"Everything. You are her host. Whatever she does is your responsibility."

"You're kidding, right?"

Wang stared at me icily while Dartmouth fiddled with a button on his jacket.

"Look: the woman travels on a beam of light. What do you expect me to do, seal her up in an unlighted room?"

They glanced at each other briefly, as if seriously considering this offhand remark. But before I could explain that this wouldn't work, Wang added, "How you do it is up to you, doctor. But we would have to make certain that no Americans are going with her."

I didn't ask them how they planned to make certain of it. "You mean anyone outside the U.S. could go?"

"We have no authority in other sovereignties," Wang reluctantly confessed. "If she wants to take 100,000 Middle Easterners, that's their concern." Suddenly Dartmouth looked up at the ceiling and began to follow something with his eyes, as if there were a tiny insect flitting around up there.

"Here's what I can do. I'll pass on your apprehension to fled. What she does with it is up to her."

"Thank you, sir. We'd appreciate that. And one more thing: we'd like for you to keep tabs on how her travel plans for the return trip are progressing. You know, the when, the where, that sort of thing. We'll take care of the rest."

I mumbled a noncommittal response. Apparently they hadn't yet heard about the proposed magazine and television ventures. Or perhaps they had no problem with those. In any case, they jumped simultaneously to their feet. Dartmouth started to fall back onto the sofa, but whirled around rapidly instead, somehow ending up facing me again. "We'll let you get on with your dinner, sir," he volunteered (I wasn't aware it was being prepared). At this point Flower ran at Wang with her squeaky fish. He immediately crouched into his defensive position, hands in chopping mode. I called her away before she could sustain some kind of freak accident.

"We'll be in touch," they cried in unison as they backed toward the door. I heard Dartmouth trip again in the entryway, but apparently Wang caught him before he crashed to the tiles.

CHAPTER THREE

The joys of (partial) retirement: Karen and I spent Tuesday morning and part of the afternoon wallpapering the guest bathroom in pastel blue and yellow flowers with dark green leaves.

When I checked my e-mail that evening I was surprised to discover more than a dozen messages requesting information about fled. The following is typical.

Hello, Dr. Brewer!

I hear you've got another visitor from K-PAX! What's she like? Can you ask her to take me and my girlfriend once around the world? Are you going to write another book about this?

Reasonable questions from interested people. I sent the same reply to all of them:

How did you know about fled's visit?

A few minutes later the responses started to dribble in.

It was on the news. They had pictures of her on top of the Empire State Building, the Eiffel Tower, the Great Wall of China, and some other places.

Obviously she wasn't keeping her presence on Earth a secret. Was she trying to get the attention of the United Nations? Or just showing off?

* * *

I hadn't seen Jerry, our matchstick engineer, for quite a while, so I came in early on Wednesday for an overdue visit. I found him where he almost always is, sitting beside his latest model, the Manhattan Psychiatric Institute itself, complete with the new Villers wing. Now in his mid-thirties, Jerry has done little else during his entire stay with us except for his amazing creations, which are scattered around not only the Ward Three (seriously psychotic patients) activity room, but on other floors as well.

I didn't say anything for a minute or two, just watched with profound admiration. His patience and the intricacy of his work are astonishing, all the more so since he has rarely been outside the building except to the big lawn facing Amsterdam Avenue, which allows him a view of only part of the hospital. Yet all the sides–the ones he has finished, anyway–are in perfect proportion, with uncanny accuracy in the smallest details. But I suppose if any of us were to virtually ignore our relationships with other people, as he (and other severe autists) does, who knows what we might accomplish.

He knew I was there, of course. Though he rarely speaks, there were little signs: a desultory humming, an occasional shuffling of feet. Ten years earlier he wouldn't have paid the slightest bit of attention to me. When I first tried to make some kind of contact with him he almost seemed fearful, and certainly resented the intrusion. More recently, he almost seems to be glad to have me around. Or at least tolerates my presence without noticeable annoyance. Maybe it's a matter of wearing down his resistance–a point for every visit that doesn't cause him undue distress. Whatever the reason, he sometimes gives me a hug when I leave him. He doesn't say anything, or even look at me, but I can often discern a hint of a smile. Whatever he feels about this superficial contact (maybe it isn't superficial to him!) I feel very good about it. As if it's a small victory of sorts. I only hope he feels the same way.

When I gave him his brief hug and said, "'Bye, Jer," before leaving the room, I expected his usual, "'Bye, Jer," in return. Instead, without taking his eyes off his newest work, he whispered, "Fled."

"You want to meet her?"

A pause, followed by a vigorous nod.

"Why, Jerry?" I asked him, not expecting an answer.

As if his throat were constricted, he stuttered, "I think she c-can fix me."

I don't know where he got this idea, and perhaps he didn't, either. "But you haven't met her yet, have you?"

He shook his head.

"Then why do you think she can help you?"

I thought maybe he didn't understand the question until he grunted, "Howard."

"Howard told you she can fix you?"

He nodded again.

I warned him that fled wasn't like prot, who had broken through Jerry's communication barrier years before. But he knew that already, or didn't care. The main thing was that she wasn't human, whom severe autists can often barely relate to. "Sure, Jerry," I assured him. "I'll speak to her." It had been, after all, the first time I could remember him requesting anything other than matchsticks.

* * *

While traipsing around the lawn looking for fled I spotted a couple of patients staring up at the sky. Curious, I ambled over. Rick was telling one of our newest inmates that the sky was actually green, though some people see it as blue. "That's why grass is green, Barney. It's just a reflection of the light from the sky."

It was a mystery at first whether Rick saw things differently from the rest of us or was simply an incorrigible liar. It now seems clear that it's a combination of both. Regardless of whether he knows he's lying or not, however, the outcome is the same: no one can believe a word he says. As if he were a used-car salesman, he is the most unpopular of all our inmates. Indeed, most patients are religious about telling the truth, at least their own truth, and they expect the others to do the same. Trust is a very important issue among our inmates, just as it is with the general public.

Prot once suggested Rick go into politics.

Rocky actually goes out of his way to avoid Rick, calling him, simply, "the fucking liar." Fortunately, for all his bottled-up anger, Rocky has never physically harmed anyone, as far as we know. Otherwise, we would have to transfer him to Ward Four, which houses the sociopaths. One of the former denizens of that floor is Charlotte, whom I spotted watering the flowers along the back wall. A confessed killer of at least seven young men, hers is a classic case of a patient who almost miraculously responded to a new medication, and she is now as docile as anyone here.

While observing Charlotte I was almost tackled by Georgie. With an IQ of forty, which is well below even most autistic savants, his interests are focused exclusively on football. For several frenetic moments at a time he kicks or tosses a ball high into the air, then runs and catches it–over and over again until he is exhausted. The rest of the time he sits and stares at whatever captures his attention: a flower, a brick, a face. Though short and wiry he is nevertheless dangerous at full speed, and the other patients try to hug the walls when he's active. When he is resting they are quite solicitous of his needs, quite unlike their attitude toward Rick.

The latter was delighted when Barney arrived at the hospital. But the ease with which he is deceived is not the reason Barney is a patient at MPI. Since birth he has never been known to laugh. He's not suffering from a pathological depression, however, like former patient Bess, for example. In fact, he seems to be reasonably happy. It's just that he sees no humor in any situation, no matter how silly. As a child he was unable even to smile at clowns, animals in human clothing, simple jokes. He made it through high school, albeit with difficulty, and his family, owners of a prominent dry cleaning establishment in the city, finally brought their nineteen-year-old son to us to see if anything could be done.

Though we don't usually accept such harmless neuroses, the blank check offered by the family was too enticing to refuse (it allows us to take on a few charity cases as well). His psychiatrist, who happens to be my own son, is stymied, as are the rest of the staff. However, we were given only a limited amount of time to come up with a drug or protocol that might help him find a bit of humor in his life. A life without which, in the eyes of most people, including his parents, is no life at all.

Apparently understanding this sad truth, many of the other patients try to help us out with Barney—making funny faces, doing pratfalls and all the rest. So far, nothing has worked, not even a talking chimpanzee.

* * *

I went in to see Goldfarb. She wasn't there, but Margie handed me a manila folder containing the information about the proposed television and magazine interviews. I flipped through the few pages inside.

As far as I could see, no harm could come from a magazine article. But the TV show was a different matter entirely. Apparently it was supposed to be a live "reality" show, with the patients going about their usual routines while interviews with the staff would be cut in wherever it was deemed appropriate. It's true that prot had appeared on one of the popular talk shows, but his segment had been taped prior to telecast and, in any case, his was a very different personality from fled's. What the hell would happen if this particular K-PAXian exposed herself live in front of millions of viewers? I didn't like the odds on that. All such considerations would become moot, however, unless she agreed to appear before the cameras. As far as I knew, Virginia hadn't yet spoken to her about it. That, apparently, was my responsibility.

"Is she here, Margie?"

"Who—Dr. Goldfarb or fled?"

"Fled."

"I don't know. Should I page her for you?"

"No, not yet. Any feedback on what she's been up to lately?"

"She's spent a lot of time playing on Dr. Goldfarb's old computer. I guess they don't have many of those on K-PAX."

"When will she be back?"

"Fled or Dr. Goldfarb?"

"The latter."

"You're already penciled in for lunch with her at 12:30. Is that convenient for you?"

"I guess so. I'll just call my wife and—"

"Want me to take care of that for you?"

"Sure. Oh, and can you see that there is a bowl of vegetables in Dr. Goldfarb's examining room?"

She flashed a lovely smile. "Any particular kind?"

"I don't know. Just have the kitchen send up whatever they have." I returned the folder to her and headed to the main lounge hoping to find fled. Unfortunately, she wasn't there. Instead, I found her on the lawn near the front wall, defecating. The patients in the vicinity ignored her. I signaled an orderly to take care of the mess.

When she was finished I motioned for her to come over. Unlike chimpanzees, who run on all fours using the knuckles of their hands, she loped over to me on two. A bit angry at her inconsideration, I started to berate her, only to realize that she wasn't a child or a trained animal, but an adult obeying her normal instincts. I did, however, suggest to her that, on this planet, we don't use the hospital lawn as a toilet.

She roared with laughter. "You mean I'm supposed to hold it in?"

"No, dammit. You're supposed to use the facilities inside, like everyone else."

"It's odd, don't you think, that sapiens are so repulsed by natural processes and not by wars and slaughterhouses and the like?" She wagged her head. "Anyway, the first rain will wash it away."

"There's no rain in the immediate forecast," I informed her. "And we have patients here who might—"

"Oh yes, prot told me there are people here who go apeshit over fecal matter. I can't see it myself–it must be an acquired taste. But in the future I'll dump elsewhere. Happy?"

"Delirious. Now how about another little talk? It looks like I'll be coming in three days a week instead of two."

"How fun!"

I couldn't tell whether she was genuinely excited or merely mocking me. But she took the stairs three at a time to Goldfarb's examining room. "I'm taking the elevator!" I shouted after her.

A very large bowl of broccoli sat on the desk. Perhaps, I hoped, it would take her mind off her preoccupation with sex, at least for the duration of our discussion. We sat down in our usual chairs and she dug in, but not before scrutinizing a stalk and carefully peeling off part of the outer layer.

I had made a mental list of the topics I wanted to cover in the conversation, paramount of which was her promiscuousness. After she had stuffed her mouth with the broccoli I laid down the law. "No sex in this office. Agreed?"

She looked up in apparent shock. "Are you sure? I guarantee you'll have no problem 'getting it up.' Agreed?"

"NO!"

"Okay, coach. But if you change your mind . . ."

"You're wasting your time."

Fled shook her head. "There's that time thing again. For your information, time can't be 'wasted,' gino. It just *is*, and there isn't a damn thing you can do about it."

"Never mind that. Do we have an understanding?"

"It's your loss. But I can't force you–we K-PAXians aren't rapists."

"I'm relieved to hear that. Next thing on the agenda today are some invitations we've had for you. Did anyone tell you about these?"

"Yes, I saw Virginny not more than twenty-six minutes ago. Sounds interesting."

"You have no problem with going on a live television show?"

"Why should I?"

"And you would agree to behave yourself?"

"You mean according to human standards."

"Exactly."

"Oh, what the hell. I guess I could try to be dull and stupid for a little while."

"Then it's okay if we accept the invitation? And for the magazine article as well?"

"Why not?" She burped softly and politely covered her mouth with the back of her hand. "Excuse me," she whispered politely, batting her eyes. I wasn't sure whether to laugh or cry.

"Okay, next thing: Uh . . ." I looked over the sketchy notes I had compiled for the meeting. "Is there anyone in particular that you came to Earth to see?"

"You mean like Robert Porter—somebody like that?"

As usual, she was way ahead of me. "Well, yes. How did you know about—oh, prot told you."

"Not everything. I read your books in the library. Fascinating." She paused and stared at me, her mouth full of ground-up florets. "Did you ever decide whether he was from K-PAX or not?"

"Very funny. But let's get back to the question, shall we? Did you—"

"I heard you the first time. Nope, there are no Robert Porters up here." She pecked on her cranium.

I had no reason to doubt this. On the other hand, there could well be personalities she wasn't aware of. "All right, let me ask you this: It occurs to me that I really don't know much about you except that you're an orf, one of the evolutionary stages before the dremers, and more specifically a trod, the final step in that process. Am I right so far?"

"Close enough." She peeled another piece of broccoli, bit off the stem and proceeded to crunch it, baring her teeth and sluicing it around in her mouth as if it were a hot potato. As she chewed, she vigorously scratched her ribs with another stalk. A bit of green saliva dripped from her protruding lips. So much for etiquette.

I tried to disregard her repulsive table manners. "Okay. So tell me the rest."

"The rest of what?" she mumbled through the macerated vegetable.

"Where you were born, what your childhood was like, what sexual experiences you've had, do you have any children of your own—that sort of thing."

"Ah. You want an autobiography."

"Well, not minute by minute. Just the highlights."

"All right, I'll sum it up for you. Without going into any of the tiresome details, of course . . . ." With a fingernail, she picked at the bits of broccoli stuck in her teeth and facial hair.

"Fine"—I waved my hand impatiently—"please proceed."

She flung her feet onto the desk and began. "First, we trods aren't as nomadic as the dremers. We like the woods or, more correctly, the little clumps of trees here and there. There isn't enough water on K-PAX to support the kinds of forests you still have on B-TIK. That is, if some fernad hasn't burned them all down overnight."

"Fernad?"

"Anal orifice. Anus. Or asshole, if you prefer. You know—like your president and his wealthy corporate cronies."

"Thank you for clearing that up."

She paused for a moment, apparently deep in thought. "On K-PAX, childhood is wonderful for everyone. All our species interact from the beginning, and none would think of hurting any of the others. I rolled around with korms and homs and— Oh, you probably want EARTHLIKE equivalents, right? Well, we have all kinds of primates, reptiles, insects, every kind of land creature you can imagine, and a lot more. No sea beings though. For that you need a sea. And birds of every size and color. All of us can communicate with everyone else, so we chatter about whatever comes to mind. Your children start out this way, too, equal to and with empathy for other animals, but it's quickly driven out of them. You tell them the other species are 'dirty,' or 'dangerous.' But on K-PAX, everyone enjoys every minute of his or her life, you see, without fear of dirt or danger. You probably can't imagine such a situation, total freedom from fear of any kind, can you?"

I declined to comment on that. "Does everyone speak the same language?"

"Well, some creatures don't speak, of course. Not in the way you mean. But for those who do, certainly. On EARTH, even the humans have several hundred languages among them. It's as if no one wants to communicate with anyone else."

"Go on."

"So early on we find out what's good to eat and where to find it, why there are stars and galaxies, where babies come from, and so on. You know—the important things. And of course we learn to share everything. We aren't taught to take whatever we want from someone else, like certain beings I could spit on."

"Let's try to focus on—"

"Yes, I didn't think you'd want to talk about that. Anyway, on K-PAX it's different. As I started to say before the rude interruption, as children we spend a lot of our time, together or individually, just sitting and looking at the fields, and the mountains, and the sky, and all the things that are going on there—you know, the *totality* of it. How it's all related, and how the littlest thing would change the balance and ruin everything. We absorb that at a very young age. And when it gets dark, which doesn't happen often because of our two suns, practically everyone on the PLANET lies down and contemplates the sky. It's probably the most beautiful thing there is. Most of the beings on your WORLD, on the other hand, can't even *see* the sky, your cities are so polluted by your streetlights and neon advertising and all the rest. Not that it matters: hardly anyone would look anyway. Have you ever noticed that your fellow sapiens don't care about much, doc? Except themselves, of course. Not their fault—that's how they've been taught. Anyhoo, on K-PAX we never get enough of the sky. I suppose that's why we start wandering around the galaxy at an early age—it's such a natural part of our existence." She paused to take a breath. "I don't know which is more fascinating to the children of K-PAX: the sky or sex."

Ah, I thought. Now we're getting somewhere. "Your *children* are interested in sex? When does puberty happen?"

"At birth."

"Birth?? Good God! And you remember that occasion, right?"

"Of course."

"Do you recall your first sexual encounter?"

"I remember everything."

"No lapses. No sessions with a krolodon (a memory-restoring device)."

"Nope. Never needed one."

"Who was your first experience with?"

"A little boy I knew."

"Knew? You don't know him now?"

"I see him once in a while. But he's not a boy any more."

"And do you remember him fondly when you see him?"

"Not especially. It was just a brief encounter. Not one of your 'love affairs.' We don't have soap operas on K-PAX."

"Well, do you remember *all* of your sexual encounters?"

"Not in intimate detail, I suppose. But basically, yes. Don't you?"

"No."

"Pity."

"And nothing traumatic happened during those early years? Unpleasant? Frightening?"

"You mean sex-wise?"

"Any-wise."

"Not really. Unless you count my mother leaving me when I was weaned."

"How old were you then?"

"About one EARTH year, give or take a few weeks. She just got itchy feet, as you sapiens so descriptively put it."

"And you never saw her again?"

"No." She stopped chewing for a moment and stared off into space. Thinking about the good times with her mother before she disappeared, I presumed.

"And your later years? Anything traumatic, unusual?"

She snapped back to attention. "Not really. Some extraplanetary adventures, nothing to e-mail home about."

"Just sex and more sex, is that it?"

"Whenever possible."

An interesting, if rather distasteful, thought suddenly came to me. "Fled, you don't have sex with *all* those other K-PAX species, do you?"

"Well, not with spiders or worms, of course. But with other species, sure. And if the genus is different, there can never be any children to complicate the issue. No pun intended. Didn't you ever have a biology course, gino?"

"Not one on K-PAXian biology," I replied, with some exasperation.

"Well, that part's the same as it is here. And on all the other PLANETS I've visited, too. Of course the shoe has to fit before you can wear it . . . ."

"The shoe—ah, I see what you mean. All right, then, tell me: do you experience any pain when you have sex?"

"Are you kidding? Do I look like a masochist to you?"

"Can you tell me why the dremers have that problem?"

"No idea, coach. Why didn't you ask prot?"

In fact, that's one thing I didn't ask him—whether he knew why it was so physically painful for his species. I've kicked myself every day for that little oversight. "So you've had sex with how many partners? Of whatever species."

She scratched her head. "Well, let me see. There was oker, and rabo and—"

"Not all the names. Just—"

"Oh, I don't know—ten thousand, maybe."

"And with members of your own species? No pun intended."

"Who knows? A few thousand, probably?"

"Good God. And how many—uh—children do you have?"

"None."

"None?"

"You're playing deaf again, gene. You're a psychiatrist; why do you suppose you do that?"

I chose to ignore that comment. "You mean you use contraceptives?"

She grinned, perhaps amused by my ignorance. "No, it's just the opposite. On K-PAX, in order to produce children, you need to add something to the recipe that stimulates the fusion of sperm and egg. If you don't have that ingredient, nothing happens."

"How fortunate for you. And what is this magic potion you need for procreation on K-PAX?"

"It's not an 'potion.' It's a fruit."

"What fruit?"

"Sugar plums."

"And you've never had a sugar plum?"

"Once or twice. They're delicious! But then I abstained from sex with another orf for a while."

"Does this mean you don't want any children?"

"No one on K-PAX wants any children, boss, or very few. Otherwise, we'd soon be overwhelmed with adults. That's a no-brainer, wouldn't you say? Everywhere but on EARTH, anyway."

"How old are you, fled?"

"Twenty-three, in EARTH terms."

"So from the time you were born until now, you've had sex innumerable times, and with any number of other species, correct?"

"Pretty much. But why this sudden prurient interest?"

I paused for a moment before asking, not certain that I wanted to know the answer, "Have you had sex with anyone since you've been on Earth?"

"Of course."

I had to ask: "Any humans?"

"A few."

I paused again before following up with: "Any of the patients?"

"One or two."

"For God's sake, fled! That's one of the rules here—no sex with the patients!!"

"Oh, the rules! The rules! When are you people going to loosen up?"

"Dammit, which ones?"

"I don't screw and tell. You'll have to ask *them*."

"Thanks a lot."

"Welcome."

"Uh . . . did you happen to have a sugar plum at the time?"

"Not to worry, dear sir. I didn't bring any yorts with me this trip."

"I'm glad to hear that. All right—I just have one or two more questions."

"Ah, your endless questions. Prot warned me about those."

"Never mind prot. It's you I'm concerned with right now. You seemed to imply that you had a simple, delightful childhood on K-PAX, full of sex and skywatching. I just want to ask you one last time whether there were any—uh—serious issues back then."

"Like bathing a stranger in a hollow log with a fallid leaf?"

"Or any other unexplained incidents that have happened to you."

"None that I can remember. And I have a pretty good memory."

"Even so, I'd like to put you under hypnosis the next time we meet. That okay with you? Do you know how it works?"

"No, and neither do you. But why the quackery? What are you looking for?"

"If I knew that, I wouldn't have to look for it, would I? I just wanted to know if there's anything significant you've forgotten."

"Why would I forget anything significant?"

"That's what I'm hoping the hypnosis will tell me."

"Sure. I'll play your silly little game." Her head fell suddenly and she seemed to fall asleep.

I had to chuckle at this. "Okay, fled, you can wake up now. We'll do it on Friday. Will you be here then?"

Her eyes came open slowly. "Is— Is it over?"

"Yes, except for one or two more things. I was wondering whether you're planning another trip to Congo or elsewhere. Will you be here Friday or not?"

She grabbed another stalk of broccoli and bit off the head. "Let me consult my calendar." She went for the one on Goldfarb's desk, pretended to check it. "As it happens, I'm free that morning." She tossed it back to where it had been lying.

"No more trips until then?"

"Did I say that?"

"Not really."

"Has my obligation for today been satisfied, then?"

"Not quite. You might be interested to know that the U.S. government takes a dim view of your taking 100,000 people to another planet. Especially if any of them are Americans."

"No doubt. That's 100,000 less robots to buy stuff they don't need, right?"

"Well, it's probably a little more complicated than that."

"Very little more. And how do they plan to stop me if I decide to take an American or two? That is, if I can find any who meet the criteria."

"They didn't say."

"Oooh. I'm skeered." The rest of the stalk disappeared into her maw.

"Let me tell you something, fled." I waited until the munching had stopped and I had her attention. "The government–maybe all governments–may be bumbling idiots, but they're dangerous ones, nevertheless."

"That's why we don't have them on K-PAX!"

"Yes, I know. Well, you've been warned. Ignore it at your own risk."

"Much obliged. That it for now, pardner?"

"For now, yes, we're finished."

She grabbed another handful of broccoli. "Good stuff, but how about a little more variety next time? See you Friday, doc." She strolled out of the room, leaving me to wonder about the possible consequences if she tried to leave our planet with 100,000 of us in tow. And, on the other hand, what consequences we might expect if she didn't show up on K-PAX at the appointed time.

* * *

I joined Goldfarb in the faculty dining room. We usually meet informally once a month or so to discuss administrative matters (I was acting hospital director for a while before she got the job), and she sometimes asks for what she calls my "conservative" opinon. Generally, I look forward to these meetings, especially the food, which is no longer limited to the cottage cheese of my working days. But today the subject was fled, a very wiggly worm in a whole can of them. I was already beginning to re-evaluate my poorly-considered volunteering to "supervise" her while she was on Earth.

"Too late for that, Gene," she pleasantly reminded me before whipping out the familiar folder with the information about the television and magazine interviews.

The former was to be a full-fledged network pilot for a reality series featuring various settings of interest to the public–hospital emergency rooms, police precincts, military camps, and the like. According to the attached blurb, the individual episodes would attempt to "put the viewer into intimate contact with the raw inner workings of these fascinating cauldrons of human drama." A mental hospital wasn't originally planned to lead off the series, but fled's visit changed all that. They wanted to feature her in the show as a "special guest." "Such an opportunity is not to be missed," the info sheet concluded. Nevertheless, the focus of the program(s) would be the day-to-day interactions between the inmates.

The proposal involved setting up their equipment on the lawn for a full day (June 15th, from six A.M. to ten P.M.), with an additional "roaming" camera or two keeping a watchful eye on the goings-on inside. Cassandra was already predicting fair weather for that Wednesday (otherwise the date would have been changed). Although Goldfarb was a bit concerned about the effect the program might have on the hospital's reputation, especially if anything went wrong, she was also well aware that it could be a great promotional and fundraising opportunity.

Despite the "ad lib" nature of the telecast, two or three members of the staff would be interviewed for voiceover purposes in addition to fled; those details would have to be worked out between our attorneys and theirs. Much of the air time, however, would be spent silently observing the events taking place on the lawn, in the dining rooms and lounges, with supporting background narrative (I had been wrong about the "live" aspect; it was to be "live on tape," a concept I have never understood). It sounded like another can of worms to me, with all kinds of legal and ethical considerations. Nevertheless, I agreed with Goldfarb that it was an offer we couldn't refuse. I had nothing to lose, of course; such decisions were no longer my responsibility.

The magazine interview was a different matter. It involved only the reporter and fled. "I want to be in on that," I said. "I don't want to find out the hard way that I missed something."

"Consider it done. And by the way, he wants to come next week."

After that we discussed the usual matters—old patients leaving, new ones arriving (where are they all coming from?)—and finished with a summary of what I had learned about fled's visit so far. There wasn't much to summarize. About all I knew was that she had come to Earth to "study' its inhabitants, learn what she could from them, and take 100,000 people with her when she departed, the date for which had not yet been determined. And, of course, she had to be the most promiscuous being in the galaxy.

"Try to keep your hands off her," she advised. I wasn't sure whether or not she was joking—with Goldfarb you can never tell. "Do you know how many people she's selected so far?"

"No."

"Or how many countries she's visited?"

"I don't know that, either. All she's mentioned so far is Congo."

"Maybe that's the only country she wants to visit. Maybe that's the reason she came here."

"Why would— Ah!" I mentioned Will's idea that she could have an alter ego living on Earth. "Maybe her alter is from Congo!"

"Slow down, Gene. You're getting way ahead of yourself here."

"Could be. But it occurred to me that her alter might be a prostitute. I suspect they have those in Congo just like everywhere else."

Goldfarb pondered this suggestion for a moment. "Maybe she is and maybe she isn't. Can you hypnotize her?"

"I've already arranged to do that."

"Personally, I don't think you're going to find another Robert Porter in Congo. I think she's looking for something else."

"Whatever she's looking for, the government wants in on it."

"Which government—the U.S. or Congo?"

"Ours."

"Try to keep them out of the hospital," she said.

* * *

On the way out I decided to relax a bit on the lawn before heading home. It was a wonderful day, the kind where the sun was shining brightly, the birds were singing, and everyone seemed to be in very good spirits.

I noticed that Cassandra was wandering around the "back forty," not sitting and contemplating the heavens as she usually does, so I headed in her direction. Many readers will remember her as an uncanny prognosticator. Perhaps like the autistic savants, she is somehow able to think deeply enough about a single subject to come up with patterns and connections the rest of us miss. In Cassie's case, she can somehow discern meteorological trends, for example, or extrapolate from past and present events to get a glimpse of what is going to happen in the near future. I wondered what she saw in fled's. But I knew I had only a few minutes before she retreated into her cocoon, presumably to mull over further developments.

"Hello, Dr. Brewer," she called out when she saw me coming. "Fine day!" She was neither smiling about that nor apparently even concerned with the weather of the moment, good or bad. It was the changes in store for us that interested her.

"Beautiful. But—"

"It's going to be like this for another week, and then the rains will come again. For three days. And then—"

"Thank you. I'll make a note of that. But I wanted to ask you whether you've met fled, and what you think of her."

"I try to keep out of her way, like everyone else."

"See any patterns emerging from her stay with us?"

"All I can tell you is that she'll be around for a while."

"And what does this bode for the patients?"

"It doesn't bode badly. It will take some time, but she will attract a following, just like prot did."

"Here's what I'd especially like to know: do you have any idea whether she's going to take any of you back with her when she returns to K-PAX?"

"I don't know how many. Only that some of us will be going along on the trip."

"Some? How many is 'some'?"

"I don't know exactly how many. Several."

"Several from the hospital?"

"That's right. Only she won't be leaving the Earth from here. The lawn won't hold 100,000 people."

"Any idea where her departure point will be?"

"Somewhere west of here."

That didn't help much. Far enough west and you end up east. "Chicago? L.A.? Japan?"

But she had already begun to get that faraway look, and she wandered off to find a bench. Reluctantly, I took my leave.

On the way home I pondered our brief encounter. She hadn't told me very much, but at least she hadn't mentioned anything about government interventions, or harm coming to anyone, which was something I had begun to fear. Of course her prognostications were only good for a week or two....

* * *

The next night Steve called me at home. Actually it was Abby who called and Karen answered, but after a fifteen-minute gabfest she turned the phone over to me. I always enjoy talking to my eldest daughter, who never fails to come up with something unexpected. This time it was a story about Star, who was performing in a school play. One of the scenes required him to cry, and his uncle Fred had told him that an actor doesn't sob about whatever it is that he's supposed to be crying about onstage; the trick is to recall some other sad moment in his life. Anyway, the sad event he had decided to think about for his lachrymal outburst was the death of our former canine companion, Shasta Daisy. He had watched her health deteriorate until she was nearly blind and deaf and unable to walk very well. We had talked about her impending demise at the time, and he seemed to understand that death was a necessary part of life. The good news was that Shasta had lived a long and happy one, and she would die quietly, without a whimper, with Karen and me at her side.

Nevertheless, he had wept for two days after we had her put down. It was this time period that he thought about during his performance. It worked, too. Onstage he bawled like a baby, to much critical acclaim. I could understand how he felt. I, too, get choked up whenever I think about Shasta's leaving us with such great dignity.

Freddy, who caught Star's final performance, thinks his nephew might have a great future in the theater. Of course I'm still hoping he'll think about psychiatry as a profession. That's one of the joys of parenthood (and grandparenthood): seeing how the lives of the people you love turn out.

Abby herself was as busy as ever with the many volunteer programs that constitute her repertoire. My lovely daughter continues to fight for everyone who is downtrodden or in need, including battered women and children and all the unwanted animals at the local shelter. If she had her way, spaying and neutering of all pets would be a federal law, soon followed by a similar requirement for abusive parents and spouses. After that familiar diatribe she finally turned me over to Steve.

He was not in a good mood. "When can Ah talk to fled?" he demanded.

"As soon as I have time to ask her about a meeting with you," I replied, as calmly as I could, "and as soon as she has time for it. I don't think she came to Earth just to visit with you, Steve. She seems to have her own agenda. Right now I think she's in Africa."

"All Ah need is an hour or two, Gene. Who knows how the Earth might benefit if she could just answer a few simple questions."

"I don't think she came to help out the Earth. She just wants to study us. Like she was an entomologist and we were bugs."

"Could you just find time to ask her? If she doesn't want to talk to me, well, okay."

"As soon as I get an opportunity, Steve."

"Thank you. Ah appreciate that." The phone clicked in my ear.

I like my son-in-law, but sometimes he can be a bit obnoxious. On the other hand, I could see his point. This could be a twice-in-a-lifetime opportunity for him (his brief conversation with prot had catapaulted him into the chairmanship of his department). He wasn't planning to make a lot of money on a meeting with fled, after all, he just wanted to get the answers to some very important questions. Perfectly understandable. There was a time when I would have tried as hard as he does to get them.

Is that what getting old is about? Do you just lose interest? I don't yet know the answer to that, but, like all of us, I suspect I'll find out soon enough.

CHAPTER FOUR

When I got to the hospital on Friday fled wasn't in Room 520–Goldfarb's examination room–nor was she in the game room or the quiet room, where I ran across Rocky, sulking as usual. Something about him always rubbed me the wrong way. My fault, not his. After all, he couldn't help being the way he was: endlessly offended by a perceived cross word, an unintentional negative gesture or facial expression.

In Rocky's case the problem originated not with his parents, as do most mental difficulties, but with an older brother. When he was growing up he couldn't win at anything. Ever. Games, sports, puzzles, arguments. He simply didn't have the development and experience to compete with his big brother. Yet he kept trying until he finally became old enough to outdo his sibling in something, and then the situation became even worse. Whenever it looked as if he were going to succeed, the brother would cheat. And if that didn't work, he would simply quit. Rocky literally couldn't win. The frustration became too enormous to bear. The result was that he became severely paranoid, unable to interact with anyone without looking for a card up that person's sleeve. As a result of this sibling abuse (only recently recognized for the serious problem it is) everyone became, in Rocky's mind, an older brother.

As sad as his situation is, his constant bickering and general nastiness antagonize everyone who meets him, including, I'm sorry to say, me. "What's the problem, Rocky? Who crossed you this time?"

"Why do you want to know?"

I absentmindedly checked my watch. "It's just that you seemed a little upset."

"You looked at your watch! I won't forget that!"

"Well, yes, I did. I'm sorry, I have an appointment."

He sneered, "And whoever it's with is more important than me, is that it?"

"Not at all, Rocky. But I'm not your doctor. If you believe that, you should talk to Dr. Roberts about it."

"He checks his watch, too! He's such a prick!"

"Have you asked him not to?"

"Wouldn't do any good. There's a clock in his office. He can't take his eyes off it."

"Maybe it's not about you. Maybe he just wants to know what time it is."

"He *does* want to know what time it is. So he knows how long he still has to talk to me. The fucking jerk!"

"Have you discussed this with him?"

"Wouldn't do any good. He'd just find some other excuse to look at it."

"Does it bother you that much?"

"Of course it bothers me! It would bother anyone!"

"Tell him!"

"Wouldn't do any good. But I'll get even . . . ."

"How will you get even, Rocky?"

"Next time I see him I'm not going to say a word. I'm just gonna sit there and stare at the clock. Same as him."

Unforgivably, I checked my watch again. "I'm really sorry, but I've got to run."

He assured me through clenched teeth that he understood perfectly. An afterthought: "Who is this goddamn important person you're meeting with?"

"Fled."

"See? Even an ape is more important than me! You're a bigger prick than Roberts is!"

"She's not an ape, Rock. She's a—"

But he had already turned around and was walking away. I started to call out that she was no more important to me than he was, but it wouldn't have done any good.

* * *

On the way back to Room 520 I started to think again about what might happen if I were to find an alter ego lurking in fled's impenetrable mind. What if he/she didn't speak English, for example? I remembered (primarily because I had only recently listened to the tapes of our sessions) what prot had said about the Congolese people: "Besides the four official languages and french, there are an amazing number of native dialects." What if the person spoke one of those dialects? (Or French, for that matter, or one of the four official languages, whatever they might be?)

The door was locked, but nevertheless fled was inside, apparently having just showed up. "How did you—?"

"You sapiens are constantly mystified, aren't you? Why don't you just accept the fact that you don't know everything? Indeed, if I may be blunt, you don't know much of anything."

"Really, fled? We've figured out how the atom works. What happened after the Big Bang. How life evolved from a few organic compounds into us. We know something about almost everything. And we learn more every day!"

"Really, gene? If you're such great learners, why have you been in the same rut for thousands of years? Stuck with the same tired, old religions, willing to fight any war that comes along or create one if it doesn't, constantly striving for more wealth, endlessly multiplying and subduing without any thought for the consequences. You might be learning, but it's a damn slow process, wouldn't you say?"

"Not really," I shot back. "We could probably prevent an asteroid or comet from destroying the Earth if need be."

She hooted: "How are you going to stop a comet when you can't even deal with a hurricane?"

I took a deep breath. I took another deep breath. "You may be right, fled. But today—"

"Where are the veggies?"

"Sorry, I forgot about them. Next time for sure."

She scowled, or maybe it was a pout, but said nothing.

"Today we're going to try to find out who's crawling around in your brain, remember? We're going to see what you can tell me about your past when I put you under hypnosis."

"Fine. Let's get the show on the road."

"Great. Okay, I'm going to roll my chair around the desk so that nothing will be between us. Is that all right?"

She spread her legs apart. "Whatever you say, Dr. B. Enjoy."

"No, dammit. Put your legs together. Thank you!"

"Killjoy!"

"Never mind that. Okay, we're going to start now. Are you ready?"

"Go for it."

Like prot, and unlike Robert Porter, fled seemed willing and eager to cooperate. Though this never hurts, it doesn't guarantee that anything productive will come out of the procedure. "Okay, now I'm going to count from one to five. By the time I get to five—"

"Yeah, yeah, I know all that. Get on with it."

"One . . . ." Fled's eyes had already begun to droop. I hoped she wasn't faking it. "Two . . . ." She was having trouble keeping them open. I thought I heard her murmur, "That's amazing . . . ."

"Three." Her eyes were closed. On "four" her head began to slump toward her chest, and on "five" her arms and legs completely relaxed. Clearly, she was "under."

"Fled?"

She mumbled something unintelligible.

"Okay, fled, you may raise your head and open your eyes if you want." When she did, she looked rather dreamy, like a child awakening. "All right. Now I want you to describe your first sexual experience . . . ."

Softly: "It went pretty fast. It was what you would probably call a "quickie."
"I see. And how old were you?"
"A few–uh–you call them 'months,' I think."
"Anyone else around?"
"Sure. All kinds of beings."
"They all stand around and watch?"
"Sure. Why not?"
"Your mother watched, too?"
"Naturally."
"Are you happy? Do you feel safe?"
"Of course. Why shouldn't I?"
"No reason."

For the next forty-five minutes I asked her to describe her sexual activities and any other events of note that she could remember, beginning when she was two years old, three, four, all the way up to her present age of twenty-three. She recalled nothing especially evocative or unusual. K-PAX seemed–for want of a better word–dull, even with the endless sex. Any hope I had harbored that something was going to crawl out of her closet dissipated like a drop of water in a hot skillet.

"All right. Now just relax. Close your eyes if you like."

Her eyes drooped a little, but stayed open.

"Now I'm going to speak to someone else. You may listen or not, as you wish."

She didn't make a sound or gesture, but she seemed to be listening.

"Just relax, and think about nothing. Keep your mind open, and try to accept whatever happens, whoever might appear in this room."

Not a muscle moved.

"Okay," I said, very quietly, "I'd like anyone with fled to please come forward and identify yourself . . . ." I waited. Ten seconds passed. Twenty seconds. Thirty. "Let me repeat that in case you weren't sure of my meaning. Anyone who is there with fled, please come forward at this time. I promise that no harm will come to you, I just want to talk to you for a minute."

Another ten seconds went by before fled, or whoever it was, suddenly seemed to shrivel before my eyes. She stayed that way for several minutes, sort of curled up and motionless, in the chair. It was almost as if she were hiding from someone. In my thirty-five years of practice I had never seen anything quite like this, and I was concerned that I might cause her (or him), and ultimately fled, some harm by trying to force her to reveal herself at once. Nevertheless, I decided to gently try. "Hello?"

She remained as she was, trying to seem invisible, perhaps feigning death.

"I'm a doctor. I won't hurt you. Do you speak English?"

Whoever it was remained curled in a big ball. I waited for several minutes, just watching, hoping she would relax a bit and make a move. She didn't. It was Robert Porter all over again.

Or was it? All my experience was telling me that something didn't seem quite right about the situation. The appearance of an "alter ego" seemed too pat, too calculated, perhaps too soon. It was almost as if she were overacting, faking the whole thing. But, of course, I could be wrong. In this business there aren't any rules. Whatever the case, I couldn't just leave her sitting there frozen in her chair.

I leaned back and said, a little louder, "Fled, are you there?" The apparent alter sat up a little straighter. "All right, fled, I'm going to count backward from five one. At 'five' you'll begin to awaken, and by the time we get to one, you'll be completely alert and feeling fine. Five . . ." She started to come out from wherever she had withdrawn to. "Four . . . Three . . ." When I got to "one," her eyes came into focus. On me.

"Satisfy your morbid curiosity, gene?"

"Not entirely."

"Well, how close did you come?"

"First of all, you have at least one alter ego."

"Really? Who?"

"I don't know. She—if it is a she—wouldn't talk to me. In fact, she seemed to be afraid to make an appearance at all. I was wondering whether this might give you some idea of who she might be."

"Someone who's been badly treated, I should imagine."

"Thank you, doctor fled. Can you be more specific?"

"Not without more information. What did this being look like?"

"A lot like you."

"I was joking, doc. If I had an alter ego, she would have to look a lot like me, wouldn't she?"

"Not necessarily. But let's get serious for a moment, shall we? Do you have any idea who a putative alter could be, or not? Have you talked to anyone lately–in Congo, perhaps–who might fit the bill?" I took a leap of faith here: "A prostitute, perhaps?"

"I deeply resent that implication! But if you must be serious for a moment: no. No prostitutes, as far as I know."

"Any other Congolese women?"

"I've met a few. Where is this getting us?"

"Not very far. I'll have to think about it a little more. In the meantime, let me ask you: where else have you been since you got to Earth?"

"Besides here?"

"Yes, dammit. And Congo."

"Relax, my humorless friend. You're behaving like Rocky. I've been to a smattering of other countries on that continent."

"Learn anything interesting about their life forms?"

"Plenty."

"For example . . ."

"They're all beautiful places, with a multitude of fascinating beings. Except for the humans, of course. *They're* the same everywhere."

"Okay, let me ask you this: did you find anyone who might qualify as a traveling companion when you return to K-PAX?"

"Yes, indeedy. Quite a few, in fact."

"Can you tell me who they might be?"

"They *might* be everyone I've encountered. But they're not."

"Thank you very much. Could you elaborate on that?"

"I *could*, but I won't. The walls might have ears."

I was worried about the same thing. But I proceeded, nevertheless. "Any of them residents of this institutution?"

"That's amazing! From Congo to here at light speed!"

"Care to give me any names?"

"I'll give you all 100,000 names if you like. But not until everything is lined up."

"Thanks again. Any progress on finding a football stadium or the like? Or setting a date for the trip?"

"I'm still looking into that."

"Well, will you give me a few days' notice before you go?"

"If there are a few days left when everything is set, they're all yours." She yawned. "Anything else I can do for you today?"

"Jerry would like to meet you. He's in Ward Three."

"I know where he is."

"Oh, and one more thing. Your interview for the British magazine article is scheduled for next Wednesday. Will that be convenient for you?"

"As all get out." Without another word she got up and loped out. "Don't forget the veggies," drifted back from the corridor.

After she had gone I sat there pondering what I had just seen. If fled's alter ego was for real, and she wasn't a prostitute, what about the other side of the coin: could she be someone who had been sexually abused? That would explain her reticence to come forward, her attempting to hide from me. But if she were an African woman, how on Earth would we be able to track her down so that we might be able to get help for her? The immensity of the concept again brought to mind the bigger question of whether everyone on Earth has a parallel life somewhere among the stars. It was just so overwhelming. And I had forgotten again to ask fled about Steve . . . . I told myself I really ought to consider retirement. Then I remembered that I was already retired.

* * *

Thanks to prot's influence, perhaps, my son Will, despite his lack of experience, has quickly become the hospital's expert on multiple personality disorder. Sorry–that's old-fashioned–we call it dissociative identity disorder now, or DID. I wanted to speak to him about fled and her putative alter(s), but he was with a patient, so I left him a note. While I waited, I took a stroll around the lawn, hoping to sort out what I had just seen and heard.

Fled was already there, occupying a corner with the toad man. Everyone else was apparently still keeping his or her distance. I went up to Darryl, another of the former "Magnificent Seven." The reader might recall that this patient suffers from de Clerambault's syndrome: in his case, he believes that Meg Ryan is in love with him. On the surface, this doesn't seem like an unmanageable problem. We all harbor secret desires, but with de Clerambault's the fantasy is entirely real and occupies much of one's thoughts and beliefs. Darryl's room is covered with photos of Ms. Ryan, he has all of her videotaped films (which he's watched dozens and dozens of times), and copies of most of the magazines that contain articles and pictures of the lovely film star. In fact, he was once her stalker, using every available means to find his way into her home, onto her film sets. He caused her no physical harm, of course–stalkers rarely do–but it must have been unnerving for her to find evidence for the presence of an unknown visitor to her bedroom, to repeatedly spot his face in a crowd. No one has been able to convince him that his feelings are unrequited. Indeed, it must be very difficult for anyone who is deeply in love to comprehend the reality that he or she might not be loved back.

But how did Darryl, who has never actually met the woman, get the idea that Meg was in love with him in the first place? When he attended the premiere of one of her films–*Sleepless in Seattle*, I think it was–it seemed to him that her beautiful smile (she was being interviewed outside the theater prior to the showing) was directed to him alone. He crawled under the barricade and tried to cross the street to speak with her, but was restrained by the studio's security people. For months he followed her, believing that his love was being denied her by jealous cops. One thing led to another and, after he was finally arrested for harassment, he ended up in a New Jersey mental institution and eventually with us. Drug treatments have proven ineffective, as has psychoanalysis (Will inherited him from Carl Beamish, now on temporary leave), and poor Darryl now waits impatiently for her to visit him at the hospital. In fact, he always keeps some cake or cookies in his room for just such an eventuality.

Instead, he got fled.

I sidled up to him and asked him what he thought of our newest visitor. "I'm a little afraid of her, Dr. Brewer," he replied. "We all are."

"Why? She seems pretty harmless to me."

"She's so big and strong, and kind of repulsive. It's like having a gorilla running around loose."

"But she's not a gorilla. Or a chimpanzee, either. She's not even from Earth."

"How do we know she can be trusted? If we say the wrong thing to her, maybe she'll turn on us."

Oddly, despite Goldfarb's warning, I hadn't thought about fled in quite that way. There's a well-known television show from the old *Twilight Zone* series called "To Serve Man." It turned out that the aliens had come to take some of us back as a source of protein. The eponymous, undecipherable tome they had brought along was a cookbook. Could fled have ulterior motives for her visit that we were unaware of?

"There's fled over there with Howard," I told Darryl. He doesn't seem too worried about her."

"Howard is as big and repulsive as she is," he reminded me.

* * *

I finally found Will on his way to a meeting, and I accompanied him to the conference room. "Got your note, Dad–sorry I was occupied. How long are you going to be here today?"

"Not much longer. I promised your mother we'd do something this afternoon. Go for a drive, or maybe a movie."

"You guys used to go to a lot of movies, didn't you?"

"Yeah. Your mom loved Humphrey Bogart."

"Humphrey *Who?*"

"You mean you don't–"

"Just kidding, Pop. He was way before my time, but I know who Bogie is. *Casablanca* is one of Dawn's favorite films. So–what did you want to talk about?"

"I think I found fled's alter ego."

"Really? Who is it?"

"I don't know. Whoever it is doesn't seem to want to talk to me."

"That could mean a couple of things."

"Like what?"

"Well, she could be an outlaw. Or afraid of doctors. Or maybe she's just shy. Or maybe . . . ."

"Yes? Yes?"

"Fled is a K-PAXian, right? But she resembles most a large chimpanzee. Maybe your elusive personality is an ape!"

"A chimpanzee! That's it, Will! Why didn't I think of that? That's why fled's spent most of her time in Congo. And why her alter ego seemed to be a phony. The mannerisms would be different from those of a human being!" We both pondered this possibility as we shuffled along. "But if you're right," I said, "how can I ever communicate with her? Or maybe it's a 'him.'"

My genes smiled at me. "I'd say you need someone to translate."

"That makes sense, but who do we know that can speak English and chimpan–"

"How about fled?"

"Oh. Right. But can that be done? How can we get her to speak with her own alter ego?"

"I don't know Dad. Let me think about that."

We got to the conference room. Inside, I could see the staff dropping their things on the table, getting some food for themselves. Despite the obvious advantages of retirement, I did miss the give-and-take I knew would be going on there. The camaraderie. At the same time, I didn't really want to go back to work full-time, even if I were up-to-date on the latest advances, which I definitely was not. As my wife has pointed out on many occasions, there comes a time to quit working and enjoy life before it's too late.

"I'll call you this weekend!" he shouted as he disappeared into the room.

"Enjoy your meeting," I murmured wistfully.

* * *

I was up early on Saturday dreamily munching a bowl of corn flakes–while thinking about fled, of course–when there came a gentle tap at the kitchen door. Flower started barking. Even though I couldn't see anyone at the window, I knew who it had to be. Karen was still sleeping, so I shushed Flower and stepped outside.

While Dartmouth hovered in the background, Wang sprung up and flashed his familiar badge. "Can't you shut that dog up?" he inquired politely, through clenched teeth.

"She wouldn't hurt a fly; she spits them out!" I was becoming a trifle annoyed by their nagging persistence. "Are you going to be coming here every day?"

"If that's what it takes, yes, sir!" he replied cheerfully. Then, as an afterthought, perhaps: "Sorry to bother you at breakfast."

"How did you know I was eating breakfast?"

He looked around furtively, as if for spies. "You have a flake in your beard."

I brushed it off. "Can't you at least make it every *other* day? That's how often I see her."

"Depends on what's going on, Dr. Brewer. Let's take a walk, shall we?"

"A walk? Can't we just talk here? In back of the house?"

"We prefer not to take any chances on being overheard."

Just like in the movies, I thought. But I had supposed that was fiction. "Overheard by whom?"

"By terrorists."

"You think terrorists are bugging the house??"

Dartmouth held up a sober hand. "Not to worry, Dr. Brewer. We're bugging the house, too." Wang gave him a stern look and his partner hung his head.

"The government is bugging our house? Why?"

"To catch the terrorists, of course!" Wang whispered.

"And how many have you caught by bugging the house?"

"None so far."

"Then it would seem to be a waste of time, wouldn't it?"

"Not at all, sir. As long as we're bugging the house, they're afraid to come around. You see how well that works?"

I thought about the old psychiatry joke about the elephants. "Well, do you bug every house in the area?"

"Of course. And as a result, it's one of the safest parts of the country. Bear in mind, though, that a neighbor of yours could still be one of *them*. Anyone could be a terrorist, you know. We've got it covered both ways." He smacked his hands together–hard. "It's beautiful, when you think about it."

We don't have a sidewalk, so we turned into the road. "I'm just curious–how many federal agents are there, anyway?"

"That's classified," Wang quickly replied. Dartmouth tripped over something, but caught himself before he dived onto the asphalt. "But let me put it this way: everyone you know could be working with us."

I felt as though I had eaten a portobello. "All right, let's get this over with. Exactly why are you here now?"

"We've learned that she can read minds. Is that right, sir?"

"Why? Is that illegal?"

"How does she do that?"

"She says it has something to do with electromagnetic waves. Otherwise, I haven't a clue."

"We need to talk to her. Would that be all right with you, Dr. Brewer?"

"It's not that simple. I don't run the hospital. As a matter of fact, I'm retired. And technically, she's not a patient. You'll have to speak with Dr. Goldfarb about that."

"We already have."

"Well? What did she tell you?"

"She said we should talk to you about it."

I thought: I don't need this shit, Virginia. But what the hell–I was certain that fled could handle herself in any situation. "I'll ask her if she wants to speak to you. What, exactly, do you want to get from her?"

"We need to know how she can read minds, sir. Critical to our national security. With your permission, we'd like to bring in a neuroscientist to examine her."

Dartmouth suddenly whipped out his enormous weapon and stuck it into a bush. After wiggling it around for a moment and drawing no response, he sheathed it again.

"What if she refuses to talk to him?" I asked nervously.

Wang's features hardened. "I remind you, sir, that this is highly sensitive material. We would appreciate your speaking to her about this. And it would be wise not to discuss the matter with anyone else. Do you understand?"

"No."

He sighed. "Consider this: if our enemies could learn to read our minds . . ."

I thought about Walt Kelly, but kept that to myself. "What about my wife?" I inquired. "Okay if I discuss it with *her*?"

"That's up to you, Dr. Brewer. But if you do, we'll find out about it. Now, if you don't mind, let's turn around very slowly and return to the house, shall we?"

I complied, but before I had gone six feet I heard my companions crashing through the brush.

* * *

Will called Sunday evening. He was obviously excited. I thought: that's probably the way I used to sound. "You could make a videotape of fled under hypnosis!" he suggested. "If you could get her chimpanzee alter ego—if that's what she is—to utter something, or even to make a facial expression or gesture of some kind, maybe fled could make some sense of it and identify her."

"Sounds like a good idea, Will!" It occurred to me that Dartmouth and Wang might think so, too. But I couldn't think of anything catastrophic they could possibly do with this information.

"Want me to set something up for you?"

I didn't know whether to be grateful for this suggestion or to resent it; Will knows I'm not particularly adept in the technical department. "Thanks, son. I'd appreciate that."

"Fled's gone again, by the way."

"Any idea where?"

"Probably back to Africa. She seems to like it there. But she said she'd be available tomorrow for your meeting with her. And that you should expect a surprise."

"What kind of surprise?"

"She didn't say. I suppose if she had told me, it wouldn't be a surprise."

I wasn't sure I wanted any more surprises from fled.

"What are you guys planning for this evening?"

"Not much. We're probably going to sit around and plot the overthrow of the government."

"Huh?"

"Just a joke, son. Actually, we dearly love all three branches of our leadership. Executive, legislative, judicial—they're all magnificent. And they've been keeping the elephants out of the neighborhood, too!"

"Dad, did you have some mushrooms for dinner, by any chance?"

CHAPTER FIVE

It was such a nice day when I left the house for MPI on Monday morning that I remembered again why I had retired. But for now I put the weather out of my mind–I had work to do.

As soon as I entered the building I ran into Laura Chang. It was almost as if she had been waiting for me. When she joined us a few years ago Laura was just out of her residency. Now in her mid-thirties, she's an old hand, and one of the best psychiatrists in the business. Not only because of her intelligence and insight, but because, like Virginia Goldfarb, nothing fazes her. I could well imagine that, in a few years, she would be running the hospital. At this moment, however, she seemed a tad perturbed. But it sometimes takes her awhile to get to the point.

"How are you getting along with your new patient, Gene?"

"Well, she's not really a patient, but–not so good. This time I think Virginia's bitten off more than I can chew. How about you? All your patients behaving themselves?"

"Hard to tell. They're all so focused on fled that it's interfering with their protocols."

"Really? I thought they were trying to ignore her as much as possible."

"They try to, but they can't. When she's here she seems to occupy all the space around her."

"Is that what you wanted to talk to me about?"

"What makes you think I wanted to talk to you about something?"

"I felt as if I were being ambushed when I came in."

"You haven't completely lost your, touch, doctor. It's Claire."

"What about her?"

"She's become interested in fled. She wants to examine and analyze her."

"You mean–"

"That's right. She wants to set up a regular time every week for interview sessions with fled. She seems to think our alien visitor is delusional."

"What did you tell her?"

"I told her that fled already has a doctor."

"What did she think about that?"

I thought I detected a faint hint of a smile. "She wants to replace you. She thinks you're over the hill and shouldn't be seeing patients anymore."

"She's probably right about that, though she's no spring chicken herself. Did you remind her that fled isn't actually a patient of mine? So I probably can't do her too much damage."

"Well, no. But that isn't the point, is it? I don't want to encourage Claire to believe she's competing with anyone on the staff here. She's already convinced most of the patients that she's a real doctor."

"Sometimes even I forget that she's a patient. She's very sensitive about it, though. The problem is, she might take serious offense if she's denied the opportunity to 'practice.'"

"Exactly. She already has. She's threatening to quit her 'job' here and go elsewhere."

At that moment Cliff Roberts hurried by. "Maybe we ought to encourage her to do that!" he suggested before disappearing up the stairs. As Karen is fond of reminding me, life gets sillier every day. But then it occurred to me that Cliff could be right for once. Maybe a pink slip would snap her out of her delirium. But perhaps he was only joking. "So what do you want me to do?"

"I don't know. I was hoping *you* might have a suggestion."

I tried to come up with one, but the best I could do was: "Status aside, why not encourage Claire to speak with fled on an informal basis? It probably can't do either of them any harm, and it might even be beneficial for Claire. Maybe fled can spot something in her behavior that we've missed."

"That's what I thought, too, but I thought you might want to tell fled what to expect. Thanks, Dr. B! Got to run–time for the Monday meeting. You coming to that?"

"Not unless I get an invitation from someone. Until I hear otherwise, I'm here on an informal basis, too."

"You could have fooled me!"

* * *

This time fled had left the door unlocked for me. I remember feeling, as I turned the knob, that she must have at least a tiny appreciation of human courtesy. That notion went directly to hell when I stepped inside and found her 'surprise' waiting for me. Fled had brought a visitor. I shouted involuntarily, "Jesus Christ!"

"Nah. His name is 'okeemon'. Accent on the 'o.' He's a bonobo."

I started to repeat, "A bonobo?" but caught myself in time and swallowed, instead. "Uh–hello, Okeemon."

"They're also called pygmy chimpanzees, or hippie chimps—they tend to settle their disputes through sex, rather than violence. Not very human of them, is it?" I was wondering whether I should offer a handshake, but of course fled intercepted this. "Just come closer so he can see and smell you better."

I hesitated.

"C'mon, gino, trust me. He won't bite you. Not unless I ask him to, anyway."

Reluctantly I took a little step toward him.

"C'mon, c'mon."

I stepped closer. The bonobo's eyes swept slowly over my vulnerable body, and his nostrils twitched a bit. I tried to remember whether I'd ever seen one of these creatures in a zoo. In any case, I had never been this close to one, or any other zoo animal for that matter. I began to sweat. But before I could make a sound, he reached out and grabbed me firmly by the cojones. I finally managed to squeak, "What's— What's he doing here?"

Okeemon released his grip and stepped back. I started to breathe again. Fled, for her part, grinned broadly. "I thought you might want to talk to him."

"He talks?"

"Not in English, doc. Nor any of your other human languages. I'll translate for you."

"Uh—what should I talk to him about?"

Fled gave me what could only be interpreted, in any language, as a look of disgust. "You're a human being, doc. Can't you think of anything you want to know about him and all the others of his species?"

"Oh. Yes, I see what you mean. All right, Okeemon. Uh, do you want to sit down?"

After mumbling something unintelligible to him, fled immediately answered, "No." Evidently she was saving me (and him) some time by reading his answers directly from his head.

I, however, needed to sit, and I dropped into the desk chair. "Where are you from, Okeemon?"

After a couple more guttural noises: "The forest." Fled elaborated, "The Congolese rain forest."

"Do you have a family?" Fled rolled her eyes. I rephrased the question. "How many children do you have?"

"Twelve." Okeemon's eyes showed an undeniable sadness.

"Are they all living in—uh—the forest with you?"

"No. Some of them are dead, and others have been taken away."

"Where have they been taken?"

Fled scrunched up her brow again. "Mostly to zoos and labs and restaurants," she replied drily. Apparently she was answering that one for herself. "Go ahead—ask him about his life in the forest."

I decided to cooperate; I just wanted to get the interview over with. "What is life in the forest like for you?"

"It is beautiful. I take deep breaths all the time." Fled added, "That means he is very happy living there." She mumbled something else to Okeemon, and then said, for him, "Until the humans come."

"What do the humans do?"

"They end us. They take our children."

"I see . . . . Interesting . . . ." It was hard to concentrate under the circumstances. "Fled, I really don't know what you're expecting me to ask him."

"All right, my slow-witted friend, I'll save you the trouble of trying to think. Okeemon is literally your nearest relative. Genetically, I mean. Take a good look at him. You're not likely to get this close to a bonobo again in your lifetime. Or anyone else's lifetime. There are only about 5,000 of them left in the wild. You're looking at a being with 99% of the same DNA strands as you yourself have. Even by your own chauvinistic reckoning, he has the intelligence of a five-year-old human child. You're looking at yourself! Or the way you could have been–*should* have been–had you not, through an evolutionary accident, evolved into a monster. Look at him!"

I looked. Okeemon gazed back at me. When our eyes met, I could tell, or thought I could tell, that he was thinking the same thing I was: we're not so different really. Not in any important way.

Fled interrupted our silence. "Why in the WORLD would you want to kill him?"

"I don't want to kill him!"

She stared at me coldly. "Does the word 'naïve' mean anything to you, doctor b? Get serious–you regularly go to war and kill *each other*! And everyone else is fair game, too." She spat on the floor. "One thing I've learned about homo sapiens, doc. You're all responsible for the actions of the few. You all choose the leaders who decide the policies of your governments. You all interact in whatever ways are the most beneficial financially to yourselves and to others who are already rich. You could do something about the killing of your nearest relatives on EARTH. In fact, you could stop it if you wanted to. You just have to give a fuck."

I stared at her. "Goddamn it, fled, I give a fuck!"

"Really, gino? When was the last time you put pressure on your congressman or your president, or anyone else, to do something to stop the bushmeat trade?"

"The– Oh, you mean the bonobo– All right! I haven't done that. The fact is, I didn't know about it. Not specifically, anyway."

"Not many humans do. Or want to. You're all too busy with more 'important' things. Like what's on the boob tube tonight."

"Okay, okay! I'll write to my congressman! Happy?"

"I've got a better idea: start electing congressmen who give a fuck!"

"And that's why you brought Okeemon in today? To help you lobby for the next election?"

"Not entirely. You could call it a sociology lesson."
"What about our session? We were going to continue the hypnosis—"
"We'll do that on Wednesday."
"Will Okeemon be here then?"
"I doubt it. He doesn't like cities much, for some reason. He tells me the vibes are all wrong. Too bad you can't feel them."
"So you're taking him home?"
"Any minute now. You want to go with us? See why he loves the forest so much?"
"Uh—maybe next time. . . ."

She murmured something to her guest, who briefly bared his teeth, which looked formidable. He stepped toward me. I flinched. He reached out again, and I thought he was going to give my genitalia another squeeze. Instead, he felt my face, my shirt, checked my hair for insects. I could smell him. It was a not an altogether unpleasant aroma.

"Go ahead," fled coached. "He wants you to get to know him, too."

Cautiously I laid a hand on his shoulder. His hair felt rough. I moved it down to his shoulder blades. He bent over.

"Go on—he wants you to scratch his back. This may be your only chance to do that!"

He inched closer. I thought: no more mushrooms—ever—for me! But I complied. He seemed to enjoy it, twitching a muscle here and there, though he made no sound at all. Just relaxed, with his head down.

Fled said something to him and he ambled back to where she was standing. She wrapped her own hairy arm around his shoulders. "See you later, doc," she chirped. Before I could respond, she pulled a tiny mirror from somewhere and stepped toward the window with Okeemon. In another moment they were gone.

"Wait!" I called out. "We need to talk about—"

I plopped down and sat without moving for perhaps another twenty minutes trying to digest what had happened. I hadn't even had a chance to ask her about videotaping our next meeting so she could see her alter ego for herself. The interview with the reporter for the British magazine was scheduled for that day as well. Never mind—she probably read the back of my mind and knew all about it anyway.

* * *

I was passing through the game room when I heard someone call my name. Howard came puffing over and asked whether I had a minute. I told him I was in no hurry. "I'm going to K-PAX!" he declared happily. I had never seen him like this before.

I didn't want to burst his bubble, but I didn't want him to be disappointed later on, either. "How do you know you're going to K-PAX, Howard?"

"Cassie told me. Isn't it wonderful? No one there cares that I am ugly."

"Yes it is. But bear in mind that Cassandra could be wrong in her prediction."

"She's never wrong, Doctor Brewer—you know that."

"I just don't want you to get your hopes up. She may be absolutely certain about it, but maybe the plan will fall through. Maybe fled will decide to take someone else at the last minute, or there might be a technical problem and she won't be able to take anyone at all." I didn't want to mention my prime concern—that the government might find a way to stop her.

"I'm not worried."

"Did Cassie say who else might be going?"

"Only that there will be a lot of others."

"A lot of the patients, you mean?"

"That's what she said. And a few from the staff."

"Staff?? You mean the nurses?"

"She didn't say."

I made a note to ask her—or fled herself—as soon as possible. But something else came to mind: Cassie's predictions were usually only good for a couple of weeks. Did that mean fled would be leaving within that time frame?

"Jerry's not going, though."

"What?"

"Jerry's not going."

"Why not?"

"Fled is going to cure him," he whispered. "He won't need to go."

"Who told you *that*?"

"Fled."

"I see. And when is this miraculous cure going to take place?"

"As soon as she gets back."

"Okay, Howard. Thanks for the information. And I sincerely hope you get your wish."

"It can't be any worse than it is here." He meant the Earth, of course, not the hospital. He turned to go. "I can't wait to tell everyone!"

"Just a second, Howard. You seem to have a pretty good idea about what's going on around here. Tell me (I glanced around to make sure no one could hear us): do you know if any of the patients have had—uh—an intimate relationship with fled?"

"Only one that I know of."

"Who?"

"Me."

"You mean . . . she seduced you?"

"She didn't have to work very hard at it. I've never had sex before. I was beginning to think I never would." He chortled happily. "Now I know what all the fuss is about."

Though vaguely disgusted by this revelation, I wasn't really surprised. "Thanks, Howard. We'll talk again later."

He waddled off and I headed upstairs for a brief visit with Jerry. He was working as usual. Indeed, the matchsticks were flying. But when I spoke to him he seemed unable to respond. He was grinning, and I heard some sounds coming out of him–little sighs and squeaks–but no words of any kind. Had she already told him about his imminent "cure"? His manner reminded me somehow of Stevie Wonder at the piano. He seemed to be beside himself with happiness. I only hoped his joy wouldn't be dashed by false promises from a certain alien visitor.

* * *

I had lunch in the Ward Two dining room. Charlotte was in attendance, and I asked for permission to join her. Though still routinely sedated, her drug regimen was more effective than even a few months earlier (it sometimes takes a while to determine the best medication and to optimize the dosage). As a result, she was under far less surveillance than she had been when she moved down to the second floor, monitored only by the security cameras like everyone else. Nevertheless, she would probably never leave the hospital. The difficulty with mental patients is that they can often be temporarily "cured," but sometimes revert to their former state even if they faithfully take their meds (and they often don't). In Charlotte's case we couldn't take a chance on her being set free–at least not until she had proven herself to be stable for a considerable length of time–and perhaps ending up a dangerous psychopath again.

Her gray, wolflike eyes were absolutely compelling, as they undoubtedly had been for her seven unfortunate victims in 1996-7, though they had lost much of their sparkle. But, despite her apparent malaise, I still found her to be the most beautiful patient in the hospital. I asked her how she was feeling.

"It's very tiring when no one loves you."

I was frankly stunned. It had never occurred to me that someone who found the sexual apparatus of the human male so disgusting would want someone to love her. Or perhaps her new medication had counteracted the repression of her instinct to love someone. Or was she looking for a lesbian relationship? I was reminded once again that we are all much more complex than we might seem, our wants and needs often contradictory, our totality far more than the sum of our parts.

Before I could express any thoughts about this, however, she confided to me that she "would really like to leave this place."

A perfectly normal response to being locked away for nearly a decade. But even if she were no longer deemed to be a menace to society, the courts would have to thoroughly review her case, a process that could take many more months or even years. If the victims' relatives were consulted, as they undoubtedly would be in a case like hers, she would probably remain here forever regardless of her mental state. And besides all these considerations, who knew if she was faking her improvement, a not uncommon occurrence among the mentally ill? It occurred to me that if fled were able to read minds, and I was pretty certain she could, she might be able to tell us what was going on inside Charlotte's. But suddenly I realized that fled might be even more helpful than that. If she could read *everyone's* mind, what could she tell us about the thoughts and fears of all the other inmates of the Manhattan Psychiatric Institute? If we knew this, it could be a godsend to both patients and staff! But—would she be willing to do this? And, if so, could she "analyze" everyone at the hospital within the next couple of weeks while, at the same time, scouting for 100,000 people to accompany her on a voyage to the stars?

I cursed myself for not thinking of this earlier; I might even have brought it up at the regular Monday morning staff meeting, and it would be another week before the next one. On the other hand, maybe I should ascertain fled's reaction to this notion before bringing it to everyone's attention. And maybe it was a dumb idea anyway. My wife likes to remind me that my brain isn't what it used to be, and I'm not all that sure it was so brilliant in the first place.

I left a message with Will reminding him to set up the videotape equipment for Wednesday. It had only been a week and half, and I was already beginning to get that dragged-out feeling I associated with entertaining visitors from other planets.

* * *

When I got out of the car that afternoon I heard what seemed to be a hissing sound. I circled around it looking for a flat tire, and it was only when I heard my name being whispered that I realized what it was. I stepped into the wooded area behind the driveway, where I found Dartmouth and Wang hiding behind an oak tree.

"We'd appreciate it, sir, if you didn't look our way," Wang admonished as I stepped toward them. I stopped and pretended to scan the sky for whatever interesting phenomena might have been up there. Two shiny ID badges protruded from either side of the trunk. "We won't keep you long, doctor," Dartmouth whined. Added Wang: "We just need to know what time we should send over our neurobiologist on Wednesday."

"I'm sorry," I told him, "but something unexpected came up today and I wasn't able to discuss the matter with fled. I'm not sure she will even be available on Wednesday."

Wang's head poked around the tree, like a turtle with a wooden shell. "Can't you put a lid on her?" he politely snarled. "We may not have much time."

I wasn't about to ask why the rush, perhaps because I didn't want to hear the answer. "I need to wrap up some things with her on Wednesday, and if she shows up I'll definitely schedule your guy for Friday morning unless there's an unavoidable conflict. Fair enough?"

Dartmouth whined again. Wang just stared at me. Somehow he brought to mind a vicious dog a neighbor once had. Dartmouth, on the other hand, reminded me of Goofy.

"Can you tell me his name? I'll need to clear him with security."

Both of them jumped toward me as if they had been goosed. "He doesn't have a name," whispered Wang.

"Huh?"

He snarled again. "It's classified. But don't worry—we'll take care of your security people. And he'll have a photo ID."

I forgot myself for a moment and turned to face him. "Without a name on it."

"That's correct, sir. And may I say that our military people are *very* interested in what our man learns about her. Now, doctor, would you mind turning around again?"

I presumed they wanted to slip silently away. Instead, I heard the government boys crunching through last autumn's leaves, Dartmouth grunting and crashing as he fell and got up again. Finally, after several noisy minutes, they were gone.

Neither had mentioned the upcoming magazine interview or television show. I wondered whether their sources knew about them.

* * *

I had planned to spend the rest of the afternoon catching up on e-mail, but when I signed on I was surprised to find more than a hundred messages asking for further information about fled—in particular, what brought her to Earth, when she was going back to K-PAX, and did she have room for a couple of passengers. That's the price you pay for having a website, I reminded myself.

I chose to answer only a token few, those that posed unique or interesting questions for me or fled. For example, one correspondent, who identified himself as a fourteen-year-old boy who wanted to be an animal trainer, asked, **Could I have fled for a pet?** A teenage girl said, **I made a dress for fled. Where can I send it?** An older man: **I would like to dance with fled.** An unidentified person: **I don't have many friends. Could fled be my friend?** But the ones that got to me most were from a Palestinian boy and an Israeli girl. Both asked exactly the same question: **Can fled tell us how we can learn to get along with each other?** I forwarded both of these messages to the other correspondent. Perhaps nothing would come of it, but what was there to lose?

Another, an American, requested that I ask fled to stop global warming. I already knew what she would say to that: get a new government, one that gives a fuck.

* * *

That evening we watched the first half of the 2005 version of *King Kong*, and the rest on the following night. It could've been cut by an hour or so, I thought, but it was beautifully photographed, the performances were good (especially that of Kong), and the special effects were outstanding. The thing that made it a truly great film, however, was that it illustrated remarkably well the emotional life of the gorilla, which, if accurate, isn't much different from our own, really. Even Flower seemed to enjoy it, whining like Dartmouth when Kong was captured by the money-grubbing humans, just as they used to kidnap human slaves. I wondered whether the government boys were somewhere nearby watching it, too.

We had to pause it during the second half to take a call from Will. He reported that the video camera had been set up and all I had to do was turn it on. He even told me where the "hold" button was. "I'd help you get it going, Dad, but I've got a group session tomorrow morning."

I thanked him and assured him that I wouldn't start the hypnosis unless I was sure I had the camera rolling. "Besides, I've got fled to help me if I run into any problems."

"That reminds me," he said. "She's back again. But no bonobos came with her this time."

I was suspicious. "Anyone else come with her?"

"No, Dad, not as far as I know."

After I turned him over to Karen, a ridiculous thought occurred to me: *could fled's alter ego be the bonobo chimpanzee Okeemon?* But I realized, of course, that this was impossible. For one thing, both of them were present in my office at the same time, something that had never happened in the case of prot and Robert (or any other multiple personality patient). Still, where aliens were concerned . . .

I didn't much enjoy the movie's final reel. When Kong was shot down by the military, I wondered whether we might not have seen a preview of fled's departure from this world.

CHAPTER SIX

We watched the rain dribble down the window in Room 520. "Fled, we need to talk."

She crunched down on a bunch of carrots. "I'm all ears."

I couldn't suppress a laugh.

She chortled, too, and bits of the orange root sprayed from her mouth. "There may be hope for you yet, doctor b!"

"Before we get started, though, just a quick question about a couple of e-mail messages I got the other day." I related the ones from the Palestinian and Israeli teenagers and asked her what I should tell them.

"Very simple," she said. "Tell them their governments should refrain from any form of retaliation, *regardless of what the other side does to them*, for six months. If they find they can't live without the killing, they should feel free to go back to their plan to wipe each other off the face of the EARTH."

"You think they should try to wipe each other off the—"

"Did I say that?"

"Not exactly." We listened to the rain for another moment before I advised her, "You're making *our* government nervous."

"They're always nervous. Or, more correctly, *you're* always nervous. Your government is just a reflection of your own fears and desires, isn't that true?"

"Well, theoretically, at least."

"Theoretically? Remind me again: how does a 'democracy' work?"

"All right. You made your point. But that's not what I wanted to discuss with you today."

"Okay, tell me: what's bothering them now?"

73

"They want to know how you read minds. Evidently the military people are very much interested in that."

"Should I tell them?"

I hadn't thought of that. "Uh . . . Uh . . ."

She reached over and patted my hand. "Don't worry, gino. I'm not going to spill any beans. Go ahead—send them in."

"They're not here right now." I glanced around the room. "As far as I know. But here's the thing: they want to bring in a neurobiologist to take a look at you. He'd like to conduct some tests. That okay with you?"

"Love to meet one of your high-powered biologists. Maybe I could learn something from him."

"Will you be here Friday?"

She went for a zucchini. "If you ask me nicely."

"What about Congo?"

"Oh, I'm finished in Congo for the moment."

"For the moment?"

"I'll be making one last trip to pick up a few traveling companions. Otherwise, I'm off to see the rest of your WORLD."

"Oh. Okay, I'll set something up with the neurologist. By the way, the British journalist is in town now, unless the weather delayed his flight. He wants to have that interview with you after we finish here. Any problem with that?"

"Can I fool around with the bloke?"

I sighed—disgustedly, I'm afraid. "Not unless you arrange something with him for later. I'll be there, too, by the way."

"When I meet him later on?"

"No, damn it, for the interview."

"To chaperone, is that it?"

"Something like that. Now before we discuss last Monday's meeting, how are your plans for the return trip to K-PAX shaping up? Cassandra has been—"

"Have you been on the web lately?"

"Uh—not since yesterday. Why?"

"I've set up a website listing the requirements people must fulfill in order to emigrate. If you're interested, you can check it out at *www.K-PAXtrip.com*."

"You've got a website??"

"I don't think there's anything seriously wrong with your hearing, chief. I think it may be a comprehension problem."

"I mean, how did you—"

"Why don't you just check out the site? Save yourself a lot of valuable time."

I jotted myself a little note to do that. "And what about the football stadium?"

"What about it?"

"Dammit, fled, have you got one lined up yet? That can't be an easy thing to arrange."

"Oh, you mean where am I going to get the rent money and all that. I don't think it's going to be very difficult. A lot of people are prepared to spend millions of dollars for a trip into outer space. I can do better than that. I can take one of the owners to Mars or Jupiter if he wants, in exchange for a few hours' stadium rental. No big deal."

"And how will you advertise this offer?"

"It's already on the website." Her eyes fluttered innocently. "Do you think I should mention it in the TV and magazine interviews?"

"I doubt if they'd be available in time. Of course it depends on when you're leaving...."

"Asap."

"What's the rush?"

"It's depressing here." Still munching, she stood up, scratched her ribs, farted. The phony demure act had been set aside for the time being, apparently. "Is that all you wanted to talk about today?"

"No. I wanted to discuss the results of the hypnosis we did last Friday."

The back of a hairy hand flapped against her forehead. "There are results??"

"Yes and no. There's an affliction called dissociative–"

"Identity disorder. That's what you accused prot of having, right?"

"That's right. And I think you may have caught it."

"I didn't know it was catching!"

"It's not. That was a joke." I shook my head. "You K-PAXians have no sense of–"

"I know it was a joke, you ninny. So who are my other alleged 'identities'?"

"I don't know yet. I don't even know how many you have."

"I hope one of them is male. I've always wondered what it would be like for a guy."

"I don't know what gender any of them are. Shut up and let me talk for a minute, will you?"

After swallowing the last of the zucchini, she clamped her lips tightly together and nodded solemnly.

"All right, let's cut the clowning, shall we? When I put you under hypnosis and asked if there were anyone else with you, someone seemed to come forward. For the moment I'm assuming it's a 'she.' Anyway, whoever it was seemed very timid. Withdrawn, I would say. In fact, she seemed to be trying to hide from me."

Fled waited for me to go on. When I didn't, she said, through tight lips, "Are you finished? Am I allowed to speak now?"

"Yes, goddamm it, speak. Doesn't having an alter ego like that interest you at all?"

"Okay, I'll play your little game for a minute. Why should it interest me? If you're right about all these 'alter egos,' doesn't everyone have a few?"

"No."

"How do you know that?"

"I'm a psychiatrist, remember?"

"Yes, I do remember, and I think you've said on more than one occasion that we can never be sure what is going on in someone's brain, human or otherwise. For all you know, every being on EARTH may have hundreds of these 'egos' wandering around in their heads. Eating potato chips, playing baseball, whatever–right?"

"Well, technically, that's right. However, in the absence of symptoms . . . ." But the fact is, she was absolutely correct. We still know very little about how the brain operates, and in particular, how individual personalities are formed. "In your case, though, there's a complication."

"Oh, my god!"

"Look–do you want to discuss this or not?"

"Sure." She yawned loudly. "It's fascinating."

I luxuriated in a momentary glower before moving on. "The fact that you've made several trips to Congo suggests to me that your alter ego may be Congolese. She might even be a chimpanzee. What do you think about that idea?"

"Interesting speculation."

"The question I wanted to ask you about all this is: how do I communicate with her?"

"What languages does she speak?"

"I don't know. She wouldn't talk to me. So here's my suggestion. Actually it's my son Will's suggestion: I'd like to videotape today's ses–I mean discussion–and ask you to watch it. See if you can figure out who your apparent alter is and what she's trying to communicate to me, if anything. Even a gesture might tell us something. Maybe you can at least determine whether she's a chimpanzee, an abused human being, or maybe something else."

"Sure. Tape the hell out of it."

"Fine. Then let's not waste any more time." I went to the camera Will had set up for me. There was a sign hanging off one of the switches, complete with instructions indicating which way to flip it. When I did that, a satisfying whirring sound came from the thing and I returned to fled. She was calmly waiting for me, and in less than a minute she was under.

I had spent so much time worrying about whether I was going to screw up the equipment that I forgot to think about what to do once we got started. "Okay, fled, just relax. Imagine, if you like, that you're in Congo in your favorite part of the forest." I waited for a moment. "You may open your eyes if you wish."

Her eyes popped open. She seemed to be gazing at me, but whatever she was seeing was inside her head.

"Good. Now I'm going to ask your companion to come forward. Just relax and let her come into the room with me."

As before, fled slumped down in the chair for a second or two. Suddenly, as if noticing me for the first time, she made a little choking sound and climbed down behind the desk, apparently hoping I hadn't seen her. I got up and quietly peered over it. "Hello," I said, as gently as I could. "It's okay–you're safe here."

She remained motionless for a few moments before slowly looking up at me. She blinked, but said nothing.

"Can you say something to me in English? Or maybe French? Parlez-vous français?" I waited, but she seemed content to simply watch me from her "hiding" place. "Hello? Can you just say hello?"

She either could not or would not do so.

At this point I took a chance. I padded softly around the desk, my fingers outstretched. As soon as she saw me coming toward her she screamed and covered her head with her hands. I backed away and she stopped, but she was breathing hard and making soft guttural noises. Her eyes darted here and there around the room, presumably searching for an escape route.

Slowly I raised my right hand in the universal gesture of peace. "I won't harm you," I promised her. This elicited only a flinch, and an arm came up to ward off any impending blows.

I waited patiently. She refused to move except for a slight rocking motion. There didn't seem to be much point in going further. Unless– I moved incrementally toward her. Again she became agitated and started to babble something I couldn't understand. I backed away a few steps and she quieted down a little. I wanted to touch her, but thought better of it. I think I could actually smell her fear. Realizing that this could go on for a very long time, and might be causing her severe distress, I decided to call it off for the moment. "Okay, fled, we're finished. You can come back out now."

In a minute or two she began to straighten up. Finally, her eyes came to a focus on me.

"Thank you," I said. "Now I'm going to count backward from five to one. When I get to—"

"Yes, I know." She was already back to full consciousness and waiting for me to say something.

I got up and switched off the camera. "Now let's see if we can get this thing to rewind...."

She jumped up. "Move over," she commanded. In a short while she held a tape in her hairy hands. "Well, bozo, is there a player in here?"

There wasn't. She took off and I followed–down the stairs to the first-floor lounge, where a few of the patients were napping or just staring into space. She found an unwatched television set and pushed the tape into the player. I sat down beside her on the nearest sofa and watched it with her. I had seen it all before, of course, but fled hadn't, and neither had the patients, who began to amble toward the set. As it went on, and her evident alter ego screamed, and later babbled something incomprehensible, fled's eyes got bigger. So did those of the audience.

"If I hadn't seen this for myself..." she whispered.

"What is it? Do you know her?"

"No. She's a young female chimpanzee. Probably from the mountains of Rwanda or Cameroon."

"Can you tell what she's saying?"

"Not entirely. She only spoke a few words. Something about her mother."

"If I could get her to say something else, would you be able to make it out?"

"Don't know. I'm not familiar with every dialect spoken on EARTH, you know. Or even in Africa."

"Chimpanzees have dialects?"

"Of course. All beings separated by geographical barriers do."

"So how do you suggest I communicate with her?"

"Isn't it obvious? What you need is a translator. Someone who can speak to her."

Several voices chorused, "Yeah. A translator!"

"And where do you suggest we find this translator?"

"There are plenty of captive chimpanzees who might be able to speak to her. All you have to do is find one of them."

"You know, that might work! But wait–how do I speak to this captive chimpanzee?"

"There are a few humans around who can talk to chimpanzees. In only one language, but that might be enough."

"What language?"

"I think you call it 'American sign language.'"

"American sign language . . . ?" echoed our audience.

It sounded like a good idea until I realized: "That wouldn't help. Your alter ego might not know sign language. Probably doesn't, in fact."

"No, you dummy. The primary translator would be the chimpanzee who speaks sign language with his guardian, and who also knows the languages of the jungle. Get it?"

"Yes! Why didn't I think of that?"

"No comment."

The patients all laughed. "No comment! No comment!"

"Uh–do you happen to know any–"

"Hell's bells, doctor! Do I have to do *everything* for you?"

"But there isn't enough time to find these translators. I can't travel at the speed of light, you know."

"Yes, you can."

"I can?"

"Telephone, e-mail, other electromagnetic devices."

The audience looked at one another and shrugged.

"All right, I'll give it a try. Let's take a break now and I'll go see if the reporter has shown up. Shall we meet again in, say, an hour?"

"One hour. A twenty-fourth of a day. A hundred sixty-eighth of a week. One sixty-one thousand three hundredth–"

The patients began to applaud. I didn't wait around to hear the rest.

* * *

When I got to the administrative office I found the British magazine editor waiting for me. Margie had been keeping him occupied. "I always wanted to visit England!" she gushed. "My great-grandparents were born there!"

"Come on over!" he replied with equal enthusiasm, though he was thirty years her senior. "I'll give you a pub tour!" He jumped up when he saw me, and thrust out a hand. "Smythe," he said pleasantly, with barely a hint of an accent. The rest of him, however, was thoroughly British—ruddy complexion, handlebar mustache, a tweed jacket and vest, and he carried himself in a dignified manner. "Love your weather here!"

I admired his energy, especially after a long flight and rainy taxi ride into the city. Of course he was younger than I was, I mused, but so was almost everyone I saw these days. I asked Margie whether Dr. Goldfarb was in.

"She's already met Mr. Smythe. She says he's all yours!"

"Fine." I turned to our guest. "It's a bit early for lunch, Mr. Smythe. But maybe you'd like a cup of coffee before we get started with fled?"

"I'd love a cup of tea, if you have it."

"Of course. Let's go to the dining room."

On the way there I commented on his almost nonexistent English accent. "In fact, you could almost be from the American Midwest."

"I was born in Indiana," he confided. "Name used to be 'Smith'. Never quite lost my Hoosier twang."

"How did you get to—"

"I was fascinated by British history in school. All those beheadings and the like. And when I went there, I found the people to be open and direct, unlike the impression most Americans have." He confided: "They love a good gossip."

I was beginning to detect a faint whiff of smarm. "Is that why you're interviewing fled? To get some good gossip started?"

"Not really. We don't start anything. We just reveal it. Spread it out a bit. One thing I've learned in my quarter-century in the business: you never know what juicy stuff is hiding below a person's surface."

"Fled isn't a 'person.' She's an orf."

"Exactly. That's part of the idea for the interview. Do orfs have all that juicy stuff hiding below their surfaces, just like we do?"

I could have answered that one, but chose not to. "Well, according to the rules, you're allowed an hour. Will that be enough to tease out the juicy stuff, do you think?"

If he sensed a hint of sarcasm, he didn't show it. "Shouldn't take more than an hour to root 'er out. I'm pretty good at what I do. And you should have a copy of *Life in General* in less than a fortnight."

"That's something like our *'People'* magazine," isn't it?"

"Yes, I believe it is. We usually interview well-known people—movie stars and the like." He glanced around before whispering, "You'd be surprised. They're the dullest people imaginable. We usually have to work pretty hard to get anything intelligent out of them. Still," he added cheerfully, "no matter what we come up with, our readers eat up everything we print about their faves. Which is fine with me. Otherwise I'd be out of a job."

We got to the doctor's dining room, which was empty. I found the teabags, hot water, and a carton of milk. "I'm afraid this will have to do."

He seemed a trifle disappointed by the absence of a proper teapot and cozy, but graciously accepted the substitutes and proceeded to solemnly dunk the bag for exactly two minutes before filling the rest of the mug with milk and glugging it all down in one go as if his life depended on it. Spotting a case containing doughnuts and muffins, he helped himself to a few of those as well. While he gorged on these and made another cup of milky tea, I went over the ground rules with him, which had already been worked out between the lawyers. The principle details were that Smythe could tape the interview and we would get a copy of the tape, not a transcript; and that I would be allowed to preview the article for factual errors, but not content, prior to publication. If I insisted on changes—either additions or deletions—in the substance of the story all fees would be returned, though the magazine would retain the option to publish the edited version.

Smythe had no problem with any of this, and cheerfully signed the agreement, as did I. "One question: how did you know about fled?"

"She sent us an e-mail."

"How did she know about *you*?"

"I don't have a clue. But I understand that K-PAXians pick up all our electronic broadcasts. Maybe she reads our zine online."

I checked my watch. Smythe quickly finished his third cup of tea and we headed for the lounge to look for fled, who had agreed to meet us there. She was speaking with Claire, or vice versa. I politely asked the latter to excuse us, and she graciously agreed. In fact, she seemed to be quite relaxed, a condition I didn't usually associate with "Dr. Smith." I wondered what fled had told her—that she would be out of here soon?

Smythe, too, was surprisingly at ease with fled. Of course he had been thoroughly briefed on her physical attributes, and they chatted amiably as we rode the elevator (he was in even worse shape than I—was she being solicitous of his welfare?) to Room 520. He took my place at Goldfarb's desk, and fled her usual chair. I sat off to the side, planning to observe and say nothing (not a term in the agreement, but tacitly understood).

The first part of their discussion revealed no surprises—fled was from K-PAX; she was a trod, one of the orfs; she came here to study our various life forms; she planned to take 100,000 people back with her when she returned; a departure site had yet to be determined (any owners of football teams interested?); to facilitate the selection process, she had created a website listing the requirements needed to qualify for the journey. Nothing new there. But when fled mentioned her pregnancy I shouted, "What??"

Smythe, for his part, allowed himself a dignified "Yahoo!"

"I'm expecting a child, doctor b. Aren't you thrilled?"

"You never told me!"

"You never asked!"

"Well, what the hell is he? A chimpanzee? A bonobo? What?"

"You shouldn't get so excited, gino. Did you take your diuretic this morning?"

"All right, all right. I'm calm. Now will you tell me who the father of your child is?"

"I haven't the slightest idea."

"Well, how many chimpanzees have you had–uh–intercourse with?"

"Quite a few. But he could be half gorilla."

"You had sex with a gorilla?"

"One or two. Or he could be human."

"He's *human*?"

"Could be. Now pay attention. I told you: I don't know who the father is."

"But how could you be pregnant? What about the yorts? We don't have those on Earth, do we?"

"Obviously I don't need them here. Amazing PLANET, don't you think? Must have something to do with the way your sperm functions."

The grin on Smythe's face was a foot wide. Despite the tape recorder humming on the desk, he was furiously jotting everything down. He didn't seem to mind at all that I had done half his work for him.

I didn't hear much of the rest of the interview. When it was finally over (we overshot by half an hour), I told fled, "I'll speak to you about this later."

"No doubt," she replied with a little snort.

I grimly escorted Smythe back to Goldfarb's office. Halfway there, he decided to head directly for the airport. "This is too good to keep to myself," he blurted before rushing toward the front door. "Cheerio!" he called out as he departed.

He was right: I wanted to tell someone, too. But not Goldfarb–I wanted to think about it first. It occurred to me to wonder what effect the news would have on the patients. And what Dartmouth and Wang were going to do about it.

As I was leaving the hospital, I met Chang and Roberts coming back in. Laura stopped me. "Claire discarded her stethoscope. I think fled told her she's going to K-PAX."

"I wouldn't be surprised."

Roberts added his two cents. "Maybe she only suggested that Claire retire and forget about psychiatry. Like Gene, here."

As I passed by the lawn, I noticed that some of the patients had found Claire's stethoscope and were examining each other's heads with it. I wished them luck. They couldn't do any harm, and they might even find something we had missed.

* * *

Karen thought fled's pregnancy was funny. I didn't, but her laugh is very infectious. We giggled like children. Then I told her about fled's website describing the requirements for a one-way trip to K-PAX. "Let's go take a look," she said.

On the way to my study she asked me, in all seriousness, "Would you go with her?"

"I don't know. Would you?"

"No."

"Then neither would I."

I found the site. It wasn't fancy, but it was to the point. She had listed the requirements for the journey, all right. But I almost felt sorry for her: there probably weren't many people on the entire planet, if any, who would be going along for the ride. Here's what it said:

ATTENTION! PEOPLE OF EARTH!
FREE TRIP TO K-PAX!

SICK OF YOUR LIFE ON THIS PLANET? WANT A CHANGE OF HABITAT? THE SHIP IS LEAVING SOON! SEND YOUR APPLICATION NOW!!!

REQUIREMENTS

1. **Vegan**
2. **Pacifist**
3. **Must have no more than two children (they are welcome also)**
4. **Prepared to give away any money or property**
5. **Opposed to zoos and all other exploitations of non-human animals**
6. **Willing to leave all flags behind**
7. **Able to live without TV**
8. **All religions must be left at the door**
9. **Sense of humor preferred**

HUNTERS, CORPORATE EXECUTIVES, AND POLITICIANS NEED NOT APPLY

ONLY 100,000 SEATS AVAILABLE
SEND APPLICATION TO *fled@mpi.com*
(include GPS co-ordinates, if known)

P.S. WANTED: FOOTBALL STADIUM FOR A DAY. WILL EXCHANGE FOR QUICK TRIP TO PLANET OF YOUR CHOICE

"Surely there are a *few* people out there who can meet these criteria," Karen observed. "Abby, for one."

"Do you think she would go without Steve?"

"Probably."

We giggled some more.

*   *   *

Normally I have a brief afternoon snooze right after lunch. This time, to my wife's amazement, I stayed in my study to see what I could find about the use of sign language to speak with the various apes. A number of primatologists have utilized this technique to communicate with certain of their subjects, and have discovered, for example, that they possess considerable language skills, and even the ability to create new words to express themselves when the old ones seem inadequate. Koko, a female gorilla, possesses a Stanford-Binet IQ of 85–95, boasts a vocabulary of about a thousand words, and can understand several thousand more. Moreover, I learned, all of the ape families demonstrate long-term memories, are self-aware, and exhibit rich emotional lives. I knew that of all the animals, the chimpanzees were genetically most similar to humans, but was surprised to learn that even gorillas share a whopping 97% of our DNA. Surprisingly, though, it's their Asian cousins, the orangutans, who are most like humans in hair pattern, gestation period, and dental characteristics, as well as hormonal levels, sexual physiology, and copulatory behavior. But there is no question that *all* of the great apes are truly our very close cousins. Literally, in fact, since we both evolved from the same ancestor!

There were dozens of books listed on amazon.com, but I didn't want to wait the few days it would take to get them. I told my wife where I was going. "Bring me back a good mystery," she called out. "See if you can get *Murder on Spruce Island*!"

If the "boys" were waiting for me outside, they didn't try to stop me from jumping into the car and zooming off to the library, perhaps because of the rain.

Only three of the books I had found on the Internet were available. I checked out the one that seemed most informative, as well as the mystery Karen had requested. With less than two days before my next meeting with fled, I began reading as soon as I got home, and by evening I had compiled a list of six individuals who were experts on ape communications.

But calling them would have to wait until the next morning. We had dinner guests that evening.

*   *   *

Just before the Siegels arrived, our lovely daughter Jennifer called from California. She was very excited: the HIV vaccine she had been working on had passed the initial tests for safety and effectiveness, and would be going into larger-scale clinical trials in the next few months. With all that hard work behind her, she and her partner (an ophthalmologist) were planning to come east for a short vacation in July. Unfortunately, they wouldn't be staying with us long; they would be spending most of the time in Massachusetts, the only state where they could be legally married. Though we talk to her regularly we hadn't seen her and Anne for nearly two years, and we quickly assured her we would take whatever time she could give us.

But the main reason she had called was that she was wondering what was going on with fled, whom Karen had told her about earlier. Forgetting that the government boys might be monitoring what we said, I filled her in on everything I knew. She listened silently, and when I was finished she posed an interesting question: if fled's child were half human, would he or she be treated as human or chimpanzee, i.e., would the baby be welcomed by the general public or ostracized as a "freak of nature"? I hadn't really thought about that, but her point was obvious. Just as children of mixed parentage are considered to be non-white by almost everyone, probably most people would consider fled's half-human child to be "sub-human."

But an even more frightening possibility crossed my mind, and I asked her whether she thought that some people—particularly those professing certain fundamentalist religious faiths—would want to harm fled and the child, claiming it to be the "work of the devil"? Privately, I wondered whether Wang and his partner might not reach the same conclusion.

Jenny, always the practical one, advised, "Dad, see if you can get her to leave before that happens."

* * *

Despite the fact that we shared a granddaughter (Will's wife Dawn is Bill and Eileen's daughter), and were nearby neighbors, we hadn't seen our old friends the Siegels for several weeks, mainly because they had only recently returned from a visit to Poland. "It's an amazing country," they informed us. "They are enjoying their freedom from communism tremendously, and are open to all kinds of new ideas. And," said Bill, taking a forkful of couscous, "the food is wonderful."

After they had raved about the scenery and architecture, particular that of the many well-preserved and charming old Polish towns, the conversation turned to fled, whom they had only just learned about. I reported, "She told me this morning that she's pregnant, and that the father may be human."

Bill stopped chewing. "That's a little far-fetched, isn't it? Maybe she's just pulling one of your legs."

"What motive would she have for lying about it?"

"Who knows? To get attention, maybe. To achieve a degree of sympathy or popularity with the patients. Motherhood is still a powerful force, even in a mental institution."

"And it sells a hell of a lot of magazines," his wife observed.

"Not to mention newspapers and TV programs," Karen added.

That kind of deviousness hadn't occurred to me, but it probably deserved serious consideration. I've learned never to take lightly anything Bill tells me. It was he, after all, who got me into psychiatry. Then I told them about her website.

"She's recruiting?" Bill asked, incredulously. "Why would she do that?"

"She says she's trying to help people who aren't happy here."

"But won't we just screw up K-PAX like we did the Earth?"

"Claims she's not taking the ones responsible for that."

"We're all responsible for that," Eileen pointed out.

This led, inevitably, to politics (with the Siegels, something always does). They were no more fans of the current administration and the party in power than we were (though none of us were thrilled with the opposition, either). "What we need," Bill opined, "is a third party."

"What we need," countered his wife, "are responsible news media that aren't beholden to their advertisers. Otherwise a new party, or even a new idea, doesn't stand a chance. The news has become a form of propaganda."

"Even so," I put in, "two parties would be enough if the Democrats had any guts. I don't know what they're so afraid of."

"Same thing as everyone else," Karen answered. "Losing their jobs."

Perhaps I shouldn't have had a second glass of wine, but I found myself telling the Siegels about Dartmouth and Wang, and their theory that the best way to protect us from terrorists is to bug every home in the country. "In fact," I confidently assured them, "they could be listening to every word we're saying."

Bill raised his glass. "To Dartmouth," he toasted.

"And Wang," seconded Eileen.

I took part in the toast and merrily carried on. "They suggested that any one of our neighbors could be working for them, keeping their eyes open for the terrorists." I couldn't resist the urge to ask, with a stupid little laugh, "You guys aren't spying on us, are you?"

Bill, who possesses an arid sense of humor, made no response to this, but pulled out a little notebook and jotted something into it. Without putting it away he asked, "What is your opinion on the nuclear weapons programs in Iran and North Korea?"

I hoped he was joking.

CHAPTER SEVEN

Karen and I had planned to do some gardening on Thursday, but the rain was still coming down so I spent most of the day (after the hangover wore off) trying to track down the primatologists I had found. Two of them worked for state universities, another at a primate sanctuary for retired chimpanzees. (For those who don't know what a chimpanzee can be "retired" from, many have spent most of their lives living in research institutions, the subject of various stressful medical experiments.) The others were retired or deceased. I didn't reach any of them at first–they were all teaching classes or out in the field–but one of them, Dr. Ellen Tewksbury, an ethologist from Texas, returned my call within the hour. As luck would have it she had read the *K-PAX* trilogy, and she proclaimed that she would give a "limb" to speak with fled.

I explained the situation: our visitor apparently harbored at least one alter ego, who appeared to be a chimpanzee, and we needed a primate who could both speak with another ape and use sign language to communicate any messages to Dr. Tewksbury, who would then relay the information to me.

She seemed barely able to contain her anticipation, so I asked her if she could get to New York by Monday.

"Filbert and I will be on our way tomorrow!" Though she seemed older, the enthusiasm in her voice reminded me of Giselle Griffin, the former reporter who was now on K-PAX with prot and the others.

"Good! You can stay with my wife and me if you like. We need to preview the session you'll be participating in, as well as discuss your expenses and so forth."

"Well . . ."

"Yes?"

"I'm not sure you want to accomodate a chimpanzee in your home, Dr. Brewer."

"Oh. Yes, I see what you mean."

"But that's not a problem! I have a friend in Jersey who would be happy to put us up. He's quite familiar with chimpanzee behavior. I'll have to drive the van, though, so it will take us a couple of days. I'll call you when we get in, okay?"

"Are you sure this isn't too much trouble for you?"

"Are you kidding? This is my job. If I passed up an opportunity like this, I'd never forgive myself!"

How I wish the people down at Wal-Mart felt that way about theirs.

* * *

The government-appointed neurobiologist came early, and was considerably annoyed when Officer Wilson at the gate wouldn't grant him entrée until I could get to the hospital. As a symbol of protest, I suppose, he stood in the drizzle like a statue until I arrived. He was bald as an egg, the man, and wore a soaking wet knee-length lab coat as he waited in the rainy street clutching an ancient medical bag as if he were planning to do a few house calls after seeing fled. Presumably it contained whatever equipment he needed for her neurological exam. He was still fidgeting and seething as I escorted him into the building. Though I had been told he was 'nameless,' he nevertheless glumly introduced himself as "Dr. Sauer," which, he hastened to inform me, was an alias. "I find that people are more comfortable when they can call someone by a name," he noted, by way of official explanation. "Even a fictitious one. Like your bogus construction barricade," he added approvingly.

Judging by the speed with which he crossed the foyer and took the stairs (I took the elevator), it is probably safe to safe to say that he enjoyed his job. But, of course, so did the people who did medical experiments on humans in Nazi Germany, I suppose. When I got to the fifth floor I found him taking pictures of the empty corridor. As soon as he saw me he stuffed the camera (disguised as a toy giraffe) back into his "medical" bag.

Fortunately, fled was waiting for us in her usual place in 520. Though he had undoubtedly been apprised of the subject he was going to examine, Sauer was noticeably shaken by her appearance. In contrast to Smythe's interview, I wasn't permitted to stay and observe—if I had, I suppose I might possibly have learned some secrets that were certain to become classified. I didn't mind; he gave me the creeps. Anyway, I was confident that fled could take care of herself in this, or any other, situation, and would probably be only too happy later on to share them with me.

I left them alone and returned to the first-floor lounge, where I discovered Phyllis invisibly sitting by herself. When I spoke to her she pretended, as always, that she hadn't heard me. In fact, though she was looking directly at me, she didn't move a muscle.

Whenever I come upon Phyllis, or any other difficult and perplexing patient, I am reminded of how tenuous is the line between sanity and mental illness. A seemingly minor insult to the brain, particularly to the frontal lobes, can result in all kinds of bizarre consequences for the rest of one's life. A mild viral illness, an encounter with a doorknob, a subtle age-related deterioration—virtually anything can cause the structural or chemical damage that changes the way a person perceives and deals with his surroundings. In the extreme, a woman might seem perfectly normal one minute and become Joan of Arc the next. Sometimes these metamorphoses can be reversed with treatment, or even disappear on their own, but usually they are intractable. And such afflictions, like the various forms of cancer, can happen to anyone, regardless of social standing, intelligence, or anything else.

Cotan's is one of the oddest and rarest syndromes in the annals of psychiatry. A patient with this condition believes that nothing exists. In a bizarre variation on this theme, called Cotard's Syndrome, a person might think that some of his body parts are missing. In a kind of worst-case scenario, Phyllis believes that *all* of them are missing, i.e., that she is totally invisible. Thus, she thinks she can get by with stealing others' food, clothing, or the like without being detected. Never mind that the clothing would be recognized on her "nonexistent" frame; with disorders of this sort, logic takes a back seat. But why in the world would a minor incident produce such a fantastic aberration, especially when none of the thousand other functions are in any way impaired? Or perhaps in Phyllis's case it has nothing to do with brain damage. There may have been other events in her background that we don't know about. It's quite possible that she only feels safe if she can't be seen by anyone.

She got up to go somewhere, at which time she farted quite noticeably. Any normal person would be embarrassed by this, or would smile sheepishly or apologize in embarrassment. Not Phyllis. In fact she gave her fernad a good scratching before shuffling off. Obviously there are certain advantages to being invisible.

I wondered again whether fled might somehow be able to help this unhappy woman and all the other patients, and I reminded myself to ask her whether she could, in fact, read their otherwise inscrutable minds. But I was getting the feeling that it had better be soon.

At this point several of the inmates came barging in, chatting animatedly in small groups and nearly knocking over poor Phyllis, who was still making her way across the lounge. Even some of the antisocial patients were participating. They were so engrossed in their conversations that they didn't seem to notice my being in their midst. The subject of their discussions was fled. A few days ago they were leery of her; now they were excited and happy—all because of her pregnancy.

It's rare that a mental patient conceives while confined to a hospital, though it does happen occasionally. Sometimes, too, a patient who is already pregnant arrives. Our most recent such case was Lou, now the "mother" (thanks to a sex-change operation) of a ten-year-old girl and living in another city. It's amazing how solicitous the other inmates can be of a new "Mona Lisa," giving her extra food or helping her with certain tasks and so on. Suddenly it appeared that fled would be reaping the benefits of everyone's care and concern and—yes—love. For all we knew, in fact, she might have been planning this from the beginning as a way of gaining the patients' sympathy and trust.

Or, as Bill Siegel had suggested, she might be faking it, perhaps for the same reason.

* * *

I had allowed an hour for Dr. "Sauer" to examine fled. Since we already had her EEG on file, I presumed he wanted to check her ability to identify playing cards or to describe certain pictures he held in his head, or maybe even to photograph any "auras" or the like encircling her own, in order to determine how she might be able to read his mind.

The subject of paranormal phenomena is likely to raise the hackles of any respected scientist. Contrary to popular belief, it's not that they are biased about such matters. It's that science is based on evidence (and nothing else), and there is very little that supports the occurrence of paranormal events of any kind–UFOs, ghosts, feelings in plants, and, yes, auras–and what little there is is shaky at best. Yet, belief in such phenomena, like that of religion, is often strong, and unsettling claims sometimes arise. Are all these reports merely manifestations of wishful thinking, or are the scientists missing something? My personal opinion is that the subject is not yet closed, but until I see (or feel) the evidence for any of these events myself, I will remain unconvinced. (I would be happy to take part in any legitimate study of paranormal events but, to date, no one has asked me, including "Sauer" upstairs at this very moment with fled.)

Because it was still raining outside, Darryl and Georgie began to toss the latter's worn football back and forth in the lounge. I started to tell them they couldn't play inside, then I thought: what the hell–I don't work here anymore. I was heading for the dining room to get a cup of coffee when Rothstein came by. Kathy is one of the most intense, and certainly the most reserved, of the MPI staff, tending to keep her thoughts and opinions to herself. I have no problem with that; she performs her duties conscientiously and well, and her methods and her personal life are her own. So I was quite surprised when she sought me out to discuss a couple of things that were bothering her. I thought: here's someone who doesn't think I'm over the hill! "Sure," I told her. "What's on your mind?"

One of her patients was Mrs. Weathers, now over a hundred years old and barely able to see or hear. Both of those conditions are treatable in her case, yet she refuses to have anything done about them. "I'm more than a century old," she once told Dr. Rothstein. "I *should* be blind and deaf!"

That isn't quite true, of course. There are some 15,000 centenarians living in the U.S. today, and many are healthy enough to experience a considerable measure of enjoyment of their lives. A few even continue to work. Their effectiveness might be open to question, but the point is they are still able to get to the office and perform whatever functions they are capable of. And, of course, the numbers are increasing all the time. But a hundred-year-old woman was almost unheard of when Mrs. Weathers was growing up, so she's certain she's going to keel over at any moment. In a real sense, though, it's her *mindset* that's old, more than her body. Indeed, she could well live another decade or more.

Kathy wanted me to speak to Mrs. W about her defeatist attitude, which included conserving her energy by barely moving all day. I demurred. Who knows–perhaps the old bat's right: whatever her program, it's worked for more than a century. And what if we encouraged her to start running laps around the back forty and she dropped dead on us? I suggested we let nature take its course. Her only comment was: "I hope I never get that old . . . ."

The other matter she wanted to discuss was more problematical. She had just had a session with Rick, and felt she might be on to something. She had asked him whether he wanted to go to K-PAX with fled. It was a variation on the old conundrum, "I am lying." If this statement were true, it would also be false, and vice versa. This created a dilemma for him. If he lied and said he didn't want to go with fled, he would have to stay on Earth. She had hoped he would become flustered and confused, and see, perhaps for the first time, the difference between the truth and fiction. But Rick, who's no dummy, replied, "Please tell fled that I want to go to K-PAX." In fact, Kathy had been trying to catch Rick in the truth for some time, only to be thwarted again and again. She confessed that she was at her wit's end.

I commiserated. No one knows better than I that it's not easy to outsmart a mental patient. But before I could say another word, she pleaded with me to speak to fled about Rick–not to ask her to cure him, or even read his mind, but to take him to K-PAX! Then she scurried away, perhaps embarrassed to have finally given up on a very difficult patient. Was she shirking her responsibility? Or was there a different motive? Did she simply think Rick would be genuinely happier there and, as a good doctor, badly wanted that for him? Or was she suggesting that *anyone* who was having a hard time coping with his life might be happier on K-PAX, including, perhaps, herself? Was she one of the staff members who was thinking of applying for a spot on the roster? Did she fit any of the criteria outlined by fled for passenger status? I was surprised to discover that I knew absolutely nothing about this young psychiatrist, and really very little about what made most of my former colleagues, especially the newer ones, tick.

At this point Dr. Sauer came running down the staircase, his tie askew, his wet lab coat hanging limply out of his bag. When he spotted me he lurched to a stop and laughed crazily before taking off again through the lounge and out the front door, back into the endless rain. The patients and I watched him go without comment, though some of them emitted an uncertain chuckle or two.

A moment later fled came roaring into the lounge. If this was laughter, it was far different from the neurologist's, and it produced a few genuine guffaws among the inmates. "You humans are hilarious!" she exclaimed.

"Why?" I asked her. "What happened?"

"Your government agents had told him that I might be able to read minds. But of course he wanted to experience that for himself."

"And?"

"He didn't waste any time. As soon as he got there, he asked me tell him what he was thinking about."

"Well?"

"What a mess his head was! There was breakfast, his mother, a teenage daughter, his ex-wife, a few girlfriends, Jesus Christ, something about flaying, shooting rabbits with a BB gun, and a hundred other things—you name it. But those were only the surface thoughts. Underneath all that he was masturbating like a teenager, visiting whorehouses, undressing his sister, screwing a nun, and all kinds of other weird fantasies. If that's what they were. Someone should write a book about him!"

"So you told him all this?"

"When I described, in intimate detail, what his deepest desires amounted to, he freaked out and tried to rape me!"

"Did he succeed?"

"Not exactly!"

"You mean—"

"Let's say I offered no resistance."

I was pretty sure I was going to hear about this from Dartmouth and Wang. "What about the examination?"

"He said I passed . . . ." She threw back her head and emitted a loud "Harrrrruppp!" Everyone roared with her, except for Barney, unfortunately. Whether they all knew what they were laughing about was another matter.

Before fled could disappear again I took her aside and asked her point blank whether she could find the time to read the minds of each of our patients while she was still here, try to find anything we didn't yet know that might uncover the deeply-buried roots of their problems.

"You mean their sexual fantasies?"

I couldn't tell whether she was joking or not. "Not just that. I mean everything that's in there. To find out what the fundamental causes of their mental problems might be."

She hooted again. "Prot warned me you'd try to trick me into doing your job for you."

"I don't have a job. I'm retired, remember?"

"Relax, dr. b. I just have a few more places to visit and I'll be finished with my study of your life forms."

"What about your list of travel companions?"

"That, too. And I need to check out a few possible departure sites. After that, I'll see what I can do for your patients."

* * *

On the way home I got to thinking about Mrs. Weathers, and aging in general. It's tough to get old. You tire more easily, and when you rest it doesn't help as much as it used to. Everything is more difficult except for losing your balance, and things you could once eat with impunity now give you heartburn. You don't even think as well as you should. And it all comes on so gradually that it's barely noticeable at first. But eventually there comes a time when you ask yourself: what's wrong with me? And there inevitably comes another time when it finally hits you: you're old! Your only consolation is that you've lived long enough to get to this state.

At this point you get philosophical. You're lucky. You have a nice home and family, you've got enough money to be reasonably comfortable, you'll probably live several more years. You can't do everything you used to, but there are plenty of things you still enjoy. Life is good. Then you remember: in another twenty years or so (an instant!) you'll be in a nursing home with a batch of feeble old farts like yourself, and this goes on for another few years, until finally you will get sick and die. It makes you wonder what was the point. Then you realize that there is actually one good thing about growing old–you finally know the answer to that question: there isn't any! There's only one secret worth knowing: have fun while you can!

At that moment the sun came out and, as always, I forgot about my morbid ruminations.

Later that evening, while I was enjoying myself with a sudoku puzzle (the damn addictive things), Fred called. After his mother got through with him we had a good talk. At last he was taking the plunge! A date hadn't been set, but this time it was definite. "Which one is it?"

"The ballerina."

"But you've been with her off and on for as long as I can remember . . . ."

"That's just it–I finally realized that I always come back to her. And we're not getting any younger, you know."

"Tell me about it!" I said, and proceeded to unload on him my current thoughts on aging.

After I had gone through it all, his only comment was, "Enjoy myself? Well 'duh,' Dad. I've known that all my life." So much for the wisdom of one's elders.

Our perceptive son went on to tell me about his latest film role in which he would be playing, ironically, an old man, with flashbacks to his past dissolute life. But the main reason he had called, besides announcing his pending engagement, was that I had mentioned Darryl to him at some point, and evidently it stuck with him (I think he's a little in love with Meg Ryan himself). In any case he had run across someone who looked a lot like Ms. Ryan, and he wondered whether he should send her over to the hospital to meet Darryl. She was a good extemporaneous actress, he said, and could make herself so unpleasant that it might turn him away from the object of his affections forever.

"How soon could she get there?" I asked him.

"Probably sometime next week."

I don't know why I hadn't thought of this myself. "That's a great idea, Freddie. But it may be too late."

"Why?"

"Fled is going to read all the patients' minds. Try to find out what's really bugging them. Maybe we'll already know what's wrong with Darryl before your friend gets there!"

"That's terrific, Dad. But that doesn't necessarily mean you can cure them, does it?"

That hadn't occurred to me, either.

* * *

Goldfarb called me at home on Saturday (I'm beginning to consider having the phone disconnected). So did Will and Laura Chang, Jerry's staff physician. They all had the same message for me, though they expressed their concern in different ways.

Laura, the first to call, actually sounded angry. "Please tell your patients to leave mine in the hospital where they belong."

"What patients? I don't have any patients."

"Fled. She's disappeared again, only this time she took Jerry with her."

"What? Where'd they go?"

"I have no idea, Gene. I thought maybe *you* could tell *me*."

"Try to calm down," was my unasked advice. "Tell me what happened. Did anyone see them leave?"

"No, but several people saw her come to visit Jerry. Next thing we knew, they were gone."

"Are you saying she *kidnapped* him? Or did he leave of his own accord?"

"Who knows?" I could see her frowning in that disarming manner she has. "Don't get me wrong," she quickly added. "I don't mind her talking with Jerry. It's taking him on a joyride that concerns me. Who knows what it might do to an autistic patient. It might be too much for him. Or maybe he won't want to come back . . . ."

"All right, I see your point. In the first place, fled isn't really a patient. In the second, she's left the hospital several times before, and she always comes back. I think we should just play it cool until Monday. She's supposed to be meeting me and a translator who can speak with chimpanzees through sign language. I predict she'll show up right on time."

"And Jerry?"

"Jerry, too. And he'll be fine. Don't worry."

"So until then he's your responsibility?"

"Well—okay, yes. He's my responsibility."

Virginia and Will were also concerned, as was most of the other staff. Again, all I could do was try to maintain calm. Privately, I, too, was as concerned as hell. I wasn't particularly worried about the outcome of fled's latest escapade, but I hadn't a clue what she had in mind for Jerry (who was my own patient for a brief period several years earlier). I didn't even know where they had gone! Goldfarb invited me to the Monday morning staff meeting to further discuss the problem of fled and her "patientnapping."

I consoled myself with the thought that, even though he had rarely even left Ward Three, Jerry might actually enjoy getting out of the hospital for a while. After all, who knows what goes on in the mind of a severely autistic patient? Perhaps all those inward thoughts are of marvelous adventures, incredible sights, and he might finally get a chance to actually experience some of those for the first time.

But soon enough (I sincerely hoped), we could all ask him this ourselves.

* * *

Dr. Tewksbury, the chimpanzee whisperer, called me on Sunday afternoon while I was watching a Mets game. She and "Filbert" had arrived in Jersey and were safely ensconced in the home of the friend she had mentioned earlier. Both were well, she informed me, and "rarin' to go." I summarized what she should expect from her visit with fled, and instructed her on the best way to get to the Institute, which would involve a drive across the GW Bridge and a short hop over to Amsterdam Avenue. If she found this to be an imposing journey, I offered to meet her somewhere and drive in with her.

"No problem," she assured me. "I've been here before."

"To MPI??"

"No. To Jersey and the Big Apple. In fact, I was born here."

"Where?"

"Hoboken."

"Do you know a Joyce Trexler, who–"

"The world isn't *that* small, Dr. Brewer."

"No, I suppose it isn't," I replied wistfully. I assured Dr. Tewksbury that the security people had been informed and would be waiting for her at the gate, see that her van was parked, and she and Filbert would be escorted into the hospital. "You won't need an ID," I told her. "Filbert will probably be the only chimpanzee at the gate all day."

"I can't wait!" she gushed.

"Great," I replied. "I'll see you tomorrow." I almost included Dartmouth and Wang in my farewell.

By the time I got back to the game the Mets were six runs behind.

* * *

They phoned later that evening from God knows where. Karen and I were in the kitchen putting away the dishes and discussing a possible Christmas trip to visit

Jenny and Anne in California. Karen took the call, rolled her eyes, and handed me the mobile phone. "Hi guys," I said cheerfully. There was a pause, perhaps because they didn't know what to make of the unaccustomed familiarity. Wang patiently explained who he was, and apologized for disturbing me at home on a Sunday. But they had learned somehow of fled's website, and weren't too happy about it. In fact, they tried to shut it down, but every time they did, it popped back up again. I asked him how they discovered it. "That's classified," he snarled. "The point is, we can't let her suggest that only vegans are welcome on a trip to K-PAX, can we, Dr. Brewer?"

"What's wrong with vegans?" I asked weakly (as a result of prot's visit, I was a vegetarian myself, at least most of the time).

"Everything. Do you realize what this would do to the nation's economy?"

I reminded him that I was a doctor, not an economist.

"Sir, we'd like you to inform your friend that we cannot, and will not, tolerate an alien coming down here and telling us what to eat. Do you understand my meaning?"

"I'll pass along your message."

"Thank you. Now about our neurobiologist—do you recall his visit to your hospital?"

It had only been two days before. "Yes, I do. Dr. Sauer."

I could hear muffled laughter. "Is that what he called himself? Har, har, har. That's rich . . . . Anyway, he tells us that the results of his study are inconclusive. He'll need several more visits to reach any definite conclusions about her mindreading capabilities."

"I see."

"And Dr. Brewer?"

"Yes?"

"Based on his preliminary observations, he'd like to line up several colleagues to join him in performing further tests. Do you think that can be arranged?"

"I'll ask her."

"Thank you, sir. And according to Dr. 'Sauer,' the sooner the better."

The dial tone came before I could say "You're welcome" or "Good-bye." I thought I heard a noise from above. "I think they were on the roof," I told my wife.

"Maybe it was Santa Claus," she said.

If the "boys" knew anything about the upcoming visit from Ellen Tewksbury and Filbert, they didn't mention it.

CHAPTER EIGHT

There was an unusually long construction delay on I-78 and, unfortunately, I missed the Monday morning staff meeting. By the time I got to the hospital Dr. Tewksbury and Filbert were already inside somewhere, according to Officer Wilson at the gate. "What's going on, doc?" he called out as I waved past him. "There are apes all over the place!"

"One of our patients thinks she's a chimpanzee," I shouted jokingly.

"Gawd, I think she might be right!" he yelled back.

The lawn was in an uproar. I thought it was probably because Filbert was running around loose, stirring up trouble. But it wasn't that—he and Tewksbury were nowhere to be seen. It was Jerry, having just returned with fled, who was causing all the commotion. But this wasn't the Jerry that I, or any of the inmates, knew. He was standing against the front wall contemplating the grounds as if he had never seen any of it before. A group of patients were milling nearby, watching, whispering among themselves, waiting to see what he was going to do. He turned to look at them, as if noticing them for the first time. Slowly his arms came up and he ambled toward the group. Some of them backed away, apparently unsure of his intent. Howard, however, lifted his arms as well, and the two of them embraced. At this point the patients came up to him, one by one, to give him a hug and get one in return. He didn't avoid their gazes, and he spoke a few words to each of them. When everyone had made contact, the entire group headed toward the back forty to greet the other residents of MPI. The excitement was contagious. Once they were sure who he was, they were all genuinely happy for Jerry, who had been one of their own. But I suspected that underneath the obvious warmth and affection they were all thinking the same thing: if fled can make such a radical change in the character and demeanor of someone who may be worse off than I am, why couldn't she do the same for me?

Though most mental patients live in worlds of their own, they are nevertheless perfectly well aware that something about them isn't quite right, and they certainly don't enjoy their private hell. For the most part they try very hard to follow instructions, take their medications, get better. Despite our best efforts, however, we sometimes can't help them. The Manhattan Psychiatric Institute is more tragic than most hospitals in this regard because we take in so many unique and difficult cases, often after other institutions have already treated them and made little progress with their ailments.

Now we seemed to have one less of those difficult cases, thanks to fled, who stood along the back wall watching the proceedings like a proud parent. I could see she was grinning, and even from a distance I detected a little twinkle in her eye. She saw me and loped over. "You can tell me later what happened here," I said. "Right now we have an appointment with your alter ego."

* * *

I asked fled to remain for a moment outside Room 520, where I found Dr. Tewksbury patiently waiting with Filbert. Virginia, too, had missed the Monday meeting because she had met them at the gate, brought them up, and remained with them until I arrived (Laura Chang chaired the meeting in her absence). As soon as I came in she excused herself.

"Are you sure you don't want to stay for this?" I asked her, certain she would love to witness the proceedings (though she would never admit it).

"No, thanks. I've got a hospital to direct." She went for the door before turning to add, with a hint of a smile, "Or is it a circus I'm running here?"

Filbert's appearance didn't surprise me. We had, after all, only recently enjoyed the company of one of his cousins–Okeemon the bonobo (not to mention fled herself). Filbert was a little bigger and more agitated than the hippie chimp, but otherwise I probably wouldn't have been able to tell them apart. Consequently, I kept an eye on his hands.

It was the appearance of Ellen Tewksbury that shocked me. On the phone she sounded much like Giselle–young, petite, attractive (yes, it sometimes shows in the voice, which often reflects the confident feeling one has in her appearance). Dr. Tewksbury ("Tewks" I learned to call her) was none of those. She was, I would guess, in her early seventies, and considerably larger than I would have thought. Not fat, just huge. More than six feet tall and built like a tackle. Even her teeth were big, as were her heavy horn-rimmed glasses. I supposed one would have to be pretty hefty to handle animals as strong and unpredictable as chimpanzees. Her hair, on the other hand, was a strikingly bright red, and her hands were surprisingly small and soft.

Filbert seemed to be having a good time. Though all the papers had long been pilfered from Goldfarb's desk and strewn everywhere, he delighted in opening and closing the drawers, sometimes reaching into one of them to pull out a forgotten pencil or paper clip, hooting to announce each new discovery. Finally, Tewks placed a gentle hand on his shoulder. That's when he noticed fled standing in the doorway.

He ran for her. Neither his guardian nor I tried to stop him. He jumped into her arms and screamed with pleasure, as if she were his long-lost mother. Finally she whispered something in his ear, and he began, finally, to quiet down.

Tewksbury herself was unable to take her eyes off our alien visitor, as if a lifelong dream had come true. I managed a brief introduction and they clasped their hands together warmly. Filbert, though trying to remain calm as instructed, was obviously beside himself with joy, whirling and clapping and hanging onto one or the other's arms, ignoring me altogether.

I reminded them why we were there, and suggested we get started on the procedure. Fled took her usual chair. I indicated that Tewks should take the one to the right of the desk. For his part, Filbert leaped onto the desk itself, facing fled. Finally, I sat down behind it and glanced at all three of them. "Are we ready?"

Fled and Tewksbury nodded. Filbert looked from one to the other, and he nodded, too.

I reminded the ethologist that we already had fled's permission for the hypnosis procedure, that there was no risk of a perilous outcome, etc. She and Filbert nodded again. "Okay, then, here we go. Fled, I'm going to count forward from one to five, and when I get to five, you will find yourself in a deep–"

I didn't hear her counting to herself, but her head slowly fell to her chest, and immediately she was "gone." I tried to repeat exactly what I had done the previous time (I had reviewed the videotape at home), hoping for a similar result. "Just relax," I whispered. "Close your eyes if you like. Now I'm going to speak to someone else. You may listen or not, as you wish. I'd like anyone with fled to please come forward and identify yourself . . . ."

We waited for what seemed like a full minute before fled began to withdraw. Finally she shrank down as usual, apparently trying to make herself invisible. She seemed to take almost a fetal position, and became excruciatingly quiet.

At this point Filbert jumped off the desk and edged his way toward fled, who remained completely motionless. He inched closer until he was crouching right beside her. Gently he reached out and touched her face with a finger.

Fled, or whoever she was, seemed to relax a bit. Her hand came up and she stroked Filbert's arm. He began to make some guttural noises to which fled's alter ego did not respond. But he persisted with a kind of cooing and caressing of her face with the back of his hand, and then he circled around and began to groom her, picking imaginary insects from her back and shoulders. "Fled" responded with some clucking sounds of her own. This went on for several minutes until Tewks reached over and touched Filbert. He turned to her and began to sign a few words, and she relayed the message: "He says she's afraid."

"Can he ask her what she's afraid of?"

She signed something to him, and he repeated it verbally to fled's alter. We all waited for a minute or two before the hushed response came to Filbert to Tewks to me: "I'm afraid of the growl creatures." The alter's eyes darted around wildly.

"He means the dogs," Tewksbury translated.

"Tell him to ask her what dogs she's afraid of."

Filbert's head swiveled between Tewks and the alter as he translated the question and the response. "The dogs of the naked beasts who come to hurt." He continued to groom the alter.

I had some idea of what she meant, of course, but what I really wanted to hear about was her relationship to fled. I asked Tewks, "Can you tell where she's from? She's not a bonobo, is she?"

(For the sake of brevity, I have omitted the various back-and-forth signing that ensued.) "No, she's not a bonobo. She's a lowland chimpanzee, probably from Congo, like Filbert. Otherwise, they would have a more difficult time communicating."

"How old is she? Does she have a name?"

"She's between two and three, and her name is Naraba."

"Does she know where she is?"

"Yes, she's been here before."

"When?"

"She goes with fled."

"She's traveling with fled?"

"Yes, but she doesn't like it here and prefers to hide from us."

"Why did fled bring her here?"

"She found her in a cage."

"Does she want to go back to Congo and live there as before?"

"Not unless the dogs go away."

"What did the dogs do to her?"

The chimpanzee began to wail and pound the desk with her feet.

"Never mind," I said. "We'll come back to that later. Can you ask her if she knows who fled is and where she came from?"

"She knows fled has come to help her, but she doesn't know where she came from."

"Does she want to go with fled when she leaves us?"

"She would rather go back to her own home if it was safe to be there. Otherwise she will stay with fled."

I contemplated the possibility of hypnotizing Naraba via Tewksbury and Filbert, as I had done with Robert Porter, but realized it would be virtually impossible to accomplish under the circumstances. But how else to re-visit her terrible childhood, her capture and removal from her native habitat, without seriously traumatizing her? Indeed, Naraba already appeared to be showing signs of mental stress: she had covered her head with her hands and started to rock back and forth. I called a temporary halt to the proceedings.

"Please take Filbert away for a moment while I speak to fled."

Tewks called the chimpanzee back to her and hugged him while I brought fled back from under hypnosis. She blinked her eyes and waited for me to fill her in. "Fled, you have an alter called Naraba."

"She's not an alter. She's a friend who travels with me sometimes."

"Where did you find her?"

"In a roadside zoo."

"What do you mean by 'roadside'?"

"Anyone can build cages anywhere they wish and keep almost any animals they want in them. They charge admission fees and make money from them. They don't even have to feed the animals. The patrons toss them marshmallows and candy and other shit like that. People are so fucking stupid!"

"These things are legal?"

"Quite legal, in every one of your states. The people who consider animals to be mindless 'property' are still in the vast majority, you know. It will be a while longer before that changes."

"But what I wanted to know was, how did you find her? And has she been with you since then?"

"It's only been a few days, gino. When I went to your west coast for a look at the beautiful pacific ocean, I landed near this goddamn roadside thing."

"So why didn't you tell me it was Naraba you saw on the videotape?"

"That wasn't Naraba."

"It wasn't? Who was it?"

"Not a clue."

"Then guess what—you have *two* alters. At least."

"I told you before: these alters are filberts of your imagination."

"Then please explain to me where they came from."

"How the hell should *I* know?"

"Okay, we'll get back to that later. Right now I'd like to return to your own childhood for a minute."

"Haven't we been over that?"

"I must have missed something."

"Fyi, doctor, you miss almost everything."

"Thanks, I'll take that under advisement. For now, a question: when you were a very young trod, was your mother killed by another being? And did you witness it?"

For the first time since her arrival, her cocky demeanor vanished. She stared at me and her eyes suddenly filled with moisture. Weeping, I concluded, must be a universal phenomenon. "How did you know that?" she whimpered.

"I think your alter—your companion—told me. What happened to your mother?"

"It was an accident. An ap was running around and banged into her and knocked her down. The collision broke her neck and she died in an instant. No one could help her. It was just an accident...."

"That was after you were weaned, and you didn't find out until someone showed you the hologram, right? But of course it was just like being there."

Her mouth opened wide and she roared like a distraught lion. Huge tears rolled down her face and disappeared in the hair on her chin and chest.

I reached out and touched the top of her head. "I'm sorry, fled. I'm very sorry."

"Beings die, even on K-PAX," she snuffed.

So, my alien friend, I thought, you're not so different from us after all. Tewks and Filbert also tried to console her, and she finally became her usual self. "Okay, folks," I said, "I think that's enough for today." To fled I added, "But don't go very far. I want to talk to you about Jerry."

She had regained not only her composure, but also her attitude. "Why not just talk to *him*?" she snorted.

"Him, too," I snorted back.

* * *

Filbert had a wonderful time on the lawn and so, for the most part, did the patients (except for those who are afraid of *everything*). He swung from the limbs of the big elm tree, went after Georgie's football, ran all over the back forty. It's remarkable how people, especially those who are institutionalized, respond to animals. We had cats a few years ago, but one of them bit an abusive patient, resulting in an infection and a lawsuit, and Goldfarb decided to call a halt to the feline companionship program. (The patient's family lost the suit; he has since departed us, and is missed by no one.)

Even some of the staff joined in the fun, running around the lawn as if they were children again. When it was time to go, Howard, who sometimes acts as spokesperson for the patients, requested that I please let Dr. Tewksbury come back soon with Filbert.

"Is tomorrow soon enough?" I asked him. "We'll need him for at least another visit."

I escorted Tewks and her companion to the nearby garage where the van was parked. By that time Officer Wilson had been apprised of the situation. "Good-bye, Doc. Good-bye, Filbert." I informed him that they would be back tomorrow. "I'll be watching for youse," he promised.

Filbert, holding our hands and walking between us, hardly elicited a stare from passersby. There probably isn't a New Yorker who hasn't seen something at least as weird. On the way to the van I thanked Tewks for coming and asked for her opinion on how we could do something to help Naraba.

"I think she would be a terrific candidate for a sanctuary," she said. "There are some good ones in the warmer states. Want me to look into it for you?"

"That isn't what I meant." I explained my hypothesis that fled's alter ego was actually a part of her, and they would probably be going back to K-PAX together. "I was hoping that you and Filbert might be able to tell her something to ease her fears while she's here."

"We could tell her that no one can harm her as long as she stays with fled."

"Yeah. That's all I could come up with, too." I declined to mention that I wasn't so sure of that anymore.

I didn't know what Filbert would do when I said good-bye. I thought he might wrap his arms around me for a big hug, as he had done for some of the patients. Instead, he stuck out his hand. I flinched reflexively, but he only wanted to give mine a shake, not grab my gonads. "I didn't teach him that," said Tewks. "They do that in the wild, too. It means he reveres you more than the others."

"Is that so? Well, thank you, Filbert. I consider that—"

"No, it's not that kind of compliment. It's because of your age. Chimpanzees respect their elders."

"Oh. Well, I appreciate that just as much," I lied.

"Sometimes they part with a kiss."

"Does that show respect, too?"

"Nope. *That* indicates friendship."

* * *

Back in the hospital I went immediately to look for Jerry. He wasn't in his room, and his matchstick sculpture of the Institute was sitting on its pedestal unfinished and unattended. It seemed sad, in a way, as if the sculptor had died. It reminded me of the final works of Michelangelo, chipped stone blocks with only a hint of the ultimate figures still trapped inside.

I finally found him in the quiet room. He was reading an architecture book. Where he got it is anyone's guess—it didn't come from the hospital library. He was so engrossed that he didn't even know I was there until I spoke to him.

"Hi, Jerry."

He barely looked up. "Hi, Dr. Brewer. How are you?"

"Can't complain. Especially after seeing you this way. There's something I'd like to ask you, though."

He was still poring over the book. "Mmmm?"

"We both know that autism isn't a minor affliction, Jerry, and it's never been cured. You clearly had demonstrable neurological damage. Nothing fled might have told you or showed you could have fixed that. Yet, you appear to be perfectly normal. What happened when you went off with her?"

"You're right, Dr. B. It wasn't anything she said that suddenly cured my affliction. It was what she did."

"Really? What did she do?"

"I haven't the slightest idea. She took me to a laboratory somewhere. It was the middle of the night, so no one else was around. There was a laser gun. In fact, there were several. She had me lie down on a table. No, it wasn't a table, it was a lab bench—she had to clear off some equipment first. That's about all I can tell you. She zapped me in several different places with the lasers, and when she was finished, I suddenly understood things I never had before."

"You mean like math and so on?"

"That was the easy part. No, it had to do with people. Before this, I could never figure out the interactions people had with each other. Those needs were utterly meaningless to me. In fact, I didn't care. People were no more important than trees, and somehow repulsive as well. But all of a sudden I was able to figure it out. *I* am people, if you see what I mean. Interacting with other people is like interacting with myself. For good or bad, I'm one of *us*. I never understood that before."

"Which do you think it is–good or bad?"

"I think it's both. My head is flooded with new ideas, and I want to find out what I've missed all these years. I want to talk to people, see how they operate. See how *I* operate. I don't have to go somewhere inside myself to have a sense of meaning anymore. But there's a tradeoff, of course."

"What's that?"

"I can't remember how to do the matchstick sculptures."

I couldn't help but smile, which segued into a happy chuckle. "That's all right, Jer. We'd rather have you than another sculpture, even if it's a masterpiece. Welcome to the real world!"

"Thank you. I think."

"It has its good points. Uh–fled didn't say anything about what, exactly, she did with the laser beams, did she?"

"I didn't ask her."

"Tell me one more thing."

"If I can."

"What was it like–traveling at the speed of light?"

"I didn't feel a thing. It's like nothing happened at all, except there's a little flash of light and then you're somewhere else. There's no sensation of movement whatever."

"Would you do it again?"

"Depends on where we're going."

* * *

Before I could find fled again, I was paged by Will. I phoned him from the lounge. Besides being curious about how the session with Tewks and Filbert had gone, he reported a message he had taken from his brother-in-law Steve, who requested a return call from me. I told Will I'd fill him in later on the recent episode with fled, though I did give him a preview: "She has a heart, after all."

Then I called my astronomer son-in-law. "Hi, Steve. Returning your call. How are Abby and the boys?"

Steve was in no mood for chitchat. "Damn it all to hell, Gene, when can Ah talk to fled?"

"Oh, God, Steve. So much has been going on here that I forgot to ask her about it."

"Well, can you do it today?"

"I'll try. What's the rush, anyway?"

"We don't know when she's leaving, right? Ah don't want to miss my only chance to talk to her."

"Well, she won't be leaving for . . ." I was amazed when I realized he was right: fled had already been on Earth for more than two weeks, and the first window would come open in a matter of days. "I'll ask her today. Matter of fact, I was looking for her when you called."

"Abby and Star want to talk to her, too. And Rain called from Princeton. He's willing to cut classes for a day if he can be included."

"Why don't we just have a picnic and make it a family affair?"

"Great idea! Thanks, Dad-in-law–Ah appreciate it."

"No, I was jok–"

But he had already hung up.

* * *

Fled was still enjoying the benefits of pre-motherhood. Everyone wanted to bring her a glass of water, a cucumber, a chair. For her part, fled ate it up. Whether it was all an act remained to be seen, but for the time being she seemed to become less belligerent and more fragile. The patients quickly picked up on this. They do live together, after all, and even subtle changes can be quite noticeable. A mental institution is much like a big family and, despite the intense focus on themselves, the inmates sincerely care about one another.

In a sense, I suppose, it wasn't fled herself whom the patients were so solicitous of, but the unborn child, regardless of its nature. Of course it's the same after they're born: who doesn't google at an infant in a stroller? Studies have shown that a person is captivated not only by the innocence of the little creature, but by the remembrance of one's own purity, now irretrievably lost. Perhaps this little fella will not be so unfortunate as I was, one hopes. Fled, like all mothers-to-be, basked in the sunshine of this yearning.

I watched her for a while from the other side of the lawn. Darryl was sitting near me gazing at his pocket-size photographs of Meg Ryan. When a sudden burst of laughter came from the back forty, he looked up to see what the uproar was about. I took the opportunity to ask him what he thought of fled.

"I didn't like her at first. She was so strange. I thought maybe she was going to take us somewhere and stick things into us–you know, do medical experiments like the aliens in the UFOs. Make guinea pigs out of us. Then Howard told us she wasn't so bad, that we should give her a chance. Didn't help much, though. She was so loud and obnoxious that nobody wanted to. But the more she hung out, the more she seemed to belong here, you know? I guess you can get used to anyone if you're around them long enough. Except for the fact that she's so–well, ape-like–Howard was right. She's okay. Not that much different from the rest of us. I don't mean she's somebody I'd want to live with on a permanent basis. But she's very smart. She seems to see things the rest of us miss. And she's really not that bad looking, either, when you think about it. I mean, she's got hair all over her body, of course, but her eyes are big and brown, and her voice is nice when she speaks softly, don't you think? And now that she's pregnant . . . I kind of like her now." He sighed and glanced again at the photos. "Of course, she's not Meg."

"No, Darryl. There's only one Meg. And there's only one fled, too, and everyone else, for that matter. Thank you for sharing your feelings about her." Which probably went for most of the other patients as well. I excused myself and crossed the lawn to speak with "Mama" fled.

"Dr. b!" she called out when she saw me coming toward her. "I've missed you!"

I had only left her an hour before, so I assumed she was joking. "Let's talk."

"What–again? Don't you ever get tired of the gum-flapping?"

"I'm beginning to. Especially since I never get any answers." Several of the patients were standing around, waiting, listening. "Let's go somewhere else, shall we?"

"She's not really pregnant, you know."

"Thanks, Rick. That helps a lot."

Since we were already on the back forty, we went into the nearby Villers wing, which I hadn't visited for some time. I asked fled whether she had ever been in it before. "Sure," she said. "Had sex with a guy right on that sofa over there."

Maybe she was lying about all the sex, too. Sometimes very shy people do that in order to cover up their lack of experience. Of course fled had shown no evidence whatever for shyness. "Really? Who?"

"I told you before–"

"Yeah, I remember. You don't screw and tell." I directed her to the solarium, which has a nice view of the rear lawn. In a corner stood Jerry's sculpture of the Taj Mahal. "Let's sit here."

"Sure, boss." She plopped down in one of the plastic chairs.

"All right. This time I want some answers."

"Then I want some questions."

"Okay, here's the first one. what did you do to Jerry?"

"Oh, not much, really. He just had some loose wires that needed to be connected."

"Which wires?"

"Sorry, doc. If I told you that, you'd be drilling into all the heads in the hospital. Worse, your government would be zapping all their secret prisoners."

"Secret?"

"Wake up and smell the feces, gino."

"I think I'm getting a whiff of it already. You're a phony, aren't you? You don't know a damn thing about neurology."

"Really, gene? Why don't you have a little chat with jerry?"

"And you're not really pregnant, are you? This is all a ruse to get the patients to listen to you, am I right? What are you planning to do—talk all of them into going to K-PAX with you?"

"Don't have to. Most of them have been waiting years for me to pick them up."

"But why do you want a bunch of crazy people on K-PAX?"

"They're not 'crazy.' They're damaged."

"And what about Naraba? Are you faking that, too?"

"What would it take to make a believer out of you, gino? You want to go for that ride in the sky now? Or would even that not convince you? I fixed Jerry's circuits, I'm pregnant, and naraba wants to stay away from human beings of all races, creeds, and countries of origin. If you can't believe any of that, we might as well discontinue our little talks, don't you think?"

"You're right. On one level I believe everything you've told me. But there's never any proof. You have to admit it's a lot for a person to swallow."

"Yes, for a small-throated sapien I suppose it is. But every word is true, regardless of whether you can digest them or not. Next question."

"If I told you that Naraba and the chimpanzee from Rwanda or Cameroon are alter egos, and that they live in your head and nowhere else, would you be able to swallow it?"

"No."

"Why should I believe you when you don't believe me?"

"Because, for humans, beliefs are mental concoctions that help you cope with a cruel and stupid WORLD. They have nothing to do with the truth. Prot already pointed that out to you, remember?"

"All right, let's change the topic. Is Naraba going with you to K-PAX?"

"If she wants to. That leaves 99,999 seats. You want one of them?"

"Not just yet. Now tell me the truth: how many of those 99,999 have you lined up already?"

"Most of them. But don't worry—all the rest will be ready when the time comes."

"And that time is fast approaching, right?"

"Still another week to the first window, gino. I won't know until the day before."

"I'd appreciate a little more notice than that."

"Why?"

"Let's just say I don't like to be left in the dark."

"You're already in the dark, my friend. I've concluded you must prefer it that way."

"Thanks again."

"No prob."

"Now about your pregnancy: would you be willing to undergo a test to confirm that?"

"Sure. I'll pee on your paper if you like. But it might not work. Our hormones aren't exactly the same as yours, you know." She was right; the lab results had come back and, though her DNA pattern and blood profile were similar to ours, they were not exactly the same. And they were different, as well, from those of her friends, the chimpanzees.

"But your blood and urine tests already gave us the baseline values," I countered. "It's the changes we would look for. Can't you give us a just little more?"

"Oh, all right. But you're a bloodthirsty lot–do you know that? And urinethirsty, too."

"And can you make a list of everyone you've had–ah–sex with since you've been on our planet?"

"I already told you–"

"All right, no names, just how many and what species."

"Sorry, doc, I really haven't kept any records."

"Yes, but you remember them all, right? So how many have been in total? Approximately."

"Fifty-seven. So far . . . ."

"And out of that fifty-seven, how many were human?"

"Four."

"Who were they?"

"You don't know them. Except for the patients, of course."

"How many patients?"

"Two."

"Who besides Howard?"

"You're wasting your precious time."

"Okay, one final question before I forget again: would you like to come to my home–or my son-in-law Steve's–for a picnic?"

"No, thanks."

"Why not?"

"Are you familiar with the word 'booooooooring'?"

"Oh. Well, would you be willing to talk briefly with Steve and his family anyway? Without the picnic? You could consider it part of your study of life on Earth–typical Homo sapiens and all that."

"From what I've heard, they're not so typical."

"All right, atypical Homo sapiens."

"What would we talk about?"

"I think Steve wants to ask you about the universe. I don't know what the rest of them want to know."

"I told you: that stuff doesn't interest me."

"You mean you don't know anything about the subject?"

She stared at me for a moment before wagging her head and sighing loudly. "Oh, all right–I'll try to work them into my busy schedule . . . ."

"And finally, the TV people are coming Wednesday morning. That's the day after tomorrow, if you haven't been keeping track. Will you be here then?"

"Maybe. If there are plenty of veggies around."
"I'll have tubs of them everywhere."
"Very kind of you."
"No prob."

* * *

I was exhausted by the time I got home late that afternoon. Not only had it been a very stressful day, but I had gotten up early, only to be thwarted by highway construction, and there were further delays on the way back. I hoped tomorrow would be different.

So it was with considerable chagrin that I was intercepted by an unmarked car with a flashing light that pulled me over next to an open field about half a mile from the house. I might have been going a little over the speed limit, but not enough to warrant a ticket. I wondered whether my license plate or inspection tag had expired.

One police officer came to the driver's side of the car, the other to the passenger side. I opened the window. He showed his badge. "Dammit, Wang, couldn't you wait until I got home?"

"Just doing you a favor, sir. We don't want your neighbors to get suspicious, now do we?"

"Suspicious of what? What do you want this time?"

"A certain individual read our neurologist's report."

Dartmouth abruptly pulled his weapon from a concealed holster and took a shot at a sparrow sitting in a tree next to the field. He missed both the tree and the bird, which shat on the hood of my car as it took off.

A bit unnerved, I replied, "What individual?"

"Let's just say you'd recognize the name. He'd like her to come down to Washington to answer some questions. Would you ask your friend about that?"

"What kind of questions?"

"He wants to see for himself that she can read his mind."

"I don't think she'd be interested."

"We'll make it worth her while."

"How do you plan to do that?"

"We'll put her up in the best hotel we have. Swimming pool, tennis, championship golf course. What more could she want?"

"Right. I'll pass that on to her. Anything else? I'm tired. I'd like to get home now."

The steely eyes locked onto mine. "We've heard that there are three windows for her departure. Can you tell us which one she's using?"

"No, I can't. I don't think she knows yet herself."

They whirled simultaneously and jogged back to the unmarked car, throwing gravel all over mine as they wiggled and sped away in a cloud of dust. I imagined I heard the strains of "The Love for Three Oranges" and a voice shouting, "Hi-yo, Silver!"

CHAPTER NINE

Tewks and Filbert were waiting for me in the lounge when I arrived on Tuesday morning. I didn't think there was much more to be learned about Naraba's or the Rwanda chimp's backgrounds, especially in the short time we had left, but I hoped they would be able to help me with the related question: how many other alters were lurking in fled's brain, and were they all chimpanzees?

Filbert, of course, was having a fine time swinging from the central chandelier, and generally galloping around among the patients, to their unending delight. Old Mrs. Weathers was enjoying the playtime as much as anyone, chuckling toothlessly at the silliness around her, even though she could see and hear very little of it. Even a couple of the faculty members, Cliff Roberts and Hannah Rudqvist, were taking everything in with childish grins on their faces.

I sidled up to Hannah and asked her what she thought of the proceedings. She observed that "If more people swung from chandeliers once in a while, I think we'd have far fewer mental problems."

"But far more broken limbs," Cliff pointed out.

"A good trade, don't you think?" she countered.

Roberts turned to me. "Come to visit us again so soon, Dr. B? Afraid you won't wear out your welcome?"

I could never think of a good comeback for a stupid comment like that. "Not really. How are you, Cliff? Enjoying the show?"

"Up until now." He turned back to Hannah. "See you later, sugar. How about lunch somewhere quiet?"

Blushing deeply, she answered, "Maybe," and quickly departed. For some reason this annoyed me. Was he coming on to her? Was she too shy to say no? "Been meaning to ask you, Cliff–how did you get into psychiatry?"

"You know the answer to that better than I do, Gene: it beats working for a living."

While I was trying to think of a good comeback for that, fled appeared. When Filbert spotted her he ran and jumped into her arms. She flipped him around to her back and headed for the stairs, to the disappointment of everyone in the lounge. "Can't he live here, Dr. B?" Rocky pleaded.

"Sorry, Rock," I said apologetically, "he has to go home tomorrow."

"He's not an asshole like everyone else here. Can't we get another chimp?"

"You'll have to speak to Dr. Goldfarb about that," I called back as Tewks and I headed for the elevator, only to see the door close with Roberts inside. Reluctantly we followed fled and Filbert to the stairs.

They were already waiting for us in Room 520. Both seemed quietly serious, as if they, too, realized that the foolishness was over for the time being. Filbert nibbled on a tomato, though "he likes fruit better," Tewks informed me. I apologized for the oversight. Fled, on the other hand, had no trouble enjoying the cornucopia, stuffing her huge mouth with a variety of tubers while she had the chance. When she was finally finished, she picked at her teeth and sighed happily.

"Ready?" I asked her.

"Always."

She cooperated fully when I coaxed her into hypnosis. It didn't take long: even before I could ask anyone to come forward another alter appeared, screaming. Immediately I shouted for fled. The squealing stopped and I found her gazing at me stoically.

"All right," I said, "let's try it again. Filbert, would you come over here, please?" He complied immediately. With him standing close to fled, I invited her to close her eyes once more, and asked Naraba to come forth. Before she could shrivel into a ball and try to slither under the desk, Filbert began to groom her.

Through the two translators I determined that she was indeed the former roadside zoo attraction, and I asked her immediately whether she knew of any other beings in the immediate vicinity besides fled and us. It seemed to take her awhile to understand the question, but finally she answered, "Yes."

"How many?"

Tewks reminded me that chimpanzees don't do well with counting, but she forwarded the question. The answer came back: "Many."

"Do you know all of them?"

Again there was a pause while Naraba apparently tried to make sense of the question. "Some."

"Can you tell us who they are?"

She became confused again and couldn't answer.

I asked her whether they were like, or different from, her.

Answer: "They are like me."

"How long have you known the others?"

"Long time."
"Since you were a baby?"
"Yes."
"Did you know them when your mother was with you?"
"No."
"Did you know them after your mother was taken away, but before you were put in a cage?"
"Yes."
"Are all of them here with you now?"
"Don't know."
"Is the first one you knew here with you?"
"Yes."
"Do you know her name?"

At this point, Filbert jumped up and screeched. He pointed to Naraba, but I was pretty sure it was fled he meant. I asked her, "Is it fled?"

The young chimpanzee raised her head and looked directly at me for the first time. She made a whimpering noise, which Filbert translated as "Yes."

Through Tewksbury I asked Filbert to instruct Naraba to rest for a while and not talk while I tried to speak to the others. When he had done so, she closed her eyes and her head fell to her chest. I requested that he try to speak to Naraba/fled as though she were someone else. Change his tone, for example. Though it might have been worth the try, it failed. After several minutes I discontinued the fishing expedition and recalled fled. It might have been my last best chance to determine how many alters were involved, but I knew there were many. And we had established that another species besides human beings could somehow call up an alter from a faraway planet to help them out in time of need. Did this apply to all the animals? Were all K-PAXians alter egos for someone living on the Earth, human or otherwise? Were there other planets harboring such personalities as well? Worm after worm was slithering out of the can.

Just then the door opened. It was Goldfarb. Not knowing we were there, she had apparently come to get something from her examining room. "God's teeth!" she muttered when she saw us all huddled around her desk. Nevertheless, she came on in to retrieve whatever it was she was looking for. Was it Naraba or someone else who was freaked by the hospital director in her white coat? Whoever it was began to scream, and scurried off into a corner. "I'll come back," Goldfarb wisely decided, and exited as quickly as she had come in. The chimpanzee, however, continued to cry and refused to come out of her "hiding" place, even with Filbert's gentle cajoling. I reluctantly decided to end the session, and recalled fled. Upon seeing where she was, the latter stood up and returned, quite calmly, to her chair. I brought her out of her trance. She remembered nothing of what had transpired, of course, but nevertheless seemed more subdued than usual, as if she felt, in some unconscious way, the suffering hidden deep in her alien mind. As a former psychiatrist, I wanted to get at that pain, but for that I no longer needed Filbert or Tewks.

Before we said our good-byes, I passed around the vegetables again, even taking a stalk of celery for myself, as did Tewksbury.

"I wish we could stay longer," she confided with a crunch. "I'd like to talk to fled about K-PAX and what it's like." Then she signed a question to Filbert. He immediately became very excited and conveyed his enthusiasm to fled, who quickly signed something back. The chimpanzee immediately became calm, almost reverential, I thought, and the two of them sat down beside the desk and groomed each other for a while.

Tewks and I chatted a little more about chimpanzees in the wild, in research labs, in zoos. I was shocked and saddened to learn that the last of these held more of them than did the forests. There are a few environmental and animal rights groups working to reverse this obnoxious trend, but the handwriting already seems to be on the wall: with the growth of human populations and the poaching for bushmeat of the few remaining wild apes, it won't be long before there won't be a single chimpanzee left in his/her natural habitat. It sounded like the initial dire warnings about global warming, which very few paid attention to, and many still don't, to the detriment of all of us.

"And that's only the beginning," she added. "Soon there won't be any rhinos, hippos, giraffes, tigers—you name it—in the wild. Unless there's a radical change in mindset among the human populations of the world, there will be more and more of us, and fewer and fewer of them, until someday there won't be anything left on Earth except Homo sapiens and a few token animals—their cats and dogs and horses—all in captivity. Would you like to live in a world filled with people, and no tigers or polar bears?" she asked rhetorically, and then answered her own question: "I wouldn't. If you ever write a book about this, Gene, I hope you'll stress this point to your readers."

"If I do that," I patiently explained to her, "there might not *be* any readers. But tell me something: isn't Filbert living in captivity, too?"

She looked at me sadly. "He was a pet. Some rich bastard in Montana brought him back from Congo when he was a baby. Same guy has a bunch of cheetahs living on his ranch. They'd never seen snow before they got there. Anyway, when this jerk got tired of Filbert's shenanigans, he advertised him for sale. Then he tried to give him away. But no one wants an adult chimpanzee who hasn't learned human manners. They're strong, and they can be dangerous. But they're too tame to go back to what little forest is left. They can't survive there after living a couple of years in captivity."

I asked her what fled had told Filbert to calm him down a little while earlier.

"I suggested he ask her if he could go with her to her forest in the sky. Her answer was that she had already reserved a place for him. "When I get home," she said, "I'm going to check fled's website to see if there might be a place for me as well!" She laughed. "Maybe Fil will put in a good word for me!"

At this point it occurred to me that fled had come to Earth to take the apes with her to K-PAX before it was too late. But then I remembered she had said it would be 100,000 people who would be making the trip. When I finally looked around to see what fled and Filbert were up to, I couldn't find them. Had they sneaked out when

Tewks and I were engaged in conversation? We finally found them under the desk, asleep. God knows what they had been doing before that.

When they woke up I asked fled whether she was going to stick around for a while.

"For a while," she echoed dreamily.

I escorted Tewks and Filbert down the stairs and out of the hospital to the front gate, Fil waving to everyone as he exited. They all wistfully returned it.

I profusely thanked Dr. Tewksbury, of course, and assured her that her expenses would be promptly reimbursed. After our final hugs, Filbert kissed me firmly and very wetly on the lips, and I could swear that he winked at me as he skipped down the sidewalk toward the waiting van.

* * *

Though it seemed rather anticlimactic, I followed my usual habit and took a turn around the lawn, where I found Barney surrounded by several other patients, all unsuccessfully making silly faces at him. Darryl's shirttail sticking out of his fly had no better success. From the back forty I heard Rocky shouting epithets at Rick, and I hurried over to try to calm them down.

As with most mental patients, the truth is quite simply what each of them believes it to be, and absolutely nothing will convince them otherwise. Same for Darryl, of course, who is certain that Meg Ryan will eventually come to her senses, and that they will live happily ever after, just like in the movies. And for "Dr." Claire Smith, who is perfectly willing to share with you anything you might want to know about her experiences treating the residents of MPI, which are as real to her as so many brick walls.

Yet, how different, really, are any of them from you and me? We all believe certain things to be true or false regardless of ample evidence to the contrary. That other people like or dislike us, for instance, or find us more or less attractive than we think we are, that our religious beliefs are the only true ones. Perhaps this is part of being human. Since we can never know the absolute truth about anything (quantum mechanics emphasizes this uncertainty), we all need to fill in the gaps in order to interact with other people, get through our days with a minimum of confusion and doubt. The only thing different about the patients here is the degree of self-deception, which precludes their functioning in the "normal" world.

Consider Rick, for example, who not only holds on tightly to his bald-faced lies, but tries to foist them on everyone else. He works very hard at this because, without his private beliefs, his world would collapse and he would find it impossible to cope with his surroundings at all.

But how did he get to this state in the first place? It would be simplistic to note that his childhood was a hell on Earth, but that pretty well describes it. He was one of those unfortunates who was kept locked in a dark, damp basement almost from birth by his mother (his father disappeared early on), and fed almost nothing. To keep him confined, he was vaguely warned about the vicious monsters lurking upstairs and prowling around outside. It's hard to imagine what grotesque beasts and ogres he conjured up in his mind. He nearly starved to death until, at nine, his survival instincts (and considerable bravery) drove him out of the house, where he was discovered pawing through the trash cans in the back alley. He ran back inside when the neighbor called out to him (who knows what kind of monster he thought she was), but she correctly concluded that something was seriously wrong and had the good sense to call the police.

This situation, and others like it, occurs more often than you might imagine. Some parents, having been badly treated as children themselves, attempt to "get even" with the world by mistreating their own children. If they were physically or mentally abused, they are often equally abusive themselves. Some even hand their son or daughter over to molesters or pornographers in an attempt to "make up" for their own abuses, acting as pimps for their own children.

You might think that Rick would be unable to see the reality of food on the table, and would refuse to eat. Fortunately, it doesn't work that way, not in his case, at least. It's true that after years of eating dirt or peelings to stay alive, a slice of warm bread or an orange are as unreal as a unicorn. But whatever they are to him he accepts implicitly because they have to fit the bigger picture already painted on the canvas of his life. He might believe he's eating rubber balls, for instance, or wooden pegs. So when he tells Barney that the sky is green, he probably believes it himself. To think otherwise would mean starting down the slippery slope toward the realization that the world is as horrible as his childhood experience suggested it was. Who knows what would happen to him if he were to begin that slide?

A similar fate might have befallen Phyllis, but it's impossible to get any information from her. Whatever her background, she is unable to face up to it or anything else, even her very existence. Her early life must have been quite horrible indeed, maybe even worse than Rick's or any of the other patients'.

Thus, with Phyllis, as for many of our residents, there is little meaning in the concept of a cure, which could actually be far worse than the affliction. How do we restore these Humpty Dumpties of the mind that were crushed and broken years earlier? Even fled, I suspected, wouldn't be able to put them back together again, to rearrange all the synapses in their brains to make them whole and functional once more.

Suddenly I had a brainstorm. Would it be possible somehow, through surgery or medication, to create a kind of amnesia in patients like these and start them over with clean slates? Perhaps fled couldn't fix them, but maybe she could do this much, give them a new lease on their miserable lives.

* * *

I wanted to touch base with Will, but he wasn't in his office. His desk, I was pleased to note, was piled high with books and papers just like mine used to be. On the wall hung a photo of him and Dawn and their daughter Jennifer. As I gazed at my granddaughter's pretty face, I suddenly found myself feeling very sorry for her. What if Tewksbury and others were right: in a century or so, by the time Jennifer left this planet, would the Earth be stuffed with human beings, devoid of most other life forms, and, as if that weren't enough, a veritable hothouse? Or worse—would we survive even that long without making some hard choices, as prot and fled have suggested. I didn't like to think about that.

On Will's calendar I spotted a scribbled note: coffee with Hannah, 11:00. I headed dismally for the doctors' dining room, where I found them huddled closely together at a table in the corner. My first thought was that if it had been anyone else but my son, I might have suspected they were having an affair. My second thought was about the same. When they saw me they quickly straightened up and Will (unenthusiastically, I thought) waved me over. Hannah's face was so red that I wondered whether she, in fact, suffered from a serious circulation, rather than an emotional, problem. I brushed off my unwelcome suspicions as the paranoia of a concerned parent.

They said they had been discussing Jerry, who was neither Will's nor Hannah's patient. Apparently Laura Chang had told the latter that, although there was no reason to keep him in the hospital any longer, the former autist didn't seem to be in any hurry to go anywhere. Feeling a bit out of place, I took a seat and asked them why they thought Jerry was suddenly so reluctant to get on with his life. "If it were me," I remarked fatuously, "I'd be eager to get out of here and see what I've been missing."

Hanna, still blushing noticeably, related that "He spends most of his time studying his matchstick sculptures, trying to understand why he doesn't know how to do them anymore."

"In fact," Will added, carefully studying his empty cup, "he took some of the matches away from his Eiffel Tower, and when he tried to put them back in, the whole thing collapsed. Now all he has is a pile of sticks."

"What is Laura doing about this?"

"Just as you might expect," said Hannah. "She wants to give him more time. It's like a blind man who is suddenly able to see. You would think it should be easy, but it takes him awhile to adjust."

"Sounds reasonable."

"She's going to present his case at the staff meeting on Monday. You want to come?"

"I'll try to be there."

Will stood up. "Maybe we should invite fled, too. Right now, I've got to run. Patient time!"

"Me, too!" said Hannah, who quickly jumped up and followed him out. The hospital equivalent of Dartmouth and Wang.

* * *

It was already approaching noon, and I had planned to be home for lunch. But I wanted to speak with fled before I left, particularly since the television people would be at the hospital the next day with all their cameras and other paraphernalia, which might make a simple discourse with her, or anyone else, more difficult than it already was. If, in fact, she showed up for the taping.

I searched for half an hour and was beginning to think she had left the premises. She had promised to stay around "for a while," but to an alien that could mean anything. The last place I looked was Room 520, where I had left her. Surprisingly, she was still there. She seemed a bit morose. "Is something wrong?" I asked her.

"Prot was right," she said. "But I had to come and see for myself."

"Right about what?"

"If anything characterizes your species, besides your greed and your violent nature, it's your amazing indifference to damn near everything outside your immediate experience. For someone from another PLANET it takes some getting used to."

"Dammit, fled, I told you I'm worried about the Earth, too. But right now there are more pressing matters to discuss."

"That's exactly what I said."

"Please listen to me. The television cameras are coming the day after tomorrow. You gave me your word that you would be here for that. I expect you to honor that commitment, and I need to know: are you going to keep your promise?"

"No one taught me to lie, my dubious friend. We don't even have a word for it on K-PAX. That's a human thing."

"Maybe you could be lying and you don't even know it."

"Maybe this is all fiction, and I don't really exist."

"We'll have to discuss that some other time. So you're sure you're not going off to Africa or Asia or anywhere tomorrow?"

"And miss my chance at television stardom? Don't make me laugh."

We stared at each other for a while. "Here's an idea: why don't you tell the people of Earth about our indifference during your TV interview?"

"Will there be editors? Sponsors?"

"Of course."

"There's your answer."

"All right. Have it your way. Right now I need to ask you about some of the patients."

"I'm listening."

"You somehow rewired Jerry. He's having a hard time coping with that."

"Who wouldn't?"

"Do you have any suggestions?"

"Perhaps he'd like a free trip to K-PAX."

"That the best you can do?"

"Do you have a better suggestion?"

"No."

"I didn't think so."

"The point is, you turned him into a 'normal' human being. For that we are all grateful, even though it might take him some time to adjust to the idea. What I want to know is whether you can do the same for the other patients."

"I might be able to fix some of the other autists. The rest are a little more tricky."

"Why is that?"

"You know why. Their problems aren't about wiring. They're like a chess game that went wrong on the first move. You'd have to turn back the clock and start them all over again. With different parents, preferably."

"That's precisely what I wanted to know: can you somehow erase their memories and start the games over?"

"No one can do that, doctor b. If you erased everything, there'd be nothing left to build new memories *on*. The brain isn't like a videotape. Memories are an integral part of the structure itself. If I erased everything they'd be zombies." She must have noticed my dejection, because she quickly added, "But I'll talk to them if you like, see if I can find out if there's something you missed."

"Thank you. Now about your alters . . ."

"What 'alters'?"

"You've got several. Maybe hundreds. It's impossible to know."

"Is this your first attempt at humor?"

"I wouldn't joke about this."

"No, I suppose you wouldn't. Let me further enlighten you, doc. You may think you have evidence for a thousand of me, but forget it. I'm it."

"Do you mean that after reading my books about prot–"

"He doesn't buy it, either."

"But what about Naraba? You admit that she's–"

"She's a friend and a travel companion."

"But you saw the first alter, remember? Rwanda or Cameroon? And you didn't even recognize her!"

"She must have been hiding somewhere when we got here."

"All right, I give up. You win. Uh–"

"Oh no, please don't ask me again whether the travel list is finished yet."

"Well–"

"Or whether I've found a football stadium to leave from."

"You're reading my mind again, aren't you?"

"Yes, and may I say you're as sick as the rest of the sapiens."

"What–"

"Don't pretend you don't know what I'm talking about. You've got Margie half-undressed, and who's that you've got tied to the bed–why it looks like Dr. Rudqvist! And Meg Ryan is with her! What's your wife going to say about all of this, mister hyde?"

"All right! I'm human! Surprised?"

She wagged her head and grinned/grimaced. "You poor sapien," she said as she headed for the window.

"When will I see you again?"

"Never fear, dear gene, I'll be here in time for makeup call." From somewhere she pulled out a flashlight.

"Wait! I wasn't finished."

"Finished with what? Your obscene daydream?"

"Dr. Sauer and a few of his colleagues want to see you again. As a group."

"Sounds like fun, but I'm pretty booked."

"And the government wants you to come to Washington for an interview with an unnamed high-ranking official. Maybe the highest one of all. Would you be willing to do that?"

"Please convey my apologies for passing up this great honor. And I hope you'll tell your boys not to try to stop us from leaving. That could be bad for everyone concerned. Especially the boys."

"If there's anything I've learned from you, dear fled, it's that no one can stop you from doing whatever you want."

"Should I take that as a compliment?" She got up and headed for the window, where she gave her tush a good scratch.

"If you like."

"Will that be all for now?"

"They aren't happy that you're promoting veganism, either."

She wagged her hairy head. "Bad for the economy, right? Are *all* you people mere corporate puppets?"

I declined to answer that. "There's one more thing."

"There always is."

"Are you taking any of our staff members with you when you return to K-PAX?"

"A few."

"Which—"

Before I could say another word, she produced a mirror. I shouted, "Don't forget about Steve!" But she was no longer in the room. Nor, quite probably, in the hemisphere.

* * *

I was exhausted again, and almost fell asleep on the drive home. The thought of Will having a fling with our newest staff member didn't relax my tired brain in the slightest. Should I tell his mother about my suspicions? I decided to hold off on that until I had talked with some of the staff, see if anyone else had taken notice of this absurdity.

On top of everything else there was another traffic delay—an accident this time, with the inevitable gawker's block—and I almost ran out of gas on the highway. The idea of never seeing MPI again was beginning to sound very attractive.

But by the time I got home I was wide awake, revived, no doubt, by unwelcome visions of government agents hiding in the rhododendrons. I discovered that I was actually sweating. It really dampens your spirit not knowing who might be watching every move you make. *1984* was a couple of decades late, perhaps, but it seemed to me that it had finally arrived.

Before I got out of the car I listened carefully, and my eyes probed every tree and bush. But nobody jumped out from anything. Of course that didn't mean they weren't in there, along with half the neighbors.

Karen, who had kept a pot of hot soup on the stove, was way ahead of me. "When are you going to get out of the psychiatry business?" was the way she put it. "It's turning into a full-time job again."

"If it makes you feel any better, I was thinking of hanging up my yellow pad for good when fled leaves. Permanently. Irreversibly. My old noodle isn't up to it anymore."

"It's still up to a lot of things. But a complete change of perspective might do it some good. Summer's almost here. What are we going to do about it?"

I took a spoonful of soup. "No doubt you've already got something in mind."

"I was thinking of sitting on a lake somewhere and watching the fish jump."

"Where?"

"Canada, maybe."

"Flower would like that. But can we afford the gas?"

"Maybe we can get fled to drop us off before she goes."

"How would we get back?"

"Maybe we won't want to come back."

You see why I love my wife? Forget Margie. Forget Hannah, and even Meg Ryan. I don't know what fled and Filbert had been doing under that desk, but I suspected what it was, and was getting similar ideas myself. I may be getting old, but I'm still not too old for *that*.

Then I remembered Dartmouth and Wang. Who knew what sort of devices they had set up in the bedroom? And were they looking in on Will and Hannah as well? "By the way," I said. "I think Will may be having an affair."

"With fled?"

I couldn't tell whether she was joking or not. "No. With Hannah Rudqvist."

She gave me the look that said: did you get off the mushroom wagon again? Then, to my great amazement, she asked, "Did you ever have an affair?"

"Yes," I answered immediately. "A lifelong one. With you . . . ."

She came over and kissed me. To hell with Dartmouth and Wang, I thought, as we headed for the bedroom.

* * *

Later that afternoon I took another look at fled's website. **HURRY, HURRY, HURRY! ONLY ONE MORE WEEK!** it proclaimed. There were no other changes.

There was plenty of new mail as well. Many people asked: is this a joke? Others begged me to put in a good word for them—they had been waiting ten years to go to K-PAX and were afraid this might be their last chance.

Two letters came from scientists. I don't know why they didn't just call the hospital; perhaps they thought that communicating through my website would be more expedient. In any case, one of them, an otolaryngologist, wanted to examine fled's vocal cords to compare them with those of both humans and chimpanzees. **Do you realize what it would mean if we could find a way to get apes to speak?** I forwarded it without comment to Tewksbury.

The other came from a biologist who wanted to teach fled sign language so she could communicate with the great apes. That one I deleted.

Karen came in to remind me that we had a bridge date with the Siegels. "I hope you aren't going to spend the rest of your retirement sitting at that thing," she said with an amused frown.

"Don't worry," I assured her. "After fled is gone, the mail will stop coming." As usual where alien matters are concerned, however, I was wrong about that.

CHAPTER TEN

When I got to the hospital on Wednesday there were trailers all along Amsterdam Avenue. The lounge and lawn (the only places the network was allowed to film, except for the Ward Two cafeteria) were a mess. Cameras and cables were everywhere. I was concerned about possible lawsuits if any of the patients were to trip on something. But I needn't have worried–Goldfarb had seen that the studio's insurance policy covered every conceivable happenstance, and had advised the staff to help the inmates cope with the disruption and to keep an eye out for any sign of trouble.

To everyone's surprise, the patients loved it. Most of them strutted around flaring their nostrils and looking like movie stars, some with scarves tied around their necks, or puffing unlit cigarettes in holders made from whatever was at hand–hollow sticks or straws or the like. And the poses! Bette Davis and Katharine Hepburn could have learned a lot from them. Claire, for example, had retrieved her stethoscope, and strode here and there with it dangling from her neck, listening to hearts pound and lungs wheeze, jotting notes onto scraps of paper, while Rocky shadowboxed the world. Darryl, on the other hand, made no such pretenses. He was too busy frantically searching the building and grounds for his favorite star on the "movie set." Howard, on the other hand, preferred to remain in the shadows.

The cameras themselves stayed put, for the most part. They weren't attempting to follow every bit of action; they were merely watching whatever happened in front of them. But even the psychotic get used to cameras hanging around, and it wasn't long before the patients returned to their normal activities. Which was, I suppose, what the director was looking for.

As part of the agreement between the studio and the hospital, Jed would be formally interviewed as a "special guest," during which time her thoughts on the afflictions of the inmates, as well as her opinion of the human race itself, would be ascertained. In addition to this, Virginia and I were scheduled for more informal discussions to be used as voiceovers throughout the program as deemed advisable by the editor or director.

Mine was to take place at 11:00 with the hostess, a woman called Priscilla, whom I had never heard of, after Goldfarb and before fled. A corner of the lounge had been reserved for the makeup man, a bouncy Greenwich Village hairdresser. In the meantime, a few would-be reporters were circulating among the patients, speaking off-camera to anyone they wished. Looking for interesting stories, I suppose, though they probably had no idea how compelling some of them really were. Mainly, I think, they wanted sound bites to fill in the "dead spaces" in the show—which, someone said, wouldn't be aired until late the following fall.

As I was wandering around, taking it all in, there was a page for "Dr. Brewer." I answered the call only to discover that it wasn't me they were after, but my son Will. While I was feeling sorry for myself for being a generation older than I used to be, a second call came. This one I ignored, only to discover it was for me. The proofs for the magazine article had arrived with an urgent request that I check them and return the approval form immediately. I picked them up from Margie, who was excited about becoming a "TV star" (though the offices were off-limits to the cameras), and read them over in the lounge while waiting for Virginia to be interviewed. The only thing I found there that I didn't already know was that the editors were initiating a contest to name fled's child. The winner was to receive a hair of fled's head (Smythe had asked for one during his visit) and a framed star map indicating the position of K-PAX in the sky. And, of course, a lifetime subscription to the magazine, *Life in General*. But there were no factual errors, so there was no compelling reason for me to hold up publication.

I approached Goldfarb and handed her the pages. She leafed through them and shrugged. "Should I sign the damn thing?" I nodded. She did so and I hauled it back up to her office, where I instructed Margie to go ahead and fax it to London.

"Thank you, Dr. Brewer," she said breathlessly, leaning invitingly toward me in her open-top blouse—in case a crew member happened to be around, presumably. In any case, I hurried on back to the lounge.

Trying not to trip over anything, I stood off to the side to watch Virginia's ten o'clock voiceover interview, much like Tiger Woods might observe a competitor's putt before stepping up for his own.

She was still sitting in her director's chair like a patient nervously waiting for the doctor, looking years younger with the professional makeup (she doesn't usually wear any) and proper lighting, or perhaps it was because I had never seen her at rest before. It was her job to present an overview of the hospital's rich history, its physical layout and philosophy, and its superlative staff, including the kitchen and janitorial personnel.

Priscilla (who insisted everyone call her "Prissy") appeared, cheerful and smiling. She was practically emaciated—surely anorectic, I thought—and had obviously gone through several facelifts, to the point that she appeared to have been hanged. She and Virginia began to chat informally. At some point this became the actual interview, though Prissy didn't indicate a transition as far as I could tell. There were questions about a few of the patients, but primarily she wanted to talk about fled–why she was here, when she was leaving, what she was planning to do in the meantime. Goldfarb didn't know all the answers but, overall, she acquitted herself with grace and wit, and once again showed why it was she who was directing the Institute, particularly in the aplomb with which she deflected the difficult questions about fled to the hostess's later discussion with me.

The only reason I had been selected was that I happened to be the liaison between fled and the rest of us. Well, okay, that should have made it easy; at least there were no facts or figures to memorize, nothing to prepare, and when I was summoned before those awful klieg lights everything went quite smoothly at first. I was just beginning to enjoy the experience when, out of nowhere, Prissy asked me about "life out there," as if I were an expert on extraterrestrial intelligence. All I could do was relate what I had gleaned from our alien visitors: there were myriad life forms permeating the galaxy, and presumably all galaxies throughout the universe, but there were probably very few humans among them.

"Why is that, doctor?"

"Well, according to prot, and fled, too, humans tend to destroy themselves wherever they arise."

"Do you have something against human beings, doctor?"

"No, of course not. As a matter of fact, I'm one myself." When not even a smile ensued, I went on. "They were just reporting their observations and suggesting that we ought to take better care of our planet."

"Well, are you saying that we should stop making cars and trucks until we solve all our social and political problems?"

I didn't like the direction this thing was going. Nevertheless, I tried to remain calm and cool. "Not at all. But prot might have agreed with that."

"What about fled?"

"You'll be interviewing her soon. Why don't you ask her?" Trying to lighten things up a bit, I added, "I haven't made a car or truck in years!"

I thought rather smugly that I had done rather well up to that point. But Prissy suddenly took another tack. "We've heard from an anonymous source that our special guest might be pregnant. How did that happen, doctor?"

Though a bit annoyed by this unforeseen line of questioning, I still tried to keep it light. "In the usual way, I imagine."

"And who is the father–another chimp?"

"I don't know. And I don't think she knows, either. And she's not a chimp!"

"You mean she sleeps around?"

"I didn't say that."

"Dr. Brewer, we have reason to suspect that the father of fled's child is a human being. Maybe even one of your patients. What can you tell us about that?"

Ordinarily I would have declined to answer such a leading question. But her know-it-all attitude somehow made me want to defend the accused. "Whoever he is," I retorted, "he must be quite a man." I regretted it as soon as I had said it.

"A lot of our viewers are going to be quite upset to think that someone half human and half ape is going to come out of this visit. What is your considered opinion on that, doctor?"

As calmly as I could, I reminded our host that fled wasn't an ape, but an orf.

"Well, that's what she'd like us to believe, isn't it? How do we know she even came from outer space? Some people think she's nothing more than a talking chimp. Maybe she ran away from the circus."

"They're entitled to their opinion."

"You don't care whether humans start breeding with apes, doctor?"

"I didn't say that, either!"

"How about humans and gorillas? Does that sound appealing to you?"

A final attempt to stay calm. "Most gorillas wouldn't appeal to me, no."

"Would human-pig liaisons be next? Human-skunk? Human–"

For a second, it occurred to me that she must be joking. Then I realized she was panting and, quite possibly, insane. "Not anytime soon," I responded quite evenly, hoping to calm her down and maybe prevent a stroke.

At that point a peal of laughter erupted from some of the patients milling about the lounge. I don't know what triggered it, but it must have interrupted her train of thought. When it died down Prissy was smiling brightly and the feverish look in her eyes was gone. She jumped up and shook my hand. "Good cover for the fled segments," she assured me. "Thank you very much, doctor."

I still wasn't certain whether or not to suggest she get help. Or, indeed, whether all television hosts might not be hovering on the edge of sanity.

* * *

Hoping to get away from the cameras for a while I had lunch in Ward Two. I had forgotten they were set up in the dining room as well, watching, presumably, for abnormal behavior of any kind, or maybe a food fight or the like. But at least no one was interviewing the patients while they toyed with their food.

Though she was supposed to take her meals in the Villers wing, Phyllis hovered around the tables, helping herself to whatever she wanted from the plates of those who didn't care whether they ate anything or not. She never took a seat, though, afraid that someone else would drop down on her (being invisible has its drawbacks). The cameras watched as she tried to pilfer something from Rocky's plate, and he went into a rage. Not at her, of course–perhaps he really can't see her–but at his absent brother, who used to do the same when they were children. An orderly quickly intervened, and decorum was restored.

I sat across from Cassandra, who had managed to stay focused on the present for a while, perhaps because the television cameras were everywhere and her natural desire to make a good impression had gotten the better of her. It occurred to me that this might be a possible therapeutic approach to take with patients like her: if she had something to occupy her time more intensely in the present, she might not want, or need, to spend so much of it contemplating the future. Such a thought might have fascinated me at one time, and I would have pursued it enthusiastically. But now, at the very end of my career, what could I do but mention the idea to my colleagues and trust that they would look into the possibilities.

Since she was merely eating, and quietly at that, no one was taping our end of the table, as far as I knew. Not wanting to pass up an opportunity, I asked her, "Is there anything you can tell me about fled and the patients that I don't know?"

"That would take a lot more time than we've got," she said in all seriousness. I thought I saw Barney smile a little, but, if so, it certainly wasn't a laugh.

"Do you know when fled's leaving?"

"Yes, I do."

"When?"

"June twenty-second."

I already suspected the approximate date and this confirmed it. "And do you know who she's taking with her?"

"Yes."

"Who?"

"A hundred thousand people."

"Can you be more specific?"

"A large contingent will be from the hospital."

I sat up straighter. "A contingent? Do you know how many?"

"All of us who want to go."

"All? Well, do you know how many want to go?"

"Yes."

"How many?"

"All of us."

"I see. And that includes you?"

Matter-of-factly, without even a smile, as if it were a trip to the next floor, she answered, "Yes. It was Howard who convinced her to take us all."

I heard one of the TV people say, "Who's Howard?"

Cassie was beginning to look a little agitated. "I'm finished here, Dr. Brewer. May I go?"

I got up and escorted her out the door. "What else can you tell me?" I asked, when we were out of earshot.

"You're going for a ride yourself!"

"I'm going to K-PAX??"

"Not that far."

I heard someone shout, "WHO'S HOWARD?"

One of the patients shouted back, "THE TOAD MAN!"

"Go find him!" the assistant something-or-other ordered a member of the crew.

"I meant, do you know where you'll be leaving from?"

"Fled wants to tell you that herself."

"She already knows where it is?"

But she had taken a seat on her favorite bench and was already dreaming of the stars.

I wondered: why would fled want to tell me where she's departing from? Was she testing me? Did she, in fact, want Dartmouth and Wang to know?"

And then another bizarre thought entered my head from God knows where. If she's taking more than a hundred people form the Manhattan Psychiatric Institute, might she be taking comparable numbers from other hospitals? *Was she taking 100,000 mental patients with her when she returned to K-PAX?*

I spotted fled lying on the grass, basking in the sun, her yellow shift hiked up to her waist as though she didn't have a care in the world. The questions could wait. I left her alone and went back inside.

* * *

Feeling a little post-prandial drowsiness I took my place in the lounge, where Priscilla was busily conversing with a man in an expensive suit–the director or a producer, presumably. I tried hard not to nod off. Most of the patients and staff had showed up for fled's interview as well (I was faintly annoyed that only a few had turned out for mine). Prissy checked her watch. It was 1:59, and fled's chair was still empty. At two o'clock she was sitting in it, and she had changed into a clean flowered garment of some kind. It almost made her look pretty.

The hostess jumped as if she'd been shot, but she recovered in time to introduce fled, "who claims to be from outer space." I, too, was completely awake now.

Her guest hooted loudly at this.

Unruffled, Prissy proceeded to engage fled in some harmless banter, apparently to get her into a relaxed frame of mind, or perhaps to lower her guard so she could come in with a sucker punch. What she didn't know was that fled doesn't have a guard. Nor was she a sucker. Nevertheless, she politely answered the questions until the interviewer got to the one about how sex would be possible between different species. Fled gently (perhaps she, in turn, was setting up the host) corrected her. "Sex between different species has always been possible. If you don't believe me, ask 80% of your farm boys. I think you meant to say that *reproduction* between most species is impossible."

"Yes, that's what I meant, of course. But first let me ask you this: are you pregnant, or not?"

"Definitely."

"For those of us who aren't familiar with alien reproduction, let me ask you: any problems so far—morning sickness or anything like that?"

"We don't do morning sickness on K-PAX."

"How nice for you. And what is the gestation period on your planet?"

"About the same as it is on yours."

"When I had my son, I was sick all the time. Worst nine months of my life!" She turned to the camera and whispered, "Some of you ladies out there know what I'm talking about."

"Not me," countered fled.

"We've heard that the father is a human being—is that right?"

"I don't know. He could be a chimpanzee, too. Maybe a certain bonobo. And there was a time with a gorgeous gorilla . . . ."

"But you're not human. And I guess you're not a chimpanzee, either. Or— Or anything else."

"You catch on quick."

"So how—"

"I'm sure all this talk about sex is fascinating to your viewers," fled observed. At this point she turned away from the host and looked directly at the camera, as Prissy had done a moment earlier. "Personally, I prefer to *do* it, rather than talk about it. The rest of you really should get a life. But let's get on with why I'm here, shall we? I came to EARTH with a warning for all of you."

"Hey, wait a minute. You can't just—"

"There's something wrong with you people in addition to your violent natures. Homo sapiens, as a species, is psychotic. The whole lot of you should be confined to mental institutions. You're committing suicide and you're too preoccupied with your own little lives even to realize it." She paused for a moment, perhaps to let this sink in. Prissy sputtered a bit, but said nothing. "Fact is, no one on K-PAX gives a bleep (yes, she said "bleep," presumably to save the censors the trouble) whether you kill yourselves or not. We're a pretty laid-back bunch, and we tend to let beings like yourselves live or die as they see fit. But not everyone in the GALAXY feels the same way we do."

The chair I was sitting in squeaked when I sat up in it. I wondered whether that would show up on the telecast. If there *were* a telecast.

"Here is the warning." She leaned forward and her huge head completely filled the monitor. "Attention! Are you listening? There are certain beings on other PLANETS who are seriously pissed by your belligerence and stupidity. If you kept it to yourselves, they would probably leave you to your own devices. But now you're sending out feelers to other WORLDS as well. They call themselves the "bullocks." But for simplicity's sake, and to give them a name you can understand, let's call them the "badguys." These beings are worried that you're going to contaminate the whole GALAXY with your cruelty and greed."

The cameraman glanced at the guy in the suit, who shrugged and nodded to keep rolling.

Fled sat back a little. "Let me tell you something about the badguys," she went on, a little less stridently. "Mercy is an alien concept to them. If they chose to do so, they could be here tomorrow morning at 5:30 A.M., and by noon your entire species could be selectively infected with an organism that you won't know how to deal with for countless millennia. You'd all be history by midnight. Hello? Do you understand what I'm telling you? If they decide to come here, *not a single sapiens would survive the day.*"

She paused again. The message had obviously sunk into Prissy's head, at least; her eyes were wide and her mouth gaping. "Here's the second part of the warning: you don't have much time left to avoid this fate. They have given you another fifteen years. If nothing has changed by the year 2020, you can say good-bye to the UNIVERSE, because you will disappear from it and never be heard of again. No more kfc, no more super bowl—you dig? And the meeker beings of the EARTH will finally inherit it.

"By now, the wiser sapiens among you are asking themselves two things: first, how do we know this alien is telling the truth? Do we take her words on faith? Well, for an illogical species, that's a reasonable question. Perhaps you will accept the disappearance of 100,000 people when I return to K-PAX as an indication that I know what I'm talking about.

"Your second question is, or ought to be: what can we do to convince the badguys that we're willing to turn things around? Another good one! It's a start! And here's the answer: prot sent a list of suggestions. But in order to prove your sincerity, I need an invitation from your united nations to bring them to the attention of all human beings everywhere. And I'll need this invitation in time to speak to that forum before our departure. That will occur in exactly—she checked an imaginary watch—six days, twelve hours, thirty-two minutes, and—uh—some seconds."

She turned back to the host. "That's it. End of warning. Thank you so much for having me on your program."

Prissy feverishly checked over her notes, but there was nothing there to cover this situation. Nor was the producer/director any help. Finally she asked, her eyes feverishly bright again, "Will these other aliens be able to have sex with us?"

Fled got up and left, and I didn't see her anymore that day. No one said anything, and no one followed her out, including me. But the TV crew wasn't finished. Having interviewed fled, the director had evidently concluded that talking with some of the "other patients" might appeal to the viewers, and he'd better seize the opportunity while he could. Another interview was quickly set up with Howard (who had been found skulking in the shadows). A second "host" had materialized by then, and he wanted Howard to describe what sex was like with an alien chimpanzee. The toad man enthusiastically complied with the request, which, if telecast, would surely have to be thoroughly bleeped. Then came Charlotte, followed by some of the others, including Jerry, who was still complaining about his lost talents, and whose bit, I was sure, would never make the cut because of the implication that "normalcy" might not be as wonderful it was cracked up to be. I didn't watch all of these, but I learned later that Cassie had been a big hit–at least with the crew, who sought her out for stock market predictions–and Darryl's impossible dream of teaming up with Meg Ryan came across as very moving. Apparently many people share such secret fantasies, a good number involving Ms. Ryan herself.

I didn't get home until late that night. Halfway there I realized I should have stayed over at the hospital, but I sure as hell wasn't going to turn around and go back. I wish I had.

* * *

Dartmouth and Wang were waiting in the dark for me, and they weren't happy. But it wasn't about the TV show, which they apparently weren't aware of. As fled's departure date drew closer, the number of hits on her website was increasing exponentially (how she could field the huge number of inquiries was a mystery to me, if not "the boys"). And there was a disturbing trend: more and more people were not only ruining the economy with their dietary choices, but were also re-thinking their religious views, reconsidering whether they were worth the price–remaining on Earth.

"We simply cannot let this happen. Giving up meat is one thing," he seethed, "but if people start to renounce their beliefs, they're going to start thinking for themselves instead of doing what they need to do. Do you realize what this means, sir? It means we can no longer depend on them to buy our products. Fight our wars. They might not even understand the joy of manual labor. It would be chaos! What kind of world would we have then?"

"Who is 'our'?"

He stared hard at me and grunted, "We need to talk to her."

"So do I," I said. "But we'll both have to find her first."

"Find her?" he snarled.

"I've told you before: I can't control her movements, even within the hospital."

"Friday midnight," he commanded. "Here."

"All I can do is ask her. I can't promise anything."

Wang sighed meaningfully. "Dr. Brewer, we've been nice to you so far, haven't we?"

"Well–"

"You're aware, of course, that things can get very rough when our national security is at stake...."

I guess I was too tired for this discussion. "I said I'd tell her!" I shouted. "If she doesn't come, there's nothing I can do about it!"

He repeated coldly, "See that she's here on Friday at midnight." They turned in unison and marched out the driveway.

I headed for the house.

"Have a nice day!" I heard Dartmouth call out (it was already past ten P.M.).

Karen was waiting in the kitchen for me. When I came in she inquired, "Who were you speaking to out there?"

We both laughed until we cried.

* * *

I don't know whether or not it had anything to do with the boys, but that night I dreamed my editor called. He had decided not to publish the fourth, and possibly the final, volume of the *K-PAX* saga. J.D. Salinger had come up with a three million-word novel/essay/autobiography/screenplay/short story/poetry collection, and everyone in the entire publishing house would be busy with that for many years.

I was awakened, thrashing and snorting, at 5:00 A.M. by the telephone. Karen answered it and handed it to me. It was Smythe, reporting that the British magazine article, the one announcing to the world that fled was pregnant, had appeared on the racks in Great Britain the previous afternoon, today in the U.S. "Sorry to bother you," he apologized cheerfully, "but I thought you'd want to know it's already sold out over here and we're rushing another edition into print."

"Couldn't this wait until later?"

"I thought you might also want to know that the calls and e-mails are already coming in, and they're two to one in favor."

"In favor of what?"

"Of the pregnancy."

"What are you talking about?"

"We expected a lot of protest letters about the mixed sex thing, but most of the people who wrote in simply asked when the baby was due, what sort of gift should they send it and all that."

"Ah, motherhood."

"Fatherhood, too."

"You mean they wanted to know who—"

"Yes, of course. We've got dozens of men already claiming to be the father. And that's just the beginning. The bloody article only just came out!"

"You're saying that they're all trying to—"

"Not exactly. I think she might actually have had sex with the lot of them."

"How is that possible?"

"She seems to get around."

"What next?" I wondered rhetorically.

Smythe answered anyway. "The naming contest. It was the biggest hit of the whole article. In another month we'll have our winner. Do you think fled will still be around then? She could make a fortune on the worldwide talk-show circuit until the time she delivers her—uh—whatever it is. It's going to be the best-selling issue (pardon the pun) we've ever had, bigger than John and Yoko, even. Remind me to send you a jar of piccalilli or something." He went on for a while about the raise and promotion he would be getting. Before he hung up he asked me: "Are you expecting any more visitors from K-PAX?"

"Who knows?"

"I hope you'll give me first crack at him. Or her . . . ."

"Better make that two jars of piccalilli," I yawned. He giggled hysterically before finally hanging up.

I tried unsuccessfully to go back to sleep. One thing was certain: if another visitor came, someone else would have to supervise their comings and goings. I finally got up at about seven and went out to get the paper. Wang flashed his badge and handed me the *Times*. There was no sign of Dartmouth. "Don't you guys ever sleep?" I asked him, annoyed but genuinely curious.

"That's classified," he replied. "But I can tell you this much: sleep is a sign of weakness."

"I must be very strong," I said. "I can't sleep, either."

He stared back without comment.

"Well," I said sourly, "what do you want?"

"I was just wondering . . ." he began, before choking up. I waited uncomfortably. He glanced around furtively before beginning again. "I wanted to speak to you privately about Mr. Dartmouth."

"Oh, I see. Do you want to come in?"

"No, thank you. I'd rather keep it private."

I tapped the paper unconsciously against a thigh. "All right. What can I do for you?"

He carefully checked our surroundings. "This is entirely off the record, of course. Agreed?"

"Agreed."

"I'm worried about his mental state. I think he's beginning to see things. Maybe it's Alzheimer's."

I considered the possibility that this was some kind of trick, but he seemed truly concerned, even desperate.

"I'm sorry, but I can't help him. I'm re—"

"Not *you*, Dr. Brewer," he snarled. "I was hoping you could ask fled to take a look at him." Though his expression and posture remained unchanged, tears were running down his face.

I patted him on the shoulder. He flinched as if it were the hand of God.

"I'll speak to her," I promised him. As an afterthought I observed, "You've been together for a while, haven't you?"

In a choked voice he replied, "A long time ago he took a bullet and saved my life. I still owe him for that." Suddenly he stood at attention, saluted me snappily, and shouted, "Thank you, *sir*!"

I awkwardly returned it. "Friday midnight," he reminded me in a whisper as I went into the house.

Once inside, I waited a few minutes before peering carefully out the front window to see if he had gone. A strange-looking vehicle with excrescences all over it pulled up. Wang ran down the driveway, disappeared into the thing, and it sped away. The possibility occurred to me that perhaps fled really was from Earth, and the government boys were the aliens.

* * *

There wasn't a trace of the cameras and all the paraphernalia when I got to MPI, and everything was as it had been. The patients were wandering around as usual, except that they seemed a bit more morose than usual. A normal letdown after the exciting time they had had the day before, I supposed. But it was more than that. Fled was gone, too. Not to K-PAX, apparently, because she left me a note informing me that she would "be away for a while." I didn't know where she was, or how long she would be gone, and neither did the boys, I hoped, but I knew what she must be doing—rounding up her travel companions, or perhaps taking the stadium owners on a joyride around the solar system. I presumed she would return for at least a final visit before leaving us, but, with a K-PAXian, one could never be sure of anything. I was comforted, however, by the knowledge that she had promised to chat with Steve and his family, not to mention the United Nations General Assembly (if the invitation came). The government wanted to see her as well, but that was their concern, not mine. And she still hadn't given us a urine or blood sample to test for her alleged pregnancy.

It's possible to get e-mail anywhere in the world, of course, and I suppose that's how she could keep up with the applications, as well as comments and questions any prospective travelers might have for her. But with the vast numbers involved, how long would it take to get a reply? I sat down at Goldfarb's office computer (with Margie's knowledge and approval) and sent a rather testy message asking her how she would know if a United Nations invitation came to her via the hospital.

To my amazement, the answer came back immediately. **You'll tell me,** it said. **And aren't we in a bad temper!**

Where are you now? I quickly replied.

Indonesia, but I'll be leaving soon.

I sent another one. **When will we see you again?**

A couple of days. I still have to talk to your son-in-law, remember?

The government wants to see you, too. Friday at midnight. Okay? And one of them needs his head examined . . . .

Got things to do, gino. Talk to you later.

Can you make it?

There was no immediate response.

At this point Goldfarb, who was still unsure about the wisdom of a television production originating at MPI, came in. "They may not even air the damn thing," she told me. "They're still thinking about it. If they don't, all we'll get is the cancellation fee."

"How much is that?"

"$25,000."

"Better than nothing."

"Not much. That'll keep us going for about three hours."

I don't think I've ever won an argument with Goldfarb, so I dropped it. "What do you think about the 'Badguys' she mentioned?"

"If it's true, we're in deep shit."

"You think it's not?"

"That's the trouble with aliens. You have to take their word for everything."

"To that I think fled would say our suspicion is part of our problem. I mean, if she were human, I'd have my doubts, too. But if she's not–"

"Why shouldn't we have your doubts anyway?"

"I'm quite confident that prot never lied to us," I told her, "and I don't really know of an instance where fled has, either."

"Maybe this is the instance."

"But why would she lie about a thing as serious as genocide?"

"Who knows? To scare us, maybe?"

"There's a flaw in your argument. I don't think she gives a fuck–you should pardon the expression–whether we listen to the warning about the Badguys or not. I think she'd just as soon see us go the way of the dodo."

"Maybe she's lying about that, too."

* * *

I hadn't realized that the patients had grown so fond of fled. In the few days she was gone they kept coming to me demanding to know when she would be back. It's amazing: one minute you're a pariah, the next a prodigal daughter. It's a shame there isn't some way to see what a whole person is like from the beginning, rather than find out a little at a time. Why does our understanding go up and down like a yo-yo? But, of course, that's part of what makes human interactions so interesting.

I sincerely believe that when you get to know someone you consider to be "different," you find that there aren't so many dissimilarities as you thought. This is particularly true of racial and religious prejudices. I'm not going to claim that I know a lot of African-Americans or Muslims personally, but the few I do know aren't really very different from me. They put on their pants like me, eat like me, laugh and cry like me. The rest of it is based, I suspect, on fear. Fear of what? You name it: job loss, property values, and all the rest. This doesn't mean that I have to like everyone I meet whose race is different from my own. Cliff Roberts, one of our most respected staff psychiatrists and coal-black, is, in my view, something of a jerk. On the other hand, maybe I just don't know him well enough to know who's really in there.

Anyway, I asked some of the patients why they were so eager to see her again, expecting them to say she was going back to K-PAX soon and they wanted to be first in line. But it was more than that. Part of it was the motherhood thing, and part was her television interview. They didn't like the host's grilling her about who she's had sex with, or who was the father of her child. Beyond that, they were concerned that there may be some Badguys who were watching us from afar, ready to step in when we got completely out of hand, and they thought she might be able to do something about that. The fact is, I think they gave a fuck.

Whatever the reasons, they wanted her back. And so did I. There were innumerable things I wanted to talk to her about. For example, I hadn't had the chance to warn her that Messrs. Dartmouth and Wang might want to see her at midnight on Friday in order to perform classified acts on her to keep her from leaving the Earth with 100,000 Earth people, particularly if any of them were American citizens who were planning to diminish the GDP. In fact, I had come to believe that these agents of the government would stop at nothing to hold on to the beliefs and values they (us?) held dear.

As far as the patients were concerned, I desperately wanted to give her one last chance to talk to each of them. If she could get to the heart of their problems, maybe some would change their minds about taking the long, and perhaps dangerous, voyage with her.

While I was dwelling on this hopeful dream, Rocky came up. "She back yet?" he asked me for about the tenth time.

"I don't think so."

"I'm going to get even with her for this."

"Get even with fled? For what?"

"She said she would look into my head and find out how to help me feel better. She hooked me up to something, all right, but she never told me what she found out. And now she's disappeared again. That was a rotten thing to do."

"She what? She hooked you up to something?"

"That's right. And most of the others, too."

"What did she hook you up to?"

"I don't know. Some cone-shaped thing."

"And she told you it would look into your head?"

"Yes. Why? Did she do something to us she shouldn't have?"

"Nothing harmful, I'm sure. Anyway, I think she's coming back, Rocky. At least one more time. But if she does, there's no guarantee she can do anything for you anyway."

"Yes there is."

"What makes you think so?"

"She told me she could."

Darryl came up. "She told me, too."

Claire, who had been taking notes on a yellow pad a short distance away, called over. "I'm not a patient," she reminded me, "I'm a staff physician. But fled said she would help me with some personal problems I've been having."

"I thought you said fled was no more alien than I am."

"She's not. She's just a lot smarter than the rest of you are."

Barney came up behind me. "You should talk to her, too, Dr. B," he advised me in all seriousness.

Rick wasn't far behind him. "She didn't tell me nothin.'" Translation: she could do something for him as well. By now, almost everyone on the lawn had turned up to assure me that when she returned, fled had a cure for everyone. I didn't know whether to believe any of them or not, except for Rick.

Or did she mean she could do something for all of them by providing them with a radical change of scene?

CHAPTER ELEVEN

The phone woke us up at 5:30 Monday morning. I thought it might be Smythe again with the early results of the baby-naming contest, and decided to let the machine answer it. My wife, however, who always thinks it might be an urgent call from one of our kids (we still call them "kids" even though the youngest one is nearly thirty), picked up the phone. In a few seconds she handed it to me and went back to sleep. It was our son-in-law. I had never heard him so excited (though he's always excited about *something*).

"What's up, Steve?" I asked him without much enthusiasm.

"Fled just left! She came last night for a picnic!"

"That's great, Steve, but couldn't it wait until—"

"Ah thought you'd want to be among the first to know that the speed of light is equal to the expansion rate of the universe! In other words, light doesn't travel at 186,000 miles per second *through* the universe at all. The universe is expanding at that rate in all directions, and photons just go along for the ride! This explains everything! Nothing can travel faster than the speed of light because if it did, it would escape the bounds of the universe, which is impossible! Einstein was right, but for the wrong reason!"

I knew what he was saying, more or less, but was a bit annoyed to get the information second-hand. "I thought fled wasn't interested in stuff like that."

"She isn't. Ah guess she just wanted to get me off her back."

I had no trouble believing that. "When did you say she came for this picnic?"

"Last night! Or this morning, actually! About two A.M.!"

"She came for a picnic at two in the morning?"

"Yep. We were in bed, o' course, but we all wanted to talk to her about different things, and we got up right away. She was hungry, so we all went out to the back yard and had some fruit and veggies."

"In the dark?"

"Not exactly. We lit some candles. It was pretty nice, actually. You ought to try it sometime."

"I'll think about it. Do you know where she'd been?"

"South America. Her last field trip, she said. Anyway, Ah asked her a bunch of questions Ah'd been saving for her. She told me enough stuff for a dozen papers. Of course everything she said needs to be confirmed experimentally. But shit–"

"Did she tell you anything else? Like where she's leaving from?"

"Well, no. Nobody asked her that. Rain happened to be home, and Star kept taking pictures of her with the rest of us, and we took some more of him and Rain with fled. I'll send you a few. She gave him a hair from her head, too. And then Abby talked to her about what might happen to the Earth and what the options were . . . ."

"Options? What options?"

"There ain't any. She said the only way we're going to survive is to evolve."

"How long will that take?"

"We're way overdue."

"Did fled tell you where she was going when she left you?"

"Back to the hospital, Ah think."

"Then I'd better get going!"

Steve doesn't always take a hint. "The other reason Ah called was to thank you for getting her to come over. It was amazin'! Think about it, Gene! Light isn't movin' at all! It's just going along with the expansion of the universe. That's why it zooms off in all directions at the speed it does. Anything else travels at a slower speed depending on its mass. Neutrinos travel a little slower than light because they have a little dab of mass. It's a little more complicated than that, o' course, but basically, the heavier a particle, the slower it goes."

"O' course."

"And get this: black holes don't just keep light from escaping. They actually stop the expansion of the universe in their immediate vicinity! Which is why no light can come from them!"

I had to admit it sounded pretty amazin'. "What did she say about superstring theory?"

"According to fled, the whole thing is a piece of shit. There are dozens of string theories. She said they're either all right or they're all wrong."

"Makes sense, I guess."

"Ah want to go to K-PAX!"

"Now?"

"Well, no. First Ah need to write a buncha papers . . . ."

* * *

I left the house early to beat the traffic, and was still in a fog when I got to the hospital. But I had been invited to the Monday morning staff meeting for the first time since my "retirement," and I wasn't about to pass up the opportunity. For one thing, I wanted to discuss an idea I had had about fled and the patients.

I wasn't the first to arrive. Goldfarb, as always, was already there, going through some notes, editing her agenda. She nodded when I came in, but went back to her business as if I weren't there.

The perfect copy of van Gogh's "Sunflowers," painted by a former patient, was still hanging on the side wall, a clear reminder that when I finally stop coming to MPI the place would go on perfectly well without me. At times like this one wonders what impact, if any, his life on Earth really has. In another hundred years who would know I had even been here?

The rest of the staff dribbled in: Hannah Rudqvist, who blushed darkly when she saw me, followed by Ron Menninger, Laura Chang, Cliff Roberts, and finally Will (Rothstein was absent–for personal reasons, Goldfarb said). I couldn't help wonder whether Laura and Will had separated their entrances for appearance's sake.

There were several topics on the table. Ron reported that Ed, a murderous psychopath who had become a lamb after a brief talk with prot, had paid us a return visit over the weekend and ran into Charlotte, another of his ilk. It was love at first sight, Ron disclosed incredulously, a storybook romance of the movie variety. Whether it was their common violent background or simply the kind of unpredictable chemistry that results in a passionate love affair between more ordinary individuals Menninger didn't know (who would?), but they were inseparable for the entire two days. Now Charlotte has announced that she is "ready" to leave the hospital. If MPI and the courts won't allow that, Ed wants to move back in!

The consensus was that Ron should prepare an assessment of Charlotte's progress over the last few years and, in the meantime, we should allow Ed full visitation rights and see what developed. The vote was 5-1 in favor (Menninger, the lone dissenter, had, himself, once been a victim of Charlotte's sadistic nature), and one abstention (mine).

Next up was Jerry. Laura reported that he had sunk into a severe depression, and had even talked about possibility of ending it all. "He's bored out of his mind," she lamented. Although she didn't think suicide was likely, it was nonetheless a serious concern: one doesn't take such threats by a mental patient lightly. She compared him to Jonathan Swift's Gulliver, who, after returning home from his visits to various other lands and their inhabitants, found human beings so repugnant that he wanted nothing more to do with them. In Jerry's case, everything about the "real" world seemed stupid and faintly repugnant.

"How can we convince him that his new–i.e., normal–existence isn't so terrible?" she asked us. Unfortunately, no one could provide a good answer to that.

"Different things make different people happy," Will offered. "It depends on the individual. The usual factors are love, religion, an interesting career, money–things like that."

Cliff, as usual, came up with a smart-ass remark. "We could hook him up with a rich, beautiful lady preacher who's always wanted to live in a house of matchsticks."

I reminded him that Jerry couldn't remember how to build matchstick houses anymore. He demanded to know if I had a better idea. I didn't, but Goldfarb contended that fled was smart enough to have foreseen what might happen to Jerry when she "re-wired" him. Maybe, she suggested, our alien visitor had something else in mind....

The rest of the hour was taken up by brief case reviews of a number of the other patients, including Darryl. I mentioned that my son Fred was planning to bring in an actress who resembled Meg Ryan, to see if an unpleasant encounter with her might snap him out of his impossible dream. There were no objections to giving it a try–what was there to lose? Most of the other issues were routine administrative matters, which droned on and on, but I just enjoyed being there, probably for the last time, gazing at the pictures, taking in the sounds of concerned people trying to come to terms with difficult mental patients, trying not to remember how short life really is. But, being human, I also glanced at Hannah and Will, sitting together in apparent innocence, pretending all was well at home. I hoped my scowl didn't show. But I realized that Karen, as always, was right. They were consenting adults who knew what they were getting into, and I had no right to interfere, regardless of who might be hurt.

I was awakened from my reverie by Goldfarb, who brought up fled. "Do we know yet when she's leaving?"

"It's still not firm, but I think it might be in a couple of days. She was in Princeton early this morning, but I don't know where she went after that. If she shows up here today, I was hoping we could set up a group meeting between her and the patients. She promised to talk to everyone at some point, and has already spoken with some of them" (I didn't mention the 'cone-shaped thing,' not knowing what it meant myself–was she making holograms for their relatives?), "but I don't think there's enough time for her to interact with everyone else individually."

"Any objections?" Goldfarb inquired. There were none. "See what you can do," she said.

Finally, our hard-working director mentioned that she had received a call from the producer of the TV program. (Actually, it turned out to be a committee of producers). They were very enthusiastic about the show, suggesting that it was on the "fast track" and the telecast would be moved up to September. But it wasn't fled's announcement–that the Bullocks were coming if we didn't change our collective habits–or even her pregnancy, which had already been scooped by the British magazine article, but the daily lives and concerns of the patients at the Manhattan Psychiatric Institute that had triggered their enthusiasm. "This is the last untapped source of human emotion that hasn't yet been explored by television," he informed her. "Until now, we've been afraid to approach it. But we were wrong. Everyone can empathize with the problems of the mentally ill," he enthused. "Certainly everyone here at the network."

Yes! I thought. If nothing else came of fled's visit, a better understanding of this serious medical (and social) problem would have made her trip worthwhile.

* * *

Fled wasn't in Room 520 so, as usual, I went looking for her. I didn't find her on the lawn or in the lounge, but I did run across Darryl speaking with–Meg Ryan. They seemed to be deeply engaged in a heated conversation, so I left them alone.

After searching everywhere else, I returned to our regular meeting place; by then fled had returned from wherever she had been. She was chewing on a potato, and there was a pile of peelings on the desk next to the basket. She took another one and began to strip it slowly with her teeth. I took the opportunity to mention something that had been bothering me all along. "Prot never peeled his vegetables. Or his fruit."

"Yes, I know. Dremers are very primitive in some ways."

"They can't even read minds!" I joked. She stared at me and continued to munch. "Before we get started," I began, "I want to thank you for visiting Abby and Steve and the boys."

"Wasn't as bad as Ah thought." Crunch, crunch, munch. "And in answer to your first question (I hadn't asked it yet), it won't be long now."

"What won't be long?"

She grinned at that; perhaps she had finally given me credit for a touch of humor.

I smiled back. "So you've got a football stadium lined up?"

"Not exactly. Something much better than *that*."

"Well? What is it? *Where* is it?"

"One moment, please." She got up and reached for the light, pulling out some sort of tiny electronic device. "'Bye, boys!" she yelled into it. I didn't want to think about how Dartmouth and Wang's ears must be feeling.

"They aren't feeling anything, my human friend. I deactivated this thing as soon as he put it there."

"He?"

"Sauer."

"While you were *here*?"

"I pretended to be asleep."

"You mean after you–and he–"

"Exactly."

"So they haven't heard anything all along?"

"No, they heard something. A fake broadcast I recorded for them. They think we talked about my baby blanket the whole time I was here." She flipped the device into the wastebasket. "Can you keep a secret, coach?"

"Nothing that I hear in this room will ever get out of it. It's been that way for thirty-five years, and I don't intend to change anything now."

"I knew that, but I also know how much you love saying it. We'll be leaving from the grand canyon."

"The Grand– I suspect that will hold 100,000 people."

"I only wish I could take more."

"Maybe someone else will come for the rest of us."

"The bullocks are coming! The bullocks are coming!"

"Uh–I've been meaning to ask you about that."

She plopped an entire potato into her mouth. "Have you, indeed?"

"Tell me: was that some kind of joke? A ruse to scare us into coming together as a world and learning to behave ourselves?"

Chomping loudly, she managed to spit out, "Why would I do that? If I were a bullock, I would've been here long ago. It was prot who asked them to give you more time. He likes your species, for some reason. Of course there's no accounting for taste." A spray of potato bits flew in my face.

I ignored them. "And they're really coming in another fifteen years?"

"Give or take a day or two."

"So you're just like prot–you don't really care if we humans survive or not, do you?"

"About as much as you care if your elephants do."

It was no use pretending I was on the front line of the save-the-elephant movement, and I didn't try.

"Anything else, coach?"

"We're having a bit of a problem with Jerry . . . ."

"Already done."

"Already–"

"Simple matter. I re-did his wiring. He's just like he was before."

"Thank you. I think. And what about the other patients? Can you see them all sometime before you go? A group session, everyone included?"

She pulled out the hologram device she had showed me when she first arrived at the house. "This will tell you more than you want to know about your patients."

I stared at the thing.

"Just set it down on its flat end, remember? And turn it to whichever patient you want to review. It will do the rest."

"You mean–"

"I'm leaving it with you. A word of advice, though, my sapien friend: when you've finished interacting with the projections, I'd suggest you don't let it get into the wrong hands."

"When did you do this?"

"Whenever I was around them. Of course they didn't know how deeply I was peering into their minds."

I stuffed the thing in my jacket pocket. "How do I keep it out of the wrong hands?"

"Do I have to do all your thinking, my dimwitted friend? When you're finished with it, just bury the thing. Like a time capsule. You could write on it, 'To be opened in a million years,'" she hooted. "C'mon. I'll take you home."

"Home?"

"You know, doc. Your dwelling."

"Uh . . ." Oh, what the hell. You only live once.

The next thing I knew I was standing on our back porch. She took my hand. "Let's go in."

Amazingly, I wasn't dizzy or, for that matter, felt anything at all. It seemed something like a movie cut. Karen and Flower were in the living room. While the latter went for a toy, fled began removing bugs from the lights, the phones, the electrical outlets—a dozen in all. "Souvenirs, anyone?" she shrieked, dropping all the paraphernalia on an end table and chasing our indefatigable canine through the house. After fifteen or twenty minutes Flower had finally had her fill, probably for the first time in her life. As she lay panting, I asked fled, "The boys got fake messages from these, too?"

"The government thinks you lead the most exciting lives on EARTH! Parties, orgies—"

"Can you give us a clue about how you did—"

"I'm going to tell you something, doctor b. You listening? You wouldn't even begin to understand it even if I tried to explain it to you. It's time you stopped asking questions and just paid attention to what you know already. Now I'm going to say it again. Slowly. You ready? Here is all you need to know: the bullocks are coming in fifteen years. Do you read me loud and clear?"

"That's affirmative."

"Good." Suddenly she clapped her hands together and screeched, "Let's go for a ride!" The light and mirror re-appeared, and the next thing we knew we were all standing on the rim of the Grand Canyon staring down into the biggest natural gorge in the world. Karen and I had never been there. "Cool" doesn't come close to describing it. It was still early morning in the West, and the brilliant sun cast long shadows on the floor of the cavern below. Wisps of fog floated above the river valley. A small herd of burros or donkeys dotted the verdant floor below. The scope could not possibly be accurately reproduced by the greatest of landscape painters, or even a wall-size photograph. I vowed to spend as much time as possible from that moment on seeing all the sights around the globe that we had never found time to take in earlier.

Another flash and suddenly we were at the bottom, standing beside a gushing river, the creator of it all. The air smelled fresh, and full of life. The burros looked up from their breakfast and sized us up before bending down again, ignoring us completely. Spring blossoms of all colors and kinds demanded our attention. The rushing water provided a paradisical background to the beautiful scene. The four of us took it all in without a word. Even Flower was awestruck, or perhaps she was just too tired to chase the burros.

"Let's come back here some day," my wife whispered to me. Fled's grin was a foot wide. In another moment we were back in our living room, and Fled was nowhere to be seen. But I knew where she was. She only had two days to gather up 100,000 people and stash them in a canyon.

* * *

That afternoon, after Karen had gone bowling with her women's league, I went to fled's website, where I found the following notice:

SORRY, THE PASSENGER LIST IS FULL
APPLICATIONS ARE CLOSED

I scrolled down to see if there were any other changes or additions. The only one appeared at the end.

COMING SOON: THE BADGUYS

Suddenly I remembered the hologram device in my jacket pocket. I retrieved it from the closet and hurried back to my study, where I carefully placed it on the floor, as fled had done earlier. To my surprise I found a three-dimensional representation of a four- or five-year-old girl at a dinner table with, I presumed, her parents. She was sitting on her hands, and appeared to be terrified. Tears had run down her dirty face.

"It's all right, Phyllis," her mother cajoled her. "Eat your chicken."

The child didn't move.

"Eat that goddamn chicken, you little slut," her father snarled.

"I don't want it. I'm afraid to."

"Daddy won't hurt you," her mother promised. "Go ahead."

Little Phyllis timidly picked up a piece of fried chicken. Before she got it to her plate the father whacked her hand with his fork. The chicken fell onto the floor, and the girl began crying again.

"GET DOWN THERE AND EAT THAT FOOD!" her father screamed.

Phyllis, her arms thrust upward to ward off blows, screamed, too. But she quickly got down on the floor and tried to pick up the wing.

"NOT WITH YOUR HANDS, YOU LITTLE BITCH–WITH YOUR MOUTH! YOU THROW YOUR FOOD ON THE FLOOR, YOU EAT IT THERE. YOU DON'T DESERVE TO EAT LIKE A HUMAN BEING!"

Phyllis did as she was told.

"And for being such a clumsy girl, you're going to get the bathtub treatment tonight," her mother added sweetly.

Phyllis cried even louder. "Please, Mommy, please no! I won't throw any more chicken on the floor! Please don't put me in the bathtub! Oh, please, not tonight!"

"And after that, you little shit, I've got a cigarette for you!" her father promised.

The girl wailed again before leaning over and throwing up on the floor.

"You lick that up, you little bitch! LICK IT UP!"

"Be more careful with that cigarette this time," the woman admonished her husband. "We don't want it to show."

Phyllis suddenly dissolved and reappeared in another scene. She was sitting in a corner of a bare room, perhaps her bedroom, rocking back and forth, back and forth. She looked to be a little older, and was no longer crying. Her face was blank, her eyes staring, as if she were a porcelain doll. Instinctively I reached out to pick her up, to give her a hug. She didn't recoil, as I had expected her to, nor did she react in any way. It was as if she were dead....

I didn't want to know what else they had done to Phyllis, and quickly turned the device a few degrees. The room turned dark, and I found myself in a dirt-floor basement. I could smell the mold, feel the cold dampness. There was an emaciated boy of six or seven in dirty rags crawling on his hands and knees—perhaps there wasn't enough room to stand up—next to a grimy window. He reached for a spider, pushed it into his mouth, and then went for a dead fly attached to a piece of the web. A mouse ran by and little Rick quickly grabbed it. Just as he was about to bite off its head it squirmed out of his grasp and disappeared through a crack in the wall. He began to cry.

I turned the damn thing again.

This time it was a boy playing Monopoly with, I suspect, an older brother. The boy landed on Park Place. Without warning, the brother slapped him hard in the face with his bare hand. Rocky didn't seem surprised. He didn't even cry. He just went on blankly playing the game....

I kept turning the device, but no matter how I set it down I found only misery and anguish. I caught a glimpse of someone who resembled Claire being laughed at, presumably by her parents and other relatives, when she said she wanted to be a doctor. And there were others. Probably all our patients were represented, but I made no effort to distinguish one from the other. There were also two staff members, whose horrible childhood explained a lot about their adult behavior, but whom I can't identify in these pages.

One last turn, hoping to find an iota of happiness, or at least a little less abuse than befell the others. A chimpanzee was holding her baby in a peaceful jungle setting. There was hardly a sound, except for leaves rustling in the trees, and perhaps the tinkling of a nearby stream. The sun came through the foliage, dappling the soft ground and the young ape. For a second I allowed myself a smile. Without warning, however, the pair were surrounded by three large mongrel dogs. Cradling her child, the mother jumped up, ran for a tree, and almost made it before their canine pursuers caught up with them. It was over in a few seconds, the adult chimpanzee's throat torn out, the little one screaming, the men with their rifles yelling at the dogs to leave the baby alone . . . .

The scene shifted without interference from me. In a brightly-lit laboratory another ape (perhaps the grownup baby) was sitting in a tiny cage, his head clamped into a vise-like tool. Electrodes connected to heavy black cables protruded from his head. A couple of women in white coats turned a dial and watched for the ape's reaction, one of the scientists or technicians jotting down the results in a thick black notebook. But the chimpanzee was long past reacting. His vacant eyes stared sightlessly ahead. I saw that he had, sometime in the past, chewed off half his fingers . . . .

I spun the thing and ended up on an icy outcropping near the ocean. Several men with grappling hooks were beating baby seals to death or kicking them senseless with their heavy boots, hundreds and hundreds of them. The bodies, already stripped of their fur (many were still alive, writhing on the ice), dotted the landscape, red with warm blood . . . .

Another turn and a huge bull was being murdered in a ring. Thousands and thousands of de-beaked chickens were crammed into tiny cages, their eggs collected on a conveyer belt, the air saturated with fecal ammonia fumes. A live pig whose throat had just been cut was thrashing and screaming on a red-stained cement floor. I suddenly realized that there was little difference between child and animal abuse . . . .

That was all I could take. Leaving Flower inside so she wouldn't dig it up later, I grabbed the terrible device and headed for the tool shed, where I picked up a shovel and, forgetting, or maybe not caring, about government agents everywhere, hiked deep into the woods behind the house to bury the fucking thing. For the first time in years I found myself weeping. "Let the goddamn Bullocks come!" I shouted to the rabbits and squirrels. "Let them take us out of existence and put a stop to this endless goddamn cruelty!"

Later, when Karen came home, I explained what had happened. Without a word she put her arms around me until, finally, after what seemed like hours, I began to feel better.

CHAPTER TWELVE

The next morning I was just getting into the car when a disembodied voice whispered, "Dr. Brewer!"

"Huh? Where are you?"

"Up here." In the oak tree nearest the garage was Wang, proffering his badge. Dartmouth was at the end of the driveway guarding the house from terrorists with his huge, ugly weapon.

"Dammit, Wang, I haven't had time to–"

"We've learned from one of our most reliable sources that your visitor is planning to send some violent aliens to wipe out the human race. Is that true or false?"

I saw no point in withholding this information, which was already on record. "Fled told us in a television interview that if we humans don't shape up and learn to share the Earth with one another and with all the other species living on the planet, some alien beings might come and–uh–terminate us. But she's not 'sending' them. She's just passing on their warning."

"What country are they working for?"

"They're not working for any country, Wang. They're aliens."

"I *know* they're aliens. Are they Russian or Chinese? What kind of weapons do they have?"

"Viruses."

"Ah. Biological warfare! I *knew* we should have put more effort into that. Somebody's head is going to roll for this one. But it's not going to be mine!"

"You can't imagine how glad I am to hear that."

"What are they going to use? Bird flu? West Nile? SARS? We can lick anything they throw at us . . . ."

"No, I think this is a new one they've produced just for us."

"Even better! A clean slate. Just give us four or five years and we'll beat this thing, no matter how many lives it costs!"

"We may only have a few hours."

"What?? We can't come up with a defense for some foreign virus in a few hours."

"That may be all we'll have."

"That's not fair!"

"Was there something else? I've got to get to the hospital."

"We'll be there afore ye."

"Huh?"

"You heard me. We have a court order to come in and talk to some of the patients. See what they might be able to tell us."

"About what?"

"About when and from where your visitor is leaving."

"What makes you think they know anything about that?"

"That's why we're going in. To find out if they know anything!" He leapt from the tree and ran down the driveway. Out of nowhere a huge helicopter roared into view above the road. Dartmouth grabbed the ladder dangling from it and started up, followed immediately by Wang, and they were still climbing toward the hatch as the chopper rumbled off toward the south. I saw Dartmouth slip once, but his partner grabbed him and pushed him back up the ladder. Perhaps they were finally even.

Karen came out of the house. "Bill Siegel's on the phone. He wants to know what the hell is going on over here."

"Tell him the elephants just left."

* * *

When I got to the hospital the empty helicopter was sitting on the lawn, its rotor blades drooping; it looked for all the world like a huge dead insect. Several of the patients were milling around it, pointing and laughing. Dartmouth stood nearby, guarding it with his massive weapon. Wang was in the building looking for fled and interviewing some of the other residents, the rest of whom were huddled together on the back forty. All except for Georgie, the football star with the IQ of forty. Dartmouth watched him suspiciously as he spiraled the ball far into the air, then ran and caught it before it hit the ground. As long as he's been here, I've never seen him miss it.

I don't know which I enjoyed more: Georgie's athletic ability or Dartmouth's fascination with it. Up and up went the football along with the G-man's dull, narrowly-spaced eyes. Over and over again—ten, fifteen, twenty times, neither of them losing an iota of interest. As luck would have it, the twenty-first toss went high into the air and plummeted straight down to where Dartmouth was standing. I could see his indecision mount as the ball came down and down and down . . . . At the last second, with Georgie running hard toward him, he dropped his weapon and lunged for the ball. There was a collision. Georgie and the football bounced a few feet away. While our athletic patient climbed to his feet, a look of surprise on his face, Dartmouth went for the ball. As he bent down to pick it up he accidentally kicked it instead. He went after it again, reached down with his hand, kicked the ball with his foot. All over the lawn the charade proceeded, Dartmouth following the football: kick, reach, kick, while Georgie watched in bewilderment.

Whether it was the size sixteen AAA wingtip shoes stabbing the ball, or his uniform: worn blue suit and red tie flapping in the breeze that produced the eruption I can't say, but suddenly from the back forty came the sound of laughter–giggles, howls, roars, guffaws–and leading the pack was Barney. Dartmouth, oblivious to the commotion, chased the football as it bounced off walls and patients, reached down for it, kicked it again. He might be out there even now but for a perfect tackle by Georgie, who grabbed the fumble and ran the entire length of the lawn for a touchdown, to deafening cheers from his fellow inmates.

By the time Dartmouth came to his senses, picked himself up, and ran for the helicopter, it was crawling with patients. There came a whine, and the rotor started to turn. The lanky agent went for his weapon, still lying where he had left it, but it flew out of his hands, end over end, seemingly in slow motion, and when he finally grabbed it he promptly shot himself in the foot. The rotor turned faster, and in a matter of seconds the aircraft was up in the air and over the wall, fled at the controls. The pilot, who had gone into the building to use the facilities, came running out, followed immediately by Wang, waving his own huge sidearm, but it was far too late–the helicopter was already circling over the Hudson. It turned southeast toward the Empire State Building, the first stop on a city-wide tour, as Dartmouth hopped around the lawn, yelping like an injured animal.

Cliff Roberts and some of the nurses appeared and began to attend to him while someone called for an ambulance. The patients who hadn't made it to the helicopter in time scrutinized the proceedings with considerable interest. Cliff was very much in command the whole time and quite solicitous toward the injured agent, who was in considerable pain and crying like a baby, and I thought: even Roberts has redeeming qualities. He may have seemed less than serious about his profession, but perhaps that was all an act to compensate for some buried neurosis or innate kindness, and when the crunch came he didn't hesitate to pitch in. This was the kind of doctor I would want if I were a patient here. I found myself hoping that the Bullocks were aware of our good points, despite the obvious negatives. Whether they came or not, I realized, we would all survive this world or perish together.

Barney was still giggling softly as he watched Georgie toss the football high into the air, run and catch it, toss it again.

* * *

That afternoon fled dumped the helicopter at LaGuardia, much to the chagrin of the traffic controllers and the FAA, and brought the patients "home" in the usual way—by light and mirror. Fortunately, Wang and the pilot had accompanied Dartmouth to the hospital, so there was no problem attending her arrival. Nevertheless, she didn't stay long; presumably she still had a few last-minute arrangements to make. Just before she left the lawn she waved at me, but whether it was just a "See you later, doc," or a final farewell, I couldn't be sure. I waited the rest of the day for her to return, and finally decided to stay overnight at the hospital in case she came back after hours.

In the meantime I took a fresh look at the patients I encountered. I saw them now in a different light, not the cold, clinical one necessary for their treatment, but as fellow human beings who had made it this far despite devastating travails, the horrible ordeals they had experienced (and, in their minds, always would) at the hands of their parents and others whom they should have been able to trust. Yet, despite the cruel and even sadistic treatment, they were still in there pitching, refusing to give up. Suddenly I felt great pride in knowing them and what they had tried courageously to overcome.

I watched Phyllis as she hid in front of a small shrub. She was no longer merely the psychiatric problem that I and the rest of the staff had dealt with, but a human being who had suffered terrible damage to her psyche, someone who hurt every single minute with never a letup. After experiencing God knows what pain and suffering, is it any wonder that she tried to become invisible, desperately hoping that no one, especially her parents, could see her and inflict further unbearable damage? What else had she gone through that even I, a trained psychiatrist, didn't know and didn't *want* to know about? How much have countless others outside these walls had to endure as the price for being born in this world? Even for those of us who escaped parental or sibling abuse, the world is a harsh enough reality. How much longer must we turn on the television set and see the faces of millions of people starving all over the world? Or count the arms and legs blown off by the weapons you and I sell to whomever will buy them? Is it any wonder that so many people want to go to K-PAX, or perhaps take their chances on *any* planet other than this one? At least a hundred thousand, according to fled's website. And with the roster filled well before the departure date, how many had to be turned away?

After dinner several of the patients came, one by one, to say good-bye. They all seemed sad, as if they might rather stay if conditions were otherwise. But perhaps they just wanted to express their thanks and hint that they would miss those of us who had tried unsuccessfully to help them. In any case they had all made the decision to go, and weren't about to change their minds. Their leader in this unified front was Howard, who summed up their feelings this way: "For the first time in our lives, we'll be able to create new memories."

When the evening finally came to a close I was almost afraid to take to my nice, soft bed. I had had nightmares the evening before; who knew what terrible dreams I would have this night, filled with barely-overcome horrors, harsh disappointments, unfulfilled desires. I was lucky to have a wonderful wife and family, and good health for my age, but was that only a hologram masking what was really lurking just below the surface? Nevertheless, I finally turned off the light and closed my eyes.

It wasn't long before I was awakened by fled. Or perhaps it was only a dream, though I hadn't had any mushrooms for days. "It's time," she whispered.

I sat up in my white hospital pajamas. "I thought you'd *never* leave."

"Keep working on that sense of humor, doctor b. And by the way, you look cute in those."

"Thank you. Everything is arranged, then?"

"Not only arranged, but the canyon is full and everyone else is in the lounge waiting for me. I just stopped in to say farewell."

"You couldn't find a way to cure any of them?"

"You saw the holograms, gene. Even if I could cure them, they'd rather be somewhere else. They don't seem to like this PLANET for some reason."

"And the other 99,900 or so?"

"Them, too."

"Can you tell me: are they all mental patients?"

She seemed puzzled. "Not to my knowledge."

There didn't seem to be much more to say. I offered a hand, which she didn't take. Instead, she leaned over whispered, "Last chance for a quickie!" I could smell her breath, which reminded me of a fresh salad.

"No, thanks. It's tempting, but no thanks."

"It's your loss." She kissed me on the cheek. It was wet and sloppy, like Filbert's, but warm and tender, too. As she turned around to leave, she called over her shoulder, "Come up and see me sometime."

After she had gone I found the blood and urine samples she had left on the little end table.

I dressed quickly, but was too late. According to the night crew, fled had reappeared briefly in the lounge, where she found Howard and the others waiting with their little traveling bags. Most were sound asleep. A moment later they were gone.

* * *

Early that morning we took stock. Missing from the hospital were all the patients (except Jerry and Georgie) I have described in this book, including old Mrs. Weathers, who apparently decided to have one last fling after all, as well as most of the other residents of the Manhattan Psychiatric Institute. All left their rooms clean and tidy except for Darryl, who had torn all his pictures of Meg Ryan into little bits and tossed them everywhere. His floor was a confetti of shattered hopes and dreams. There was no trace of the little cakes and cookies, however.

I was surprised that Barney went with them—he had finally found something to awaken his sense of humor. But maybe it wasn't enough. Maybe his deeper unhappiness, whatever its origin (perhaps underneath it all he abhorred the thought of going into the family dry cleaning business) couldn't be overcome by a few laughs. Or perhaps fled convinced him that there was far more genuine humor on K-PAX than on Earth, where most people will laugh at almost anything, even if it isn't funny, to momentarily mask their chronic sadness. Charlotte and former patient Ed went along, too. I hope they find the peace they desperately needed and longed for. What I hadn't expected, however, was that Kathy Rothstein embarked on the journey as well, along with former colleague Arthur Beamish and some of the nurses. As did our perky secretary, Margie Garafoli. Underneath her bubbly exterior must have simmered a cauldron of pain and suffering.

Despite the loss of a few of the staff members, Goldfarb wasn't disappointed with this turn of events. On the contrary she was delighted, as any good psychiatrist would have been, that most of her charges had finally found a measure of peace, and maybe even happiness, somewhere, anywhere. "Now," she calmly observed, "we have room for a few new patients. A hundred and ten, to be precise."

It wasn't until I got home later that morning that I found an e-mail message on my computer:

> **to my dear gene with love (whatever that means)**
> **thank you for putting me up**
> **your friend fled**
> **ps the door to K-PAX is always open for you**

* * *

The media reports were sketchy. For one thing, there were no reporters at the Grand Canyon in the predawn hours and no one witnessed the event except, perhaps, for a few sleepy burros (for all we know some of them might have gone along, too). For another, barely a handful of notes were left by the travelers for worried families or places of employment. Only gradually did it become clear that the 100,000 "people" fled had taken with her were almost entirely great apes: chimpanzees (including Filbert and, of course, Dr. Tewksbury), gorillas, orangutans. Most of these came from the mountains and jungles of Africa and Southeast Asia, though many of the zoos and research laboratories around the world reported missing animals as well (although fled didn't mention this to me, she must have visited quite a few of those during her visit). There was a great outcry among the researchers involved, most of whom were heavily funded by government grants, lamenting the theft of their "property." The zoos, too, loudly resented the taking of their prime exhibits, complaining primarily about the expense of replacing them.

But maybe fled had little choice. Perhaps hardly any of Earth's humans were able to fulfill the requirements for the trip. How many pacifist, agnostic vegans with two children or less are there in the world, anyway? Well, at least one. Our daughter Abby managed to be invited along on the trip, and is, at this moment, somewhere on

K-PAX. Steve was quite upset by this at first—she didn't tell him she had applied—but he soon became too busy to dwell on it. And when he finally found time to do so, he was very proud and happy for her. In any case, she left a note explaining that she would be back "in a few years." Perhaps she'll accompany Giselle and Gene when they make their promised return visit. In the meantime, we all miss her terribly.

The rest of the story we learned from fled's website, which she had somehow updated at the last minute while traveling the world accumulating her fellow passengers. To explain why she regarded her travel companions as "people," I quote directly from the site:

> ... **The great apes share between 96% and 99% of the human genome. Homo sapiens are genetically more closely related to the chimpanzees than are two species of finch! They share with you many emotions that are indistinguishable from your own: they feel pain and anguish, they intensely love their children, feel deep fears, form close friendships, and grieve the loss of a parent or sibling (sometimes to the death). By your own standards of measurement, the IQ's of the ape species are equivalent to those of human children. They are curious about their environment and hate being bored (in this regard, of course, they are different from most sapiens). And, like humans, they can sometimes be cruel and devious. Go to an ape prison [zoo or laboratory] and look into their eyes. What you will see is yourselves looking back.**
>
> **The apes are, in fact, members of your own genus (homo). They have been classified otherwise because of their physical appearance, without regard for the countless mental and physical similarities between you. Regarding them as something else merely underscores your own prejudices. You and they evolved from a common ancestor, a fact that has been vigorously denied by your religions, which unanimously insist that human beings are in a special category, elevated above every other form of life on EARTH, or anywhere else. Discounting your biological history clearly illustrates this human bigotry. Treating the great apes as "inferior" is like considering all women, all humans of other races, all those with different sexual orientations, or anyone who exhibits differences of any kind as being of less value than yourselves.**
>
> **I have left you a few thousand of your relatives, enough to maintain their species if you are willing to set aside territory which is theirs alone, and never violating it. If you were to do this, you would be taking a great step toward joining the civilized beings in**

the rest of the UNIVERSE as partners. Otherwise, it will no good on your record, which, even now, is being scrutinized ⌣ͺ bullocks.

Taking some of your cousins with me in no way suggests that beings other than humans or apes are inferior in any way to either of you. I could only take 100,000 of you with me on this trip. Perhaps other K-PAXians will come to bring some of your fellow beings to K-PAX, where we will all live in harmony with one another. If you should learn to co-exist on EARTH, of course, there will be no need. If you cannot, they will not miss you when the badguys come. Either way, their short lives of terror will soon be over, and your WORLD will again be the paradise it was before the sapiens arrived on the scene. And when that happens, those who have emigrated to K-PAX may wish to return to your beautiful PLANET.

A few days after fled and her companions departed, Dartmouth (hobbling on old-fashioned wooden crutches) and Wang paid us a final call. "We have decided to allow her–uh–child to be born," the latter informed me, "provided that she agrees to certain experimental procedures. We'd appreciate it if you would tell us where we can find her. The boss is very keen to have this matter successfully resolved in the interest of national security."

"That's classified," I told him, and went back into the house, thinking: perhaps we ought to be glad that our governments are so inept. Imagine the damage they could do if they were competent . . . .

* * *

The following Monday Goldfarb called and requested that I come in one last time for lunch and to fill in some paperwork. Karen decided to go, too. I supposed my long-suffering wife was worried that while I was there I'd find some puzzling case to become involved with, though I assured her there was no chance whatever of that.

She rolled her eyes. "All it would take would be an alien visitor or someone equally interesting and you'd be off and running again."

"I don't think I could take another alien visitor!"

We went in a few days later. The plywood barricade blocking the grounds from prying eyes had already been removed, but the lawn and lounge were eerily deserted, and there was little to see. As we proceeded to the doctors' dining room I vaguely wondered how long it would be until the hospital would be filled again with impossible patients of all possible kinds.

"Surprise!" a few dozen voices shouted. It was a long-postponed retirement party for moi.

Well, I won't go into the gory details on that. Except to say that it had been organized by Will (with the assistance of Hannah Rudqvist). But how did they know I would be hanging up my yellow pad for good as soon as fled had gone? "I knew you would consider anything that happened after she left to be anticlimactic," Will later told me. Another good indication that it's time for permanent retirement: when your family and co-workers know you better than you know yourself.

All the remaining patients were also there, including Jerry and the other autists, along with Georgie and his football. Their obvious joy served as a reminder to everyone, especially those of us who had forgotten, that being mentally ill doesn't always mean sadness and despair.

We all had a wonderful lunch, including a huge chocolate cake (my favorite dessert) with thirty-five candles on it, one for every year I had been at the hospital. There were speeches by Goldfarb, Will, and even Roberts, who openly confided, "To tell you the truth, I never liked you much."

What else could I say but, "I didn't like you much either, but now that I've gotten to know you better, I like you even less." His roar of laughter indicated that he accepted the joke in the spirit that had been intended, though it probably covered up a little unconscious prejudice on both our parts. But, of course, we're both human.

Finally it was my turn. I hadn't prepared anything, so it was pretty rambling. The easiest part was thanking everyone for so many enjoyable years as their colleague at the Manhattan Psychiatric Institute. All of them, particularly Virginia Goldfarb, had made everything about my difficult job easier and more rewarding. As much as I had sometimes complained about the workload, the frustration, and the stress of treating some very demanding patients, it had been thirty-five years of fascination and wonder. And being able to help a lot of miserable people to live happier lives than they might have otherwise was the icing on the cake. I was almost sorry I had decided to retire.

I confessed that I had been extremely fortunate, of course, in having been in the right place at the right time when prot showed up, followed by fled a few years later. It's impossible to really explain how much they have enriched my life. Until you've been privileged to know beings who represent cultures that have been around far longer than ours, it's difficult to fully appreciate how very young we are on the cosmological scale, how enormously much we have to learn. In a similar vein, we could also ascertain a great deal from our close cousins, the great apes, who have been around for at least as long as we have, and who have learned to live within the prescribed bounds that a benevolent nature allows, and never try to take more than they need.

After the yawns had died down I pointed out that MPI has a wonderful young staff, doctors and nurses who, I am sure, will give their best until their turn to exit the stage comes along, as it inevitably must. I hoped they would all have lives, both professional and personal, as enjoyable as the one I have had. If I died tomorrow I would die happily, knowing I had done the best I could with what little talent I had.

But, I added, none of it would have been possible without my wonderful wife, who unflaggingly helped me get through the difficult times with her unquestioning love and support. I don't know how many years we have left together, but I know they will be good ones, happy ones, if not very productive.

I ended with the hope that many of the staff would visit us once in a while in the Andirondacks, knowing that most would not. That's okay, too. They will have plenty of other things to do.

As would I. I looked forward to getting back to travel planning, my telescope, my rented Cessna, and to reading the vast number of books accumulating dust in my study—*Moby Dick* and all the rest.

And I had one last book of my own to write.

EPILOGUE

A short time after fled's departure I got another call from Wang. "We have reason to believe," he confided, "that she is leaving soon–perhaps from a football stadium somewhere in the Western United States. But never fear: we have every one of them staked out, and–"

I patiently explained that she had already gone.

"Gone where? The boss wants to see her. There has been an invitation from the United Nations for her to speak to the General Assembly."

"You're too late," I reluctantly informed him. "Maybe on her next visit. She was planning to tell us–"

"Hang on," he mumbled. Apparently he was trying to set up a recording device. Or perhaps looking for a pencil. "Okay, shoot."

"She had a message from prot. He wanted to give us nine suggestions for avoiding a visit from the Badguys. Unfortunately, we will probably never know what they were."

'Nine? That's too complicated. The boss isn't going to like that. Can't you make it one or two?

"There aren't going to be *any*," I repeated slowly. Fled is already back on K-PAX by now."

"But we had a meeting scheduled for midnight tonight . . . ."

"She won't be able to make it."

Another pause. "What did she say about Mr. Dartmouth?"

"He ought to see a mental health professional as soon as possible. And, incidentally, she suggested that you do the same."

"I'll have to get back to you on that." That was the last I heard from Messrs. Dartmouth and Wang.

* * *

As of this writing, everything is back to normal at home and at the Manhattan Psychiatric Institute. I get all the hospital news from Will, who tells me about the many new patients, all difficult, all interesting. Although I'm glad he enjoys discussing them, I only half-listen sometimes.

Steve and the boys show up now and then, but not very often—all are busier than ever. Our son-in-law did show us some pictures of the late-night picnic, which turned out surprisingly well despite the darkness—Star may have a future in photography as well as acting. But it was chilling to see them and remember that fled had actually been with us not so long before. She looked amazingly human in her candlelit poses with the family: smiling, with her arms draped around one or another of the boys. As a result of all this, and the hair of fled's head encased in plastic, Star was elected to the student council. Unfortunately, he couldn't stand the boredom and quickly resigned from that post.

Fred is starring in a new Broadway show and is hoping to reprise the role in Hollywood (we'll see about that—the starring role he told us about earlier had already fallen through, the film having been relegated to "development hell"). And Jenny and Anne did make the trip to New York, and we to California. Karen is planning several more trips for us, including a month-long tour of the entire Southwest with a stop at the Grand Canyon, where fortunes are being made by vendors selling all kinds of ape paraphernalia, and to the Siegels' favorite country, Poland.

I rarely visit the hospital anymore, but I did stop in to see Jerry not long after my final retirement. He no longer interacts with anyone, so he'll probably be at MPI the rest of his life. Despite this grim outlook, I believe he is the happiest patient there. I don't know whether he remembers how he was for a while, but, if so, he must be doubly happy. He finally finished the miniature MPI, and rebuilt the Eiffel Tower. His current project is a matchstick version of the great pyramid at Giza, which almost fills his room (he sleeps inside it).

I left him with the usual hug, and a "'Bye, Jer."

"'Bye, Jer, 'bye Jer, 'bye, Jer," he replied, without hugging me back. To me it sounded like music.

One other note from the hospital: last Christmas, Hannah Rudqvist married Cliff Roberts and has become an American citizen and a permanent member of the MPI staff. It wasn't embarrassment that caused her blushing problem, but a physiological response to the detergent she was using coupled with heat and perspiration. She wasn't even aware of it. Who knows—perhaps that was one of the reasons Cliff was attracted to her (besides her good looks). Or maybe it was something else. The mysteries of love should remain just that, and I wish them both well. Incidentally, her new husband wasn't really a womanizer. He started that rumor himself because of his innate shyness. People!

Freddie was also married, in the fall of 2005, though not to the ballerina but to the actress who played Meg Ryan so convincingly that Darryl dumped her. Perhaps they should have waited awhile–they're already having problems they never had for the few months they were living together before the wedding. Life is so weird!

I mentioned to Will that, while he and Hannah were meeting to plan my retirement party, I had suspected they were having an affair. "I knew you would never do a thing like that," I fatuously told him.

"No more than you would, Dad," came the obvious reply.

According to news reports, a sizable number of the people who became vegans or vegetarians in an attempt to secure a ticket to K-PAX have not gone back to eating their fellow beings. As a result, the air is a little cleaner, water shortages have eased a bit, and global warming has slowed down significantly. Encouragingly, perhaps, there is even some evidence that the general population has become fractionally more aware that our planet is but a speck in the cosmos, only one of countless trillions throughout the universe. In this sense alone, perhaps, fled's visit has had an impact of potentially monumental consequence.

It's possible that some of this apparent awakening is due in part to the telecast of the pilot program for the reality show filmed at MPI, which, in fact, included fled's warning that the Badguys could show up in 2020. I don't know whether the producers did this just to make the show more exciting to the viewers, but the end result was that some people must have heard the message. Perhaps it's a start. In any case, I did get two voiceovers on the show, including my defense of fled's mating habits and putative offspring. Freddy said I was "brilliant." I wasn't, of course, but it's nice to have a son who thinks so.

Not long after the telecast of the pilot episode, the series itself was canceled. Not just the mental hospital part–all of it. Apparently, like most popular TV programs, the reality show blueprint had already begun to run its course, beaten to death by spinoff and repetition. (The only formulas that seem to be unaffected by overexposure are the endless identical cop shows and sitcoms, which most people can't seem to get enough of.)

In other news, son-in-law Steve has been awarded the 2007 Copernicus prize in astronomy, primarily because of his work on the speed of light. Since its value is directly related to the expansion of the universe, he discovered that it is possible, in fact, to show that the rate of expansion is slowing down, rather than accelerating, as other evidence had suggested. He did this by making exquisitely sensitive measurements of the speed of light over a period of one year, and when this calculation is carried out to eighteen decimal places, the value of c is clearly slowing at an infinitesimal, though measurable, rate. Furthermore, he found that the light coming from at least two distant galaxies "winked out" as a result of the slowdown in light speed during this same time period. The awards committee favorably compared his studies to the special relativity theory formulated by Albert Einstein a century earlier. Fled's help in initiating Steve's findings was not mentioned in the citation, however.

There was considerable e-mail following her departure, much of it debating the proposal that the great apes belong to the same genus (Homo) as us, and their concomitant designation as "people." Though many correspondents disagreed, a surprising number took the view that the apes should, at a minimum, enjoy freedom from pain, invasive experimentation and incarceration, i.e., much like mentally disabled humans. Some farsighted responders suggested further that if apes should be allowed such rights, why not all the other animals?

Knotty issues to be sure. But perhaps no more so than the question of whether all of us (including the non-human animals) have alter egos living on other planets in the galaxy, or even in other galaxies. K-PAX alone harbors countless beings who might well be our mental counterparts, just as the great apes are our physical cousins.

On the other hand, there was the inevitable pack of letters from those who can't accept anything that doesn't fit their preconceived view of their world. This is a typical one: **Man didn't crawl out of the ooze or evolve from monkeys! The Bible says we were given dominion over the beasts of the fields, to use in any way we want. The animals don't have souls, therefore they don't have any feelings, therefore they don't feel pain. And we can't breed with them, either. That's why they are called animals . . . .** I wish I could be so sure of how many toes I have as some of these people are about their place in the universe.

Some correspondents wanted to know whether fled came to promote sex between the primate species, and if I agreed with this notion. Of course I don't, and I don't think she did, either. Her point was that our similarities far outweigh our differences, and appearances shouldn't be the only criteria for acceptance among our peers.

No further word from fled. I even sent her an e-note once after she left, but of course there was no reply. Yet. But who knows–the message may be floating in cyberspace and a response may come any day. Will she ever visit us again? Probably not, but maybe fled's half-Earthling son or daughter will make the journey. And if his father was human, what would the kid be like? Something like a hairless chimpanzee? Or perhaps a very hairy human, like the mechanic down at the local garage? Incidentally, the results of the naming contest came in last summer, and the winner was "edam," a cross between "adam" and "eve" for a being of unknown gender, according to Smythe. Not very original, perhaps, but did you do any better?

Beyond that, will other K-PAXians show up some day? If so, will they be taking any of us back with them as prot and fled have done? And will Abby and Giselle and Gene be making a return trip to their home planet sometime soon, as fled suggested? I hope so; I'd love to ask them some questions. For example, did Phyllis become visible when she touched down on the purple plains of K-PAX, and has Rocky finally found beings who don't rouse his ire? Does Cassandra still sit on a bench somewhere and contemplate the future, or did she find enough stimulation to keep her thoughts rooted in the present? Is Darryl in love with a Meg Ryan hologram? And did all those great apes mingle with the orfs and adjust well to their new environment? Are there ape-orf hybrids running around everywhere?

On the other hand will we, in another short decade and a half, receive a visit from the Bullocks, who seem to be some of the nastiest beings in the universe? Or was fled just trying to scare us into behaving ourselves, much like we might tell our children about the "bogeyman"? If so, then perhaps she was lying to us about everything else. But if she was telling the truth, do we have the will to correct some of our mistakes before it's too late? Again, only time will tell. All we know for certain is that the universe is an unimaginably big place, filled with surprises. How little we know of it even in the twenty-first century. I hope we will soon learn to do away with our petty, stupid wars, no matter how seemingly righteous the cause; begin to conserve and protect our common environment, which is deteriorating with far greater rapidity than anyone would have thought even a few years ago; and reduce the human population and learn to share our still-beautiful planet with the other species who inhabit it with us.

Even if we manage to survive the century under the present conditions, what kind of world will we have if it becomes an oven supporting only a few species, including ourselves and our pets, all huddled in environmentally-controlled apartments on higher ground, while the coastlines become underwater playgrounds for scuba divers? Or if we continue to kill our neighbors, with ever more dangerous and sophisticated weapons, over who owns the last of the fossil fuels or professes the wrong religious beliefs? If so, whatever the Bullocks do to us couldn't be much worse than what we've done to ourselves.

My generation may have been the last one on Earth to live without worrying about running out of space, of fuel, and of other natural resources including even air and water. But now our planet is having a tough time surviving us. Yet, even with the future in serious doubt, we're still in thrall to the world's leaders, who worry primarily about conserving their own wealth and power. How is it possible that we still support the hamburger chains, the tobacco industries, the gun manufacturers? Our very survival, I believe, depends on the answer to that and related questions.

Whatever happens, of course, won't make much difference to us old farts; we're not going to be around much longer anyway. What we're talking about is our grandchildren, and *their* grandchildren, and the world they will have to deal with. Or does that matter enough to any of us, including them? Sometimes I wonder . . . .

A DECLARATION ON GREAT APES*

We demand the extension of the community of equals to include all great apes: human beings, chimpanzees, gorillas and orangutans.

"The community of equals" is the moral community within which we accept certain basic moral principles or rights as governing our relations with each other and enforceable at law. Among these principles or rights are the following:

1 **The Right to Life**

   The lives of members of the community of equals are to be protected. Members of the community of equals may not be killed except in very strictly defined circumstances, for example, self-defense.

2 **The Protection of Individual Liberty**

   Members of the community of equals are not to be arbitrarily deprived of their liberty; if they should be imprisoned without due legal process, they have the right to immediate release. The detention of those who have not been convicted of any crime, or of those who are not criminally liable, should be

---

* from Paola Cavalieri and Peter Singer: *The Great Ape Project* (St. Martin's Press, New York, 1993).

allowed only where it can be shown to be for their own good, or necessary to protect the public from a member of the community who would clearly be a danger to others if at liberty. In such cases, members of the community of equals must have the right to appeal, either directly or, if they lack the relevant capacity, through an advocate, to a judicial tribunal.

3 The Prohibition of Torture

The deliberate infliction of severe pain on a member of the community of equals, either wantonly or for an alleged benefit to others, is regarded as torture, and is wrong.

SUGGESTED ADDITIONAL READING

Brewer, Gene: *The K-PAX Trilogy featuring Prot's Report* (Bloomsbury, London, 2003).
Dian Fossey: *Gorillas in the Mist* (Mariner Books/Houghton Mifflin, New York, 1983).
Jane Goodall: *Through a Window* (Houghton Mifflin, Boston, 1990).
Biruté M.F. Galdikas: *Reflections of Eden* (Back Bay Books/Little Brown, Boston, 1995).

ACKNOWLEDGMENTS

This work was inspired by two unique human beings. Dr. Jane Goodall was the first person to live among the great apes and study them in their natural habitat. The world owes her an incalculable debt. Dr. Oliver Sacks has written extensively on mental illness and related topics. Great inspirations, both.

visit the author at *www.genebrewer.com*